Pride Publishing books by April C. Griffith

Single Books
Electra Rex

I0658887

ELECTRA REX

APRIL C. GRIFFITH

Electra Rex
ISBN #978-1-83943-956-8
©Copyright April C. Griffith 2021
Cover Art by Louisa Maggio ©Copyright March 2021
Interior text design by Claire Siemaszkiewicz
Pride Publishing

Published in 2021 by Pride Publishing, United Kingdom.

Pride Publishing is an imprint of Totally Entwined Group Limited.

ELECTRA REX

Dedication

Thank you, Dr. Cat

Chapter One

"I am the last of my kind, and I suck," Electra mumbled to herself, throwing back another drink. On the first night of a planetary holiday, Electra Rex was drunk, scorned and looking to buy a gun. She couldn't recall exactly which holiday it was, though, since there were so many. The planet took time off constantly to celebrate a googolplex of different accomplishments, important figures and momentous occasions across hundreds of alien species. It was a wonder anyone did anything but observe holidays. She sat in a window booth, watching ships both large and small land at the valet pad while she waited.

Little of her Embarker pedigree remained after years away from the flotilla. Endless toil and nomadic life marked her people's existence, even if it didn't describe her life. She'd lived in an apartment in Authrillia's largest northern city for more than a year, which should have made her itchy to get back to spacefaring, but she wasn't. In fact, she wasn't much of anything. Apathy had settled heavily over her and it had made her careless — at least, more careless than she'd already known herself to be. To pay the bills, she engaged in the least Embarker type of work she could find — being a professional party guest. *'Come see the last known human woman, drink with her, maybe even...'* But that was over. She'd frittered away too much money on fleeting things, another Embarker no-no. A job meant to replenish her account at the last moment and save her apartment, her precious creature comforts and allow her reckless lifestyle to continue for another month hadn't paid out. Now she had only the clothes on her back and the cash in her pocket. Enough to buy a gun, she hoped.

She'd given the DJ of the club a copy of *Margaritaville*, promising a transcendent experience. Jimmy Buffet sang while a dozen different species of aliens attempted to dance on the multi-tiered dance floor to the ancient Earthling music. Electra's dad had loved Jimmy Buffet. *'The finest music in the galaxy,'* he'd said. Even with great effort and a good deal of booze in her system, she couldn't hear what he'd heard. She must not have inherited his ear for classical music. *What the hell is a flip-flop anyway?*

Normally leering over spacecraft cheered her up, which was why she'd selected a window booth near the landing pad. She wasn't into the functional caravan freighters that comprised Embarker fleets. She liked the chic, silky, beautiful spaceships that focused on form over function. The bleak, unrepentantly crappy mood that had clung to her throughout the day lightened an iota at the arrival of her dream ship in the valet station directly below her window. An oval saucer body, three hundred feet long, sleek and stylish, with three classic fins off the back, it was — it had to be — a Cadillux 1959 Dorado edition. And it was pink, the brightest, most beautiful pearlescent pink trimmed in the shiniest of chrome. Electra stood on her knees on the booth's bench and pressed her face drunkenly against the glass. She wanted to lick it. She didn't care that the thought was absurd. That ship was so gorgeous that it deserved to be licked.

The transparent arrival tube extended to the ventral port while a valet-bot lowered onto the dorsal spine above the cockpit that sat directly in the middle of the oval. Electra wanted to see what wondrous creature possessed such a magnificent spaceship. After several agonizing moments, the owner of the ship passed from beneath the edge within the arrival tube and Electra's elation turned to fury — *Weisella. Fucking Weisella.* Her need to buy a gun redoubled, not to begin a life of mercenary work — which was the Embarker way after going bust — but for murder, satisfying revenge on the woman who had thoroughly screwed her. The fact that such a heinous, underhanded creature could own such a glorious ship was a crime on par with regicide in Electra's inebriated mind.

Weisella was a Panaeus, a vaguely humanoid alien species with advanced telekinetic and telepathic powers. She was only a little taller than Electra's five-and-a-half feet. Her heart-shaped face had two enormous black, almond-shaped eyes, no nose or mouth. Frilled spines replaced what could be called hair. A cluster of five ephemeral tentacles stood in the place of an arm on each side, and instead of legs, she had what looked like a jumbo, curved shrimp tail. Indeed, the only attractive features Electra saw in Weisella were her money and her strangely perfect breasts — three of them across the center of her chest, prominently displayed since Panaeus didn't wear clothes. Weisella liked jewelry, though, and she was sporting a shiny new metal ring on her tail that was probably just brimming with expensive tech.

Electra's memory of the night before was fragmented at best. She'd been hired to attend Weisella's gala for the Panaeus New Year, partially as the spectacle of having a human in attendance and partially as Weisella's date. Electra didn't mind the escort portion of the work. Weisella was rich, enchanting, well-traveled and she'd paid extra for the pleasure. Except she hadn't actually paid. The transfer had bounced back in the morning when Electra had tried to use the money to get the foreclosure lock off her apartment door. The timer on her lien had expired and everything in her apartment had gotten incinerated while she watched through the little glass window on the door. Everything her parents had ever given her, every keepsake from Transition Island, every souvenir she'd collected in her travels was gone in a flash of white fire and a quickly ventilated puff of smoke, all because Weisella had ripped her off.

Electra had done her part. She'd danced, charmed and been better than presentable in her skin-tight Utopalex pants, knee-high go-go boots and a black corset that made the most of what she had. The Panaeus guests had loved her. Weisella had loved her. By every measurement, Electra had performed perfectly. They'd retired to Weisella's bedroom at the end of the night to continue the festivities. Things hadn't gone as smoothly behind closed doors. Electra had been intoxicated from drinks, a few drugs she wasn't familiar with and the high oxygen environment created in the penthouse, plus she'd never slept with a Panaeus before. The swell of Weisella's backside, what looked like a delightfully curvaceous butt? Nope, that was a nose and *'Please stop fondling it.'* Okay, the breasts were breasts, right? Close enough. Fondle those, lick them and fall asleep face-first in them. Was that why Weisella had bounced back the payment? Failure to consummate? It was explicitly stated in Electra's contract that sex was not a guaranteed part of any escort arrangement. It was her prerogative. Besides, she'd tried. There simply weren't obvious sex organs on a Panaeus — at least none Electra could find in her sloppy groping.

The valet-bot guided the Cadillux away after Weisella entered the club a couple of floors beneath Electra's booth. The little bot was flying the beautiful ship toward the stacks. *Not the stacks!* That was where someone parked a junker that nobody would want to steal. The stacks were for heaps with so many scratches and dents that a few more might go completely unnoticed. The Cadillux could be scraped, dinged, stolen or breathed on wrong in the stacks. Only the worst kind of philistine would park such a beautiful vessel in the holding pen for pig ships!

"That tight little butt could only belong to *the* Electra Rex," a gravelly voice sounded behind her.

Electra sat back down and glared at Fizan. Her underworld contact was a Gromphra, essentially an eight-foot-tall cockroach in every despicable sense. Fizan was too large and inflexible to actually sit in the booth, so she stood at the end of the table, inspecting Electra with her dead bug eyes. It wasn't that Fizan was a particularly vile example of the species — all Gromphra were lecherous and blunt. It was considered a badge of honor to gross out other species—at least, that was what Fizan claimed.

The seemingly transparent shell on the front of Fizan's torso opened up like a flasher's raincoat. It was clothing and body armor mixed and wasn't actually transparent. Within the shell, guns, knives and a dozen other nefarious items were concealed behind the projected image of her chitinous trunk.

"See anything you like?" Fizan asked.

Electra had enough cash on hand to afford a decent gun. A carbine worked best for mercenary work, although a small pistol would be ideal to assassinate Weisella on a crowded dance floor. Shooting anyone or anything wasn't really her style, and the reality of what she was doing rolled over her in an unpleasant manner, accompanied by a wave of nausea. Electra scrunched her nose while she considered the weapons until she spied something entirely different.

"How much for the ID-clone?"

* * * *

Access and time were all Electra needed. The ID-clone could give her the access and Weisella's party-girl attitude would hopefully provide ample time—enough time for Electra to have a few drinks of her own. The booze would help steel her nerves. Crime wasn't her thing—at least, not overt crime like grand theft starship. She liked subtle stuff, scams, white lies, a flirty wink that could grab a gift under false pretenses, a hacked communicator to collect a secret or two for later use, but nothing remotely on the scale of what she was about to do.

Desperation and betrayal had driven her to such a state, and potent cocktails containing a dozen or so cerebral inhibitors provided the necessary courage and dulled her higher reasoning. A smile, a bribe and a clever lie cleared the security guard from the maintenance tunnel for the stacks. The bouncer watching the emergency exit that led to the parking pods was flesh and blood — silicon-based, maybe. Electra didn't recognize his species. He was gray with lots of arms and eyes — and easily charmed, thankfully. She had a single flash charge on her datapad that could have stunned the bouncer, but she needed it to reboot a valet-bot for her plan to have a chance.

The tunnels wobbled with every step. She was nearly to the pod before she realized the wobble was entirely in her head. Her senses were the unstable part of the equation. Over-served or over-ordered — at any rate, she'd shot well past the point of functional, yet she was brave enough to commit a major felony, which was where she'd tried to land. She was a dangerously inebriated woman on the edge, and she was halfway up a ladder toward the beautiful pink Cadillux before she realized how far into her crime she'd actually made it and how far she'd fall if she missed a rung. How many minutes had she just lost falling into a void in her memory? Didn't matter. The ship was right there.

Wind howled through the stacks, carrying with it the familiar scents of oil, rust and industrial grime, the perfume of decrepit starships. The flotilla she'd been born and raised on had bathed her in that smell from her first breath until she'd abandoned the Embarker lifestyle forever at age thirteen.

The ID-clone scanned the ship and began a search of the galactic net for the proper code. Electra stabilized herself by resting her forehead on the side of the ship while she waited. In her inebriated state, she decided licking the vessel would be okay, even though it wasn't hers yet. Indulging her initial impulse, she licked the hull in a long, slow, lingering swipe of her tongue...and immediately threw up. The expensive, potent drinks she'd spent the last of her cash on poured through the metal grating of the platform in three massive heaves. She felt better. Licking the ship hadn't been a terrible idea after all.

The ID-clone popped open a moment later and Electra retrieved the ID, which was now a perfect copy to identify her as Weisella, for most purposes. All the money she was owed from the party, the boob massage and the betrayal, yeah, the ship would barely cover what was due after a job mostly well done.

"This area is off limits, ma'am," a valet-bot blorped from behind her. It was little more than a floating ball with four long bracket arms and a blue, glowing triangle for a face. "If you'd like your vehicle, you need to show your ID at the entrance and I will retrieve it."

"Don't 'ma'am' me in your bleepy-blorpy voice," Electra slurred. She flipped her datapad around to face the bot and hit buttons until the scramble flash went off, accidentally taking her own picture at the same time. The valet-bot spun erratically and rebooted.

"Can I retrieve your ship for you, ma'am?" the valet-bot asked convivially.

"I would like that very much, yes, and sorry about calling your voice bleepy-blorpy," Electra said, providing the bot with the new Weisella fake ID.

The valet-bot happily retrieved, scanned and returned the offered ID, along with the starship's keys.

"Have a splendid rest of the night, Weisella," the valet-bot declared before floating back down to its cradle.

"I'm really good at crime," she declared to nobody in particular.

Electra climbed into the ship, closed the door behind her and took a deep, luxuriating breath of the grandest ship she'd ever set foot in. Once she hacked the onboard computer, the Cadillux would be hers and she could take her talents all over the Milky Way and Andromeda galaxies. She'd wake up to a better life and an epic hangover after she made her getaway.

Chapter Two

"Wake up, you little sneak," a familiar voice echoed through the bedroom.

Silk sheets, pillows the size of land speeders... Why would Electra ever want to wake up? She pried one eye open to make sure she wasn't dreaming. Yep, it was the master bedroom on the Cadillux. She'd stolen it. She'd really stolen it and flown to...somewhere. She'd figure that part out after coffee. Space was big and empty. Hopefully her drunk self from the night before had found a nice spot to bunk down.

"Weisella, how did you get this number?" Electra joked as she stretched leisurely in her giant, new bed.

"It truly is unfortunate you were the one to steal my ship," Weisella said.

"Steal? Yours? I have no idea what you're talking about," Electra said. "This ship is registered to the one and only Electra Rex—a payment and healthy apology for a jilted contractor. Very generous of you."

"Didn't the security coding seem simplistic to you?" Weisella asked.

Electra bit her lower lip. She didn't remember. Blacking out wasn't uncommon for her when she over-indulged. She was a waif of a thing and had an Embarker's pitiful tolerance for any and all intoxicants. She rolled across the bed and hit the display button on the nightstand. The room was completely white, too white to even look at any of it directly with a hangover, now that she was seeing things clearly. It was like sleeping inside a light bulb. She might have to make some changes.

A holographic display of Weisella popped up at the foot of the bed.

"There you are, sweetness," Weisella said.

"The coding seemed…"

"You don't remember."

"Not exactly."

"Because you were too drunk."

"Not too drunk to get away with it." Electra laughed, immediately regretting it as the noise echoed painfully through the room and the inside of her head.

"The ship has a twenty-fold lien on it," Weisella said. "All of my debts, including the bounced payment to you and the party you took part in? It all transferred to you when you swapped the title."

Electra's head swam. If she had anything left in her stomach, she assumed it would be on its way out of her mouth. Twenty-fold on a ship the size and value of the Cadillux would be an astounding amount of money, more than Electra could reasonably be expected to comprehend in her hungover state.

"Fuck you," she managed to grumble.

"I'm so sorry. I didn't mean for it to be you," Weisella said. "Speaking of fucking, I've been looking up stuff on the galactic net, and I think I've figured out how we might... You know. Feel like taking pity on a broke girl and giving me a freebie?"

"You've got to be kidding me." Electra reached for the display button.

"Wait! I learned the swell on your lower back isn't your nose," Weisella said. "I could..." She waggled a few of her tentacles.

Electra hit the button, ending the call. "Ew, no," she said to the dead feed.

Debt was an Embarker's worst nightmare. *Never owe.* The motto was plastered on almost every wall, inscribed at the front of every book and was even used by some of the older members of Embarker fleets as a greeting.

'*Never owe, Stan!*'

'*Never owe to you too, George!*'

And now Electra owed without enjoying any of the extravagances that had incurred the debt — aside from the ship she'd stolen, but she felt that had been earned.

She cursed Weisella for outsmarting her yet again, Fizan for selling her the ID-clone at a discount, the bartender-bot for over-serving her and the Chamber most of all for enacting the law that stealing someone's identity in any fashion gave access to money and credit lines but also transferred debts. It was a whimsical way to deter identity theft, making debts transfer to would-be thieves if they picked the wrong target. The Chamber, the faceless, nameless, all-knowing, all-seeing government that was so damn clever that they'd actually tricked the whole galaxy into centuries of peace... Who the fuck did they think they were? Identity theft and fraud were dangerous vocations now, thanks to the Chamber, and Electra should have known. *Too easy.* It had been so easy that a thoroughly inebriated neonate at crime could pull off the heist, and that was why any thinking person would have known it was a trap. If the ship were free and clear, if Weisella's identity was at all worth stealing and swapping, there would have been a mountain of defenses to keep people like Electra out. If it were a honey pot, someone could do it in their sleep — or dead-drunk — and wake up thoroughly fucked.

Cursing Weisella and kicking herself for her own stupidity came to an abrupt halt when the wall slid open and a massive bot rolled into the room. It stood almost seven feet tall, a looming rectangle of metal the size of a large refrigerator and twice as shiny. It moved swiftly on two triangle tank tracks set to either side of the frame, while a nest of ten prehensile tube-arms jutted from the top, each tipped in a different tool.

"Debtor, it has been seventy-two hours since your last payment," the bot clicked.

"What's the default threshold?" Electra asked.

"One hundred fifty galactic standard hours."

"Great," Electra grumbled. "I don't suppose it'd change anything if I told you I'm not Weisella."

"It would not! That information is already logged and applied," the bot said. "Weisella's debts were transferred to Electra Rex eleven hours ago. You are Electra Rex. Mistakes have not been made."

"They were, by me...many of them," Electra said. "Can't I just transfer them back with the fake...I mean, my actual ID?"

"You cannot, as the ID was reported cloned mere hours after you ran it through the atomizing recycler."

"That was stupid of me. What am I even supposed to call you?"

"Letterman."

"What? Why?"

"It stands for Lien Enforcement Technology…"

"Yeah, yeah, yeah… Letterman's fine," Electra said. A lien-enforcement bot was serious business. Letterman was nearly indestructible, a hair below high sentient and had a nuclear core that would provide it with enough power to function independently for thousands of years. There would be no getting rid of it without discharging the debt.

"Due to the extreme sums owed and the parties to which they are due, it is considered imperative to avoid default," Letterman said. "Assistance threshold is set to one hundred percent in pursuit of repayment."

"Discharge the debt owed to Electra Rex," Electra said, glad she could at least remove what she technically owed herself for the party appearance.

"Authorizing discharge, bank fee assessed, twenty-thousand standard units has been removed from total balance, five thousand bounce fee added," Letterman said. "New balance is seventy-eight billion, nine hundred twenty-one million, six hundred thousand fifty-seven point forty-four standard units."

"Oh for fuck's sake, that number doesn't even make sense!" Electra screamed. The amount Weisella owed her for the party was so paltry, so insignificant in the scope of her total debts, that it seemed blatantly insulting not to have offered double or triple the fee, since she was just going to hand the debt off to someone else anyway.

"Would you like an itemized recounting of the debts?" Letterman asked.

"No, fuck, how long would that even take?"

"Four hundred eighty-one galactic standard hours, twenty-two minutes and thirty-eight seconds."

Electra's first instinct was to curl up in the bedding, try to vanish into herself and let the mountain of debt crush her like a hung-over little bug. She didn't suspect Letterman would let her stay cocooned in blankets and sheets for long, though. His job was to get her working, get her earning and get the debt moving in the right direction. She didn't fancy being dragged nude from her bed by the enforcement bot, so she climbed out willingly.

"I need coffee, a shower and a word with the only person who can help," Electra announced. "Ship Virtual Intelligence, what is your designation?"

"Ivy, Miss Electra," the ship's computer interface replied. She had an obnoxiously cheerful demeanor and a faint accent Electra didn't recognize. "You asked for this designation five times already."

"Is there a way to turn off your personality matrix, Ivy?"

"No, Miss Electra. You already asked that as well."

"Can you call me something other than Miss Electra?"

"Your designation was preprogrammed by master user Electra Rex."

She didn't remember doing that or why she'd chosen such an inane designation. "Is the master user password 'carbuncle'?"

"No, Miss Electra."

"Fine, whatever. It was worth a shot. Ivy, set a course for Station 51 in the Winter Triangle," Electra said. "And get a shower started for me."

"Would you like to use the Spatronic 9000Z as well?"

"The…what?"

"Spatronic 9000Z."

"Where? Where is it? Ivy, show me the Spatronic!"

"Illuminating a floor path for you now, Miss Electra."

A faintly glowing golden path zipped across the floor, fading behind her as she ran through it. A Spatronic 9000Z, the most advanced personal grooming and pampering system ever conceived, existed on her ship! Its very existence could explain a significant amount of the total debt, and Electra hoped it would be worth every monetary unit, as she'd only dreamed of such astounding opulence. If anything could wick away her hangover, soothe her jangled nerves and give her a reprieve from the ocean of stress and debt she'd been dropped into, it was a Spatronic 9000Z. Several billion standard units of luxury were about to obsess over every cell in her body with the single goal of making her feel spoiled and beautiful!

* * * *

Hair treatments, manicures, pedicures, exfoliating, teeth whitening and cleaning, body hair grooming or total removal and everything in between… The options on the Spatronic scrolled on and on down to every single detail of indulgence and appearance Electra could want or imagine and several options she had never even heard of. She set up a first-time profile, checked a million boxes on what she wanted then sat in the pod and awaited the magic. Hours, years, lifetimes passed in the heaven created by the Spatronic. The calming scents of the ocean, faint music, gentle massage and perfectly coordinated adjustment of lights drew her into a meditative state while her body was cleaned, toned and adorned from the top of her head to the bottoms of her feet.

"We have arrived in the desired coordinates of the Winter Triangle, Miss Electra," Ivy's voice pierced the soothing music pumped through the Spatronic.

Electra reluctantly emerged from the machine. She'd been buffed, massaged, brushed, plucked, painted, styled and given the exact makeup look she'd always wanted yet could never manage on her own. She looked down at the gleaming perfection of her body after the treatment and felt bad that she'd have to cover up so much glorious work.

Pulling on her Utopalex pants took far longer than usual. The material was designed to adhere to skin, which made it challenging to put on or remove any garments made of it, but beyond the simple tightness, there was the sensation. The slogan and truth were that Utopalex felt like euphoria to wear. Sensations brought on by the material felt so good that most species had to build up to wearing full garments or risk dissolving into a puddle of pure pleasure if the species was capable of turning into a puddle. Electra learned humans responded by falling into a catatonic bliss that made basic functionality extremely difficult. It had taken two years for Electra to work up to pants. With her skin completely cleared of hair, cleaned, exfoliated, massaged and given several renewal treatments that she hadn't known existed until then, it was like starting all over again in learning to wear Utopalex, since every inch of the material touched her in an entirely new way. She'd thought she'd worn Utopalex before. She'd been wrong.

She stood with only the last bit to go. Her body was already positively thrumming with the need to lie down and simply writhe. The hardest part was yet to come. She steeled herself and slid the back up over her ass, which gave her head-to-toe goosebumps and diamond-hard nipples. One more step and she'd either be ready to go or rendered completely useless for hours. She pulled open the tight front of the pants and tucked her cock and balls neatly into the pocket she'd created with the backs of her fingers. When she removed her hand, the material sucked perfectly flush against her every contour and she nearly fell over from the sensation. After she regained her senses, she pulled on a T-shirt then a vest to cover the fact that her nipples were tiny pyramids that gave no indication of calming any time soon.

"Something new to consider," she muttered to herself, feeling exceedingly hot and bothered. Her hangover was gone, worked out of her system by the Spatronic, only to be replaced by an intoxicating euphoria brought on by the Utopalex that rivaled high-quality designer drugs. It seemed like keeping the hangover might have allowed her to be marginally more functional than her new, highly aroused state.

She exited her ship on the far end of the landing platform for Station 51 feeling beautiful, pampered and stressed beyond measurable levels about her current situation. Before she could make it one step down the gangplank, she felt a metal clasp encircle her left wrist. She looked down to spot a vaguely familiar metal bracelet.

"The Lien Enforcement Bureau requires a tether if you are to leave the ship without me, and a lockdown on the vessel if you are to leave it with me," Letterman said.

"Peachy." Electra shook her hand to try to rattle the bracelet, but it held fast—snug, but not overly tight. The thing on Weisella's tail hadn't been a new accessory. It was her lien enforcement tether. She felt stupid and nauseous all over again. "Wait! Weisella didn't have one on at the party. Were you there?"

"You behaved foolishly and danced poorly."

"Helpful notes. I assume this thing explodes or something if I try to take it off."

"A massive, debilitating jolt of electricity, and I am summoned to charge you for any damage you might have done to the tether," Letterman said. "We are not monsters."

"Agree to disagree," Electra muttered on her way down the ramp.

The freighter depot platform crawled with Gromphra workers and pilots. The giant cockroach aliens scuttled around on all six of their legs to move faster over the open terrain between the pumps, ships, and amenities. Electra made a beeline for the service plaza and the glowing, red-and-white Tim Hortons sign.

Within the donut shop, a dozen different species of alien freighter captains and crews enjoyed donut holes and coffee. Electra got in line at the counter, breathing deeply of the heavenly scents of fresh-brewed coffee and breakfast foods sizzling on the griddle. Above the medley of pleasant aromas lingered the sticky-sweet perfume of warm glazed donuts.

Manning the counter was the only entity that could possibly help her—Om the wise. Om comprised several hundred swirling green blocks that ranged from the size of small boulders to tiny pebbles orbiting around a central white light but never touching one another.

"Om, it has been too long," Electra said when she reached the front of the line.

"Too long since you've eaten donuts or too long since you've visited your oldest friend?"

"I thought donuts were my oldest friends?" Electra smiled.

"You must be in some sort of trouble if you're all the way out here making jokes," Om said.

Electra held up her left wrist to show the lien enforcement tether.

"I hope you bought something good, at least," Om said.

"Sort of... Well, yes and no." Electra nodded toward her typical corner table.

Om poured two large, dark roasts and grabbed a bag of booparian berry timbits to share.

Electra polished off several of the glowing blue donut holes and half her coffee before she elaborated. "Remember the ship—and I mean *the* ship."

"You found a Cadillux?"

Electra nodded.

"A Dorado 1959?"

Electra nodded again.

"Worth the tether, I'm sure."

Electra nodded emphatically.

"So, what's the trouble?" Om asked. "You should be able to keep up, if just barely, on the payments with your appearance gigs."

"It came with a lien of its own. A huge one. A hair under seventy-nine billion units."

Om seemed to consider the number. At least, she thought that was what his relative silence meant. It was tough to tell what Om was doing most of the time, since they were a constantly shifting pile of swirling stones with no face. Electra didn't even know if there was a name for what Om was. They didn't have a gender. They were truly a 'they', as each stone contained countless other tiny life forms, and they didn't have a beginning or end, as far as Electra knew. Om, for all intents and purposes, was a small galaxy unto themselves, comprised of millions of little ecosystems that combined to create consciousness and profound wisdom, not to mention make the best cup of coffee in two galaxies.

"I have to assume you want to keep the ship but lose the debt," Om said.

Electra nodded. "Do you know a Gromphra that sells something to remove lien tethers?"

"For a seventy-nine-billion-unit lien, I don't think there is such a thing," Om said. "The creditors will find someone to connect that debt to and they already know who you are and what you're flying. You could always let someone else steal the ship and the debt, since I'm assuming that's how you came by both."

"Don't judge me." Electra groaned. "She owed me money and I was drunk. There has to be another way to keep the ship. They don't make them anymore, and this one is practically perfect in every way."

"It's pink, isn't it?"

"So very, very pink."

Again, Om seemed to consult the thousands of advanced societies within the stones of their body. "Have you heard of Bi-MARP?"

Electra shook her head.

"It's a Chamber project, all on the up-and-up, and there are some treasure-hunting jobs attached to it that pay big units."

"How big?"

"The one I've held on to for the right friend — getting a Bort Pod off a derelict ship in the California Nebula — pays a decent sized mountain of units," Om said. "The wreck is only scan-able for another week or so before it floats back into the Persei illumination field, so you'd have to act fast."

"What's a Bort Pod?"

"No clue, but it's worth twenty billion."

Electra almost took a sip of coffee just to perform a perfect spit take. If she took the job while still wearing the lien tether, the payout would be due to the preferred creditors, no matter what. If she let someone else steal the ship, she could be fabulously wealthy, but all she'd really want to buy would be a pink Cadillux Dorado 1959, and she probably had the only one left in existence, not to mention that she'd need a ship to get the Bort Pod and turn it in. Discharging the debt would be an enormous undertaking, but the Embarker in her thrilled at the prospect of tackling such a monumental job.

"Okay, give me the details," Electra said. "I'm doing this thing. Real work, no fun, no sex, minimal booze… My parents would be so proud."

Chapter Three

Details on the job didn't elaborate beyond one, thin line—find the Bort Pod on a derelict ship in the California Nebula, right near where San Diego would be. The last part of the job posting was supposed to be a joke. Electra was pretty sure about that, although she didn't get it—California and San Diego were Earthling references and she was an Embarker. A hop, skip and a jump through six wormhole relays later, she was on the edge of the Milky Way Galaxy, zipping through the nebula toward the provided coordinates.

The Cadillux 1959 ran like a dream at five times the speed of light. Over such large distances and such great speeds, the ship's onboard computer compressed the two into a workable display that allowed most species to grasp the enormity of interstellar travel by scaling it to a level comprehendible by organic cognition. What the computer displayed on the cockpit window was a projection of a vastly slowed down and miniaturized version of what was actually occurring, adjusted to match reality by compressing the distance. To top it all off, the Cadillux handled so smoothly that Electra almost couldn't tell the ship was even moving, were it not for the display. The vessels in the Embarker fleet made almost constant noise when sitting idle and a cacophony of creaks, groans, pops, screeches and hisses when flying at any sort of faster than light speed.

Electra leaned back in the white leather captain's chair, letting Ivy and the navigation computer guide the sleek pink-and-chrome vessel toward the blip on the screen. Flying, the only job on the Embarker fleet Electra had wanted to learn, was ninety-nine percent working with a navigation computer program to find the best possible numbers. The excitement of the hands-on one percent made the rest of the tedium bearable.

The derelict ship was almost two thousand years old, according to the hull signatures, and not easy to find until it passed out of the illumination field created by Persei IX star cluster. Electra tabbed through various scope settings on the long-range scanners. Aside from a few pockets, the nebula was almost impenetrable when the local star's radiation hit it. If she lost the floating wreckage in the dust, she wouldn't be able to find it again until after it circled back around to that same point. She had no idea how long that would take, but she assumed it wouldn't be in her lifetime.

"Find me an entry point, Ivy," Electra said when the ship came into view on the long-range scans. It looked like a silver edamame bean pod with a short tower on what Electra guessed to be the stern. For its age, the old girl didn't look too bad. "The nebula must have prevented a lot of bombardment from asteroids and space debris."

"The cargo hold doors are open a crack on the prow, Miss Electra."

"A big enough crack for us to slip through?"

"Barely, Miss Electra."

"Turn down the repulse engines so we don't knock all the crap off the shelves once we're through, and make sure you don't scratch the paint," Electra said. "I'll go suit up."

Electra headed down to the airlock elevator. Trying to run out the gangplank in the cargo hold might be impossible, depending on the clutter. The elevator could stop and let her off if the floor wasn't clear enough to make a complete drop, then she could float the rest of the way. She slid into the armored bio-suit she'd printed from Station 51's public fabricator terminal and locked down the fishbowl helmet. The ship had its own terminals to create items from recycled molecules, but they weren't nearly as fast at big jobs like an armored spacesuit.

"Do you require the lien tether?" Letterman asked.

"Nope, you're coming with me." Electra snagged the elevator control off the wall and guided the enforcement bot toward a red square on the floor of the airlock. "Take a deep breath and think happy thoughts." Before Letterman could reply, she hit the evacuate button on chute three and dropped him out of the bottom of the ship. A series of red flashes from terminals told her the ship was in lockdown and couldn't be moved until Letterman was back on board. The little ruse had been worth a try to see if Letterman was telling the truth about being able to lock her out of the ship's systems.

She considered the globauncher on the wall. It was more of a tool than a weapon, meant to launch balls of quick-expanding gel that would seal breaches with ten-foot by ten-foot bricks of glob. She'd heard it could also capture dangerous space junk and creepy-crawlies in a pinch. Every Embarker was trained in the use of one practically at birth, so any citizen of the flotilla could prevent a catastrophic hull breach wherever and whenever one occurred. Better to have it and not need it than need it and not have it, she decided.

Armed with her globauncher tube, she hopped onto the airlock elevator and descended into the derelict ship. She anticipated the sense of weightlessness when she passed out of the artificial gravity field created by the Cadillux, but the gravity never turned off. Letterman had landed a dozen feet away, creating a massive hole in the floor where she'd dropped him. He'd apparently had to climb out and she was a little sorry she'd missed seeing it. Letterman was her jailer, her warden and taskmaster in repayment of a debt that they both knew wasn't actually hers, and he didn't even have the manners to be apologetic for the lousy position she was in. His slavish devotion to enforcement etiquette and her inborn Embarker discomfort with owing combined to create a healthy disdain in Electra for the enforcement bot.

"Ivy, why am I not floating?"

"Sixty-seven percent of the derelict ship's gravitational cores are still functioning at better than eighty percent, Miss Electra," Ivy replied through the com in Electra's helmet. "You should have at least partial gravity through most of the ship."

"Bummer... I was looking forward to some floating," Electra said. "Come on, Letterman. Stop waxing the floors with your face. We have work to do."

"Damage to lien enforcement technology will be added to your outstanding balance," Letterman said as he followed Electra, illuminating their path with a bright flashlight on one of his tentacle arms.

"Are you damaged?"

"No."

"Then shut up."

Electra crept forward slowly through the derelict ship's cargo hold. She'd expected a ton of scrap and random junk floating around, but the whole place was picked clean. Some dust and crumbs floated through the beam of her flashlight in the warehouse-esque room, but nothing bigger than a fingernail. A green dot illuminated on the heads-up display of her helmet, provided by the link from Ivy and the scans done by the Cadillux's powerful scopes.

"That is most likely the Bort Pod, Miss Electra," Ivy said. "A faint electrical signature is coming from a metal-and-glass container at that location, and it is the only item of significant size in any unshielded room."

It would be great news if Ivy were correct, and Electra wouldn't have to do personal reconnaissance of the un-scan-able sections — poking around shielded rooms on a derelict ship was a great way to get radiation poisoning or, in rare instances, eaten by a hidden galactic beastie. Electra walked to the nearest wall and followed it to the right until she found a hallway that led in the vague direction of the glowing dot. Many of the panels on the walls had been removed, either by catastrophic decompression or an exceptionally deft salvaging team.

"I wonder what they were doing out here?" Electra mused.

"The predominant theory on galactic net deep space salvaging forums is that this was a colonizing ship from Mars sent to populate the Andromeda Galaxy, Miss Electra," Ivy said.

"Wait! This hunk of junk is an ancient human vessel?" Electra asked. "I thought we could do better than this." Humans had fallen a long way to become Embarkers in fleets of rust-bucket ships, but this was supposed to be from the pinnacle of human space exploration. It was a little disheartening to learn her species had never been particularly good at spacefaring.

Room after room, corridor after corridor turned up empty. Ivy wasn't kidding about the Bort Pod being the only item of significant size. It may have been the only item of *any* size. Judging from the torch burns in some places and pried metal in others, Electra decided it was an oft-picked-over husk that scavengers worked on whenever it floated into the scan-able range of the illumination field. Her initial hopes that there might be other valuables to grab beside the Bort Pod were dashed. She was way too late to the scavenge party for easy gains.

They entered a long room with low ceilings and several vacant mountings lined up along the floor. Letterman's light flashed over a lone pod left in the row and the green light on her heads-up display faded away. The mythical Bort Pod, twenty billion units, looked like a seven-foot long metal crate mounted onto a table.

"Okay, do your thing, Letterman."

"What is 'my thing', exactly?"

"Assist in the earning of money to pay the debt," Electra said. "Figure out how to get the Bort Pod off that table and carry it back to the ship so your preferred creditors can get their units and get off my back for another hundred and fifty hours. Why did you think I brought you?"

Letterman brushed past her to scan the Bort Pod, rolled to the other side, scanned some more and eventually tapped at a few points with a prodding arm. "There is a dedicated power source. It has kept the contents 'fresh', for lack of a better term, and maintained the mag-locks securing the pod to the bulkhead."

Electra wandered over and gave the table a light kick. "Must be why nobody was able to swipe it." Cutting out a chunk of bulkhead was well beyond what even the best-equipped salvagers could do. She chewed the inside of her cheek while she thought. "We can't just burn out the power supply, since I'm guessing what's inside needs to be in mint condition when I turn it over or there's no payout. Can you reroute the power for the freshness protocols to your own supply then cut the mag-locks off from the dedicated source?"

"It will take time," Letterman said.

"I guess I'll amuse myself staring at the walls while you work," Electra said.

"I have recorded you as the laziest Embarker in existence," Letterman said.

"I'm the *only* Embarker currently in existence, so I'm also the hardest working." Electra stuck her tongue out at him, accidentally licking the front of her fishbowl helmet in the process.

"A fleet of ten vessels is inbound, Miss Electra," Ivy said.

"What kinds of ships?"

"Raider signature, three brigs and seven skiffs, Miss Electra."

"Work fast, Letterman," Electra said. "I'll see what I can do about our visitors."

Electra walked the room quickly to count the doorways. Six in all, including the one they'd come through. At the opposite end from their entry point, and the farthest from the Bort Pod, she hit a low gravity zone and floated down toward the hallway. She righted herself by grabbing the door frame and pulling herself back into the room before she could get too far.

"Ivy, I need a layout," Electra said. "Are they boarding from the front or back?"

"Front, Miss Electra."

Electra thought for a moment. "Okay, I guess I don't know which end is the front. The one with the tower or the one we came in through?"

"The end with the tower, Miss Electra."

"Which doorway is the fastest route to where we are now from where they're coming in?"

"Illuminating it for you now."

Electra walked to the side door marked by the green dot on her Head-up Display and fired a glob into the black void. At the threshold for the door, the ball expanded into a large orange block of semi-solid gel.

"Okay, and which is the fastest way back to the Cadillux?"

"The one you came in through, Miss Electra."

"I'm lucky or good," Electra murmured. "Either way, I'll take it." She wandered among the rest of the doors, globbing them up one by one until she returned to the doorway with the gravitational dead zone. She decided against blocking it, but headed back to the doorway they'd entered through and blocked up that one. She could reopen the doors using the other end of the applicator tube. Flip the thing around, the glob ammo turned green and the shots dissolved the orange blocks into goop. She could only hope that whoever was on their way to swipe her salvage didn't have the foresight to bring their own launcher to take down her barriers. "Where are we on the Bort Pod, Letterman?"

"I have the power transfer complete," Letterman said. "Cutting the pod free now."

"Sweet, sweet, sweet," Electra chanted as she paced between her defenses, finally coming to stop before the blocked-off door Ivy had said was the fastest route for the boarding party. Lights flashed down the hallway, killing the weak hope Electra had that the scavengers weren't after the same prize she was. It had been a preposterous hope anyway. Ten ships wouldn't come all the way out the edge of the galaxy to chop up an old hull. That was the kind of fleet assembled to grab a twenty-billion-unit prize.

Question-mark-shaped reptilian aliens toddled down the hallway toward the glob block. Their bottom ends contained four toes pointed in four different directions to walk along while the opposite end contained the face with a wide mouth and tiny eyes. Splotchy gray skin with blue dots covered the rest, while belts bristling with weapons and tools were cinched in several places. Glott pirates… She'd heard of them from newsreels on the galactic net but had never actually met one. Glotts were common enough, but most of them were decent, industrious farmers and miners. The ones that turned pirate were peculiar, even in Glott society, and not often found in civilized space.

The Glott pirates gathered at the glob block in the doorway and poked at it while glaring at her. A large, almost albino Glott moved to the front of the group and bonked the orange block of gel several times with his head. Each smack sent a ripple through the surface.

"I am Sempa, Glott Raider Captain and Scourge of…" the large, albino Glott began.

"I'm Electra. Nice to meet you, Sempa. The Bort Pod is mine. Have a nice day!"

"I think I will have a nice day. Counteroffer, Electra," Sempa said. "Give me your ship, the Bort Pod, your money, become a pirate slave and we'll let you live."

"Wow, tempting, but I'm going to pass," Electra said. "A tip for future negotiations… Offer at least one outrageous thing the other side can say 'no' to easily, not a whole list of them."

"Find a way in, boys. Don't bother being gentle once you've got her." Sempa's men turned to begin searching other corridors while the Glott leader continued to glare at her through the gel. "I can see a doorway open from here, girl. Run out of glob?"

"I had enough to get the job done." Electra grinned when she saw Letterman loading the Bort Pod into his armored body cavity and sealing himself back up. "Gotta go. Lovely talking with you."

"My boys have the open door covered," Sempa said.

Electra turned back to the blocked door she'd come in through, turned the globauncher around and fired a green orb at it. The orange block immediately dissolved into murky, gray liquid and sloshed across the floor. "That should be fun for them."

She jogged ahead of Letterman and slipped in the gray sludge left by the dissolved glob, spoiling her otherwise slick-as-zero-friction-lube exit. Letterman scooped her off the floor and set her on her feet with one of his tentacle arms. When she glanced back before entering the hallway, she spotted the Glott pirates rushing blindly into the gravity dead zone. Without hands or a door frame to grab hold of, the pirates floated aimlessly, bouncing off one another until all their weapons started firing in waves.

"Whoops," Electra said, ducking behind Letterman when the bullets, missiles, lasers and flame bursts filled the room. "Are you damaged by any of that small-arms fire, Letterman?"

"Not in the slightest," Letterman said while they rushed down the hallway back toward the ship.

"I'm ambivalent about that news." Electra jumped, far too late to actually dodge the bullet that had ricocheted off the floor and Letterman's casing to skip off the wall to her right. Blind luck and one of Letterman's arms kept her from being hit. "On one hand, I don't want to pay for a scratched chassis. On the other hand, I'm essentially your prisoner, and if you were damaged beyond repair here, I could be free."

"The lockdown on the Cadillux becomes permanent if I am destroyed," Letterman said. "Another lien enforcement bot would have to be dispatched to this location to remove it and would not arrive before you were enslaved."

"I'm no longer ambivalent."

The elevator to the ship lowered on their approach. Electra waited for a lull in the barrage of lasers and projectiles to peek around Letterman's side. Once they were ready to be lifted, she fired a glob into the void of the doorway they'd come from. It would take a while for the pirates to blast their way through, and she didn't need much time.

"Keep the Bort Pod in your central storage," Electra told Letterman once they were aboard. "Protect that twenty billion units like..."

"I am a Lien Enforcement Technology..."

"I know you don't need to be told, but I'm telling you anyway, because stating the obvious to technology that doesn't care is something humans do."

She shed her helmet and suit along the way, hopping and bouncing off the walls awkwardly to try to reach the cockpit without slowing down to turn corners. From the last stair on the way up, she vaulted herself to land in the chair, spun back to the console, and readied the escape plan she'd formulated on the fly while running through a derelict ship to flee Glott pirates. The ship rotated to slide out of the crack in the doors. The engines powered up to full thrust. The repulse setting focused entirely front and back at max power. Then she punched it with the coordinates for the wormhole spawn ready to load the second she cleared the cargo hold. The Cadillux shot between the doors. She hit the activation for the full repulse engine thrust, which sent the Cadillux skittering forward even faster and spun the derelict ship into the waiting Glott pirate vessels.

"Ivy, power up all weapons and fire on the derelict ship," Electra said.

"*Whhhhiirrrrrring* noise, *pewpewpewpew, bzzzzzzzap, kaboom,* Miss Electra," Ivy said.

"This ship doesn't have weapons, does it?" Electra asked.

"No, Miss Electra."

"Someone programmed you to do that if anyone tried?"

"Yes, Miss Electra, at the factory where I was produced."

"Was that the first time you ever got to run that routine?"

"Yes, Miss Electra. None of the previous owners seemed unsure of whether a luxury vessel contained military grade weaponry or not."

Electra shrugged. It was pretty funny. *Nicely done, whoever wrote that little line of code into Ivy.* The coordinates for the wormhole spawn kicked in and the ship was gone before the pursuers could figure out what had happened.

Electra smiled at her shaking palms. *Adrenaline. So much lovely adrenaline.* That was the real flying she'd always wanted to do — the one percent of piloting work that made the drudgery and math worthwhile. It wasn't something they'd wanted to teach her on the Embarker fleet, but she'd managed to sneak in more than a few evasive maneuver modules while learning to fly.

"Tell me about Sempa, the Glott pirate, Ivy."

Ivy showed pictures, a couple newsreels, audio commentary from a documentary on alien subspecies and organized crime that was trying to prove Glott pirates weren't true Glotts. It was all pretty much what Electra had expected. He was a powerful-ish pirate of modest renown. The creditors breathing down her neck for their seventy-nine billion were far scarier and had a lot more reach in the form of a nearly impervious enforcement bot on her ship and an almost limitless army of collection drones and bots if she tried to run. Still, from what the galactic net said, Sempa seemed to hold a grudge, had a violent temper and she'd given him reasons to focus both on her. *Not the best outcome, but also not the worst.*

"You have made a dangerous enemy," Letterman said.

"I did, but the alternative of giving him everything I had and becoming a slave would prevent me from paying the debt you're enforcing. Shouldn't you be happy I didn't take the deal?" Electra asked.

Letterman stood unmoving for several seconds. "Carry on." He pivoted and spun back down the stairs and out of the cockpit.

Chapter Four

Getting to the Sol System took several long wormhole jumps on a narrow path only recently cleared for travel again. Signal markers along the way proclaimed the reopening of the Pilgrim Trail courtesy of the Chamber and Bi-MARP. Electra asked Ivy to run a search on Bi-MARP but no results returned.

The Pilgrim Trail was something Electra already knew about in theory. Sentimental humans from centuries past made the journey back to the Sol System to see the dead worlds that had spawned humanity. Earth had died before humans could be sponsored by the Appdurpins into spacefaring society. There were large colonies on Mars, a few inhabited stations orbiting Venus, a handful of holdouts on Luna and quite a few growing settlements on the moons of Jupiter when humanity was finally brought into the galactic society. Over the centuries, the Sol System faded, the colonies dwindled and humans became nomadic to take advantage of wealth and opportunities along more established trade routes. The Sol System hadn't had permanent human residents in almost six hundred years. People returned to the toxic surface of Earth to poke around for maudlin purposes on their pilgrimages, since the resources of the planet had been long since spent and nothing of actual value remained. The atmosphere was still highly acidic, and so even prepared pilgrims couldn't stay on the surface for long without risking life and limb. The Chamber had shut down the Pilgrim Trail decades before, citing safety concerns. With no humans, excepting herself, left to make the pilgrimage, reopening the route seemed like an odd move.

The wormhole spawn dropped the Cadillux on the star side of Neptune's orbit. The planetary guide on the star-chart said she'd have to wait in place for sixty or so years for the planet to make its way back around if she wanted to see it without chasing it down. She plugged in the most direct route to the Bi-MARP headquarters in orbit around Earth. On the straight line, she'd manage only a quick glance at Jupiter when she zipped past. The Sol System was the genesis point of her species, yet she didn't feel particularly compelled to see the sights. She was an Embarker, not an Earthling, and she wasn't schmaltzy about any of it.

Her curiosity lay in the mysteriously named Bi-MARP and what they might want with a Bort Pod. She planned on trying to stick around until they opened it to see what was inside. A special Earth plant or animal was her best guess, maybe corn or some fish.

The closer they got to the sun, the less Electra saw in the whole thing. It was a G-type main-sequence star, mostly white, but maybe a little yellow with some filters. All in all, it was pretty bright for a star its size, but nothing spectacular. She thought she should feel some sense of awe. She simply didn't.

On approach to Earth's orbit, she spotted hundreds of Jun'Tar construction rings working on a space station intended to encircle the entire planet like a high-orbit silver hula hoop. Electra chuckled and rolled her eyes. If the Chamber was entrusting the Jun'Tar with the Bi-MARP contract, they must not care if the job was done fast, cheap or well.

"This is Bi-MARP airspace control," a nasally voice said over the long-range communication array. "What business do you have in the Sol System, Cadillux 59?"

"This is Cadillux 59," Electra replied. "Inbound with a Bort Pod delivery to fulfill a Bi-MARP requisition contract." Under her breath, she added, "for twenty mother-fucking billion units."

"Airspace control transmitting landing coordinates."

"Do your thing with the coordinates, Ivy," Electra said on her way down the stairs out of the cockpit. "Don't get too comfy. I'm already sick of this graveyard."

"I'll keep the engines running, so to speak, Miss Electra," Ivy replied.

Electra banged her fist on the side of Letterman's armored body on her way past the enforcement bot. "Let's get paid."

While they waited for the docking sequence to complete, Electra swayed a little front to back, drummed her hands on the tops of her thighs and made popping noises with her mouth. Twenty billion units sat in the enforcement bot to her left and she wasn't going to get any of it. The whole thing made her itchy and anxious. The airlock doors slid open after three warning chimes. Two Jun'Tar security guards stood ready on the other side.

Jun'Tar were tall, nearly ten feet, but their height came almost entirely from the three slender bird legs, which pointed down from the hard, egg-like carapace of their body, which was roughly the size of a large watermelon. One hand and one eyestalk usually dangled about halfway down their height on the same slender limb-type as their legs. The security guards wore strange metal rings on their ashen spindle legs and orange helmets over their carapaces.

"Captain Electra Rex at your service," Electra said. It was a Chamber project. There was no reason to think she wouldn't get paid, yet she didn't like being there, not so near to Earth, and she couldn't name a single reason as to why.

"This way, Captain," the guard on the left said.

Electra followed the guards down the long, tall, exceedingly narrow hallway. Letterman struggled to keep up, barely fitting between the walls. Indeed, if Electra stretched her arms straight out to either side, she could place her palms flat against both walls and still have a little bend in her elbows. The fact that Letterman was scraping at every slight turn made her smile—big tough enforcement bot struggling because the walls were too close together.

Eventually the hallways opened up onto a large observation room. Earth was clearly visible outside the station. The planet was brown, dead, glowing in places from volcanic fissures and black in others for reasons Electra couldn't deduce. A Jun'Tar bureaucrat and an Appdurpin scientist approached, easily identifiable by the yellow fedora the Jun'Tar wore on top of his carapace and the white lab coat the Appdurpin sported.

"I am Cog 2, lead supervisor of Bi-MARP, and this is Doctor Baarqua, our resident human specialist," the Jun'Tar wearing the fedora said.

"I'm Captain Electra Rex, this is my assistant, Letterman and here is the Bort Pod you ordered." Electra banged her fist twice on the front of Letterman's core. Everyone waited expectantly. Nothing happened. "That means open up and give them the Bort Pod," Electra growled at Letterman.

"That was hardly made clear to me." Letterman opened up, all the same. "And I am *not* your assistant."

"You're assisting me in this, so technically you are," Electra said.

"I'm supervising your repayment of a debt, which makes me —" Letterman began.

"Middle management at best," Electra said, "and you're slowing down this whole process with your yammering."

Two Jun'Tar technicians rushed over with modified hand-trucks to accept delivery of the large metal container. Electra stared expectantly at Cog 2. She wasn't running a pod retrieval charity.

"This is most serendipitously unexpected," Dr. Baarqua said. "A marvelous happenstance."

Electra rolled her eyes. Appdurpins were bloviating doofuses as far as she was concerned. Appdurpins stood around nine feet tall and were covered in shaggy, bright blue fur, with three of almost everything — three eyes, three nostrils, three fingers per hand, three toes per foot, three nipples, etc., and they fancied themselves the experts on damn near everything, but most especially humans. They were apes, much like humans, which was probably the primary reason they had sponsored humanity all those years ago. The particular Appdurpin in question was looking at Electra, not the prized Bort Pod she'd brought. *Starstruck, most likely.* She was slightly famous among human-fanciers.

"What's Bi-MARP, anyway?" Electra asked as she meandered toward the Bort Pod and the technicians working to open it.

"Bi-Millennial Apocalypse Reconstruction Project," Cog 2 said, "a co-venture between the Chamber and the Jun'Tar Tri-Crown Construction Concern."

"Uh huh, but what does it do?" Electra asked, her eyes widening as the Bort Pod's shell opened a crack.

"We're reconstructing Earth according to the guidebooks," Cog 2 said.

The metal casing of the Bort Pod fell away to reveal an ancient cryo-stasis chamber with a glass door. A dark, fuzzy shape rested in suspended animation, encased in faintly blue ice. Electra let out her bated breath in a disappointed flapping of her lips.

"*Pff-ft*, it's just some weird ice," Electra said.

"Ice containing a perfectly healthy human male," Dr. Baarqua corrected her. "Bort Thompson of Mars."

Electra rushed over to the ice block and tried to peer into the milky surface to the hazy shape inside. "So, he's alive? A real person and not a 'for display only' type of thing?" She couldn't decide if her excitement was from maybe not being alone in the galaxy or if she wouldn't have to carry the burden of being the last human anymore.

"When we thaw him, yes," Cog 2 said.

"Yeah, that's worth twenty billion units or even more," Electra said. "Let's get him out and wake him up!"

"You're worth a substantially grander sum than that astounding amount to us," Dr. Baarqua said. "50 billion units if you will remain on the station."

"Say *what* now?" Electra asked.

"A breeding pair," Cog 2 said. "You and Bort shall be the mother and father of a new generation of humans. Before you answer, let me remind you this is a Chamber-sponsored project and we have the power of eminent domain to compel you to stay, even if you aren't swayed by the fifty billion units."

"Really? You mean it? I can become a fifty-billion-unit baby mill for you, with or without my consent?" Electra asked, dripping the words with sarcasm. "There are a couple problems." Electra walked toward Letterman first. She kicked the front door on his armored shell closed. "Problem one—this bulky bastard won't let me. I owe seventy-eight billion units and change. Even with the money for Bort and the extra for me to stay, I'm still short of paying my debts."

"The Cadillux and all items aboard could be liquidated to discharge the rest," Letterman unhelpfully offered.

"Marvelous!" Dr. Baarqua exclaimed.

"Problem two." Electra ran to the Bort Pod and swiped her hand across the front to clear the condensation that had gathered over Bort's nether region. "Me and the dude-cicle have the same genitals." She waved her hand grandly over her own package, prominently displayed by the Utopalex pants, and Bort's, which was even more obvious, due to his complete nudity.

"Is that a problem, Dr. Baarqua?" Cog 2 asked.

"I...I am unsure of the ramifications of such a revelation," Baarqua stammered.

"Let me break it down for you," Electra said. "Who came up with the price list for a human male at twenty billion but a human female at fifty billion?"

"The Chamber," Cog 2 said, "with our standard contractor markup percentages, of course."

"Of course, but you didn't stop to wonder why a female was worth more than twice as much?" Electra asked. When neither the bureaucrat nor alleged human expert could answer, she continued. "You have two producers of the cheaper part of the required equation for creating a human baby. The egg and womb are thirty billion units more valuable than the sperm."

"With markups," Cog 2 added.

"And you mean to edify us with that revelation because…?" Dr. Baarqua began.

"Keeping me here against my will and selling my ship to cover the rest of my debt won't get you any closer to creating a human baby, since he and I have the same piece of the reproductive puzzle. And, if I'm being completely honest, I'm not totally sure mine throws genetic material, so I may not even be worth the twenty billion that he is. Not every human is fertile or potent. Lot's of reproductive non-participants in my species."

"That does complicate things," Dr. Baarqua sighed.

"Problem the third," Electra said. "Two people can't make a viable population. Embarkers have known the minimal viable population for centuries. Anything under a hundred and sixty is going to fail."

"We know. We're more interested in the commercial draw of a baby," Cog 2 said. "Tourists love baby animals."

"Okay, that's a messed-up thing to do to a kid," Electra said. "Regardless, I can't carry a child, even if I wanted to, and I don't. But I found the Bort Pod and delivered it unscathed, didn't I? Maybe I can find a fertile human woman and talk her into going along with this whole forced breeding program. I could find other stuff too. I have a really good eye and nose and other sensory organs when it comes to old human junk." She didn't actually think she could, nor was she all that thrilled about selling out her species to settle a debt that wasn't hers, but she would tell them almost anything they wanted to hear if it meant leaving with her ship and freedom intact.

"There is a master list created by our scholars based on the guidebooks," Cog 2 said. "We've given it to a few select subcontractors already. One more might become problematic." Cog 2 produced a display laser from beneath his fedora and drew a green triangle in the air. "For you see, it's the classic contractor's triangle." He wrote 'fast', 'easy' and 'cheap' on the three points. "Jobs cannot be done fast, easy or cheap, so adding another independent collector to the roster could speed up the job, creating undue speed, which would result in unwanted cheapness when the contract finished ahead of schedule and under budget. Don't get me started on the ease that might result from your apparent skill."

"I'm positive that's not how a contractor's triangle is supposed to work," Electra said. It was typical Jun'Tar nonsense. Their entire society was built around inefficiency and waste. They built things but typically found a way to make it take forever and cost a fortune. Why the Chamber kept employing them was a mystery to almost everyone. Still, she thought she could use their love of inefficiency against them. "Um…oh! How about this… I already ran into one of your other collectors, Sempa, the Glott raider. We totally got in each other's way. It was a textbook example of too many people trying to do the same work and tripping over one another in the process."

"Labor redundancy!" Cog 2 said. "It is one of the pillars of good Jun'Tar contract management. Yes, you are right. More collectors should be added — as many as we can get until you're constantly stumbling over one another, grinding the whole process to a screeching halt."

"I remain skeptical of this designated course of action," Dr. Baarqua said.

"Dr. Baarqua, you're a human specialist, right? Who would be better suited to find Earth artifacts than an honest-to-goodness Earthling?" Electra said.

"You are not an Earthling. Earth-born humans have not existed in millennia," Letterman corrected her. "Bort is not even from Earth, and he is almost two thousand years older than you."

"Close enough, closer than you're going to get elsewhere," Electra said.

"Have you had the pleasure of poring over the guidebooks provided most generously by the Chamber?" Dr. Baarqua gestured grandly to a dusty old set of dark blue books locked away behind an impenetrable repulse field. "Behold the Encyclopedia Britannica, fourteenth edition, circa 1961."

"I can't say that I have, but I'd be super eager to try to read all those really dusty, really thick, really old books," Electra lied.

"Then I shall procure a digital copy and have it transmitted to your ship's computer posthaste!" Dr. Baarqua exclaimed. "Mr. Cog 2, I must insist, most vigorously, that this woman be employed by Bi-MARP."

"Again, we find ourselves in complete agreement, Dr. Baarqua," Cog 2 said. "Welcome to the team, Captain Rex." Cog 2 snapped to one of his assistants and pointed at Letterman. "Pay this woman's enforcement bot the twenty billion units she is owed."

A blue bar on the front of Letterman's core stretched less than a third of the way across the large, black display of her debt. At the end of the blue, a tiny sliver of red light appeared.

"What's the red?" Electra asked.

"That is an operational line of credit to continue your repayment work," Letterman said. "It must be paid back at ten percent variable interest compounded weekly."

"Great, a little red rope to further hang myself," Electra said.

"You are the great Captain Electra Rex, earthling and human expert, while I am lowly middle management," Letterman said. "Apparently, you're also willing to sell your fellow humans into a circus in exchange for a pink spaceship."

Electra knew Letterman was incapable of inflecting his voice to indicate any sort of emotion, but she recognized a cutting remark when she heard it and Letterman's words sliced straight to the bone. No, she wasn't sure she'd be able to do that, and she was increasingly unhappy about leaving Bort with Bi-MARP. She didn't know if she'd be able to help Bort, but she knew she couldn't if she became part of the menagerie.

Chapter Five

Against Dr. Baarqua's objections, Cog 2 had Bort Thompson thawed right then and there. Electra watched the conclusion of the Bort Pod retrieval job with a case of thoroughly jangled nerves. She'd already been paid and the contents of the pod were more or less known, but it could be a frozen corpse and she'd be back to being the last human. She'd already adopted and adored the idea that there was at least one other, and she didn't want that lovely, reassuring notion to thud dead on the floor at her feet.

The ice melted, warmed, conducted an electrical pulse to start Bort's senses again, then drained out of the bottom of the pod across the floor. Electra initially thought it was water, but it was too viscous to be water and it smelled funky, like slightly off milk or strong cheese.

Bort came around slowly and began to urinate involuntarily. The floor was already thick with the gross fluid that probably would have gone down a drain port on the original ship. Since the pod had been disconnected and flown a third of the way across the galaxy, the fluid drained straight onto the floor and mingled with the long-held contents of Bort's bladder. He finished peeing ages before his senses returned to him, which seemed fortunate to Electra. Knowingly peeing in front of a room full of aliens, a strange woman and an enforcement bot would probably be difficult for most men, and after sleeping for seventeen hundred years, Bort probably wasn't in charge of his need to urinate at the moment.

"I'm here," Bort mumbled. "The promised land of..." His eyes cleared and he got a look out the window at the planet he probably assumed was the destination point in the Andromeda Galaxy that he'd never reached. "Shii-it, why am I orbiting Earth?" He rubbed his eyes with his fists, blinked like he was waiting for the bleariness to clear and took another long look at Earth, possibly willing the planet to transform into something else. "It's worse. How is it even worse? Damn! Damn! Damn!" Bort stood around six feet tall with a slender build, short black hair and a ruddy, tan complexion.

Electra looked to Dr. Baarqua first, who stared blankly, then Cog 2, who...she didn't really know how to read Jun'Tar body language and they didn't have faces, so his inaction in that crucial moment stood as the only indication that he hadn't prepared anything to say after thawing Bort. *Bad planning all around.* Not that Electra had any helpful words, but she hadn't known what was in the pod until a few minutes ago. Not really enough time to write a, 'Hey, welcome back to reality, a bunch of shit has changed,' speech.

Bort sprang into action, apparently unconcerned by the other inhabitants of the room. First, he leaped back into the pod and frantically tried to close the lid. Either the Jun'Tar technicians had damaged the pod while opening it or the chamber was only meant to be used the one time, because the door flatly refused to close. He next rushed to the window and pounded on the glass with his fists, cursing people, governments, religious deities, himself and a name Electra suspected belonged to an ex-wife, based on context clues. Whoever Nitzi was, she had done some things Bort wasn't remotely ready to forgive, and he'd really counted on waking up in an entirely different galaxy than her.

Having a wet, angry, naked man rushing around a room in front of a hapless audience was easily the most awkward thing Electra had ever seen. Dr. Baarqua was first to avert his eyes from the uncomfortable spectacle. Soon the dozen or so Jun'Tar in attendance did the same. Electra wanted to follow their lead, but she couldn't. It was too compelling, too enthralling, too absurdly human. Impotent rage was just something humans had or did or were inherently prone to. In all her travels, the only other species she'd seen exhibit impotent rage was the Appdurpins, and it was extraordinarily rare. The emotional tempest that flowed from Bort was easily the most impotent of all rages in human history. She decided another human should bear witness to it, if only for the sake of posterity. He was almost two thousand years removed from his time, in the wrong galaxy, completely naked and there wasn't anything he could do about any of it. The shine wore off quickly, however, and she realized one of the two remaining humans should try to behave reasonably and she was far too frivolous for it to be her, so Bort needed to get his shit together.

"Stop it," Electra finally said. "You're embarrassing humanity and there aren't enough of us left for it to go unnoticed."

The statement, of course, made things worse — or might not have been understood, since she doubted Bort had a universal translator implant. Electra could only hope he hadn't understood her. He didn't know humans were on the brink of extinction or that he was the sole survivor of the ship he'd flown on. Finding that out by having it shouted at him by a complete stranger probably wasn't the best way to break the horrific news. Eventually, Dr. Baarqua produced a tranquilizer and Bort was sedated. They'd have to find a fabricator to get him clothes, as Jun'Tar only wore hats and Appdurpins didn't normally wear clothes at all. Dr. Baarqua was kind of an odd duck for donning a lab coat. Electra assumed he wore it as the eccentricity of a human expert working on a project to restore Earth.

After the head of Bi-MARP and the assigned human expert had allowed the thawing process to devolve into a grand display of public urination and impotent rage, Electra thought the least they could do was calm Bort, clean him up and give him a less chaotic environment to adjust to. She shot scolding glances at Cog 2 and Dr. Baarqua.

"Most unsatisfactory," Dr. Baarqua said, once the sedated Bort had been removed on a stretcher. "There is a prehistoric human proverb. *'We have thoroughly defecated in the slumbering apparatus.'*"

"Yes, yes you have done that," Electra said.

"This is not your kerfuffle to ameliorate, and you have already been compensated," Dr. Baarqua said. "It might be best if you took your leave."

"Now, wait a second," Electra argued. "I was hoping to talk to him some when he isn't so naked and angry."

"Perhaps later. For now, I have an admired colleague, a doctoral candidate to be precise, who has studied an astounding multitude of cultures through computer simulations," Dr. Baarqua said. "He has graciously offered to share his data with me, although he is justifiably concerned about transmitting it via the galactic network for fear it might be purloined by rival researchers. This is an item of immeasurable import to this project, and thus worth a vast quantity of compensatory units. I would implore you to dedicate yourself next to its delivery, as I feel many of the other collectors do not have genteel enough demeanors to interact fruitfully with academics and their delicate constitutions."

"Go get the data from your friend and bring it back without freaking out the scientist involved? Not a problem," Electra said. "Incidentally, what's the payout? I don't have my list yet."

"Nearly a billion standard units, nine hundred eighty million, for precision's sake," Dr. Baarqua said.

"For some saved files from a computer game?" Electra said. "Consider it done, Doc."

"You are so gracious, Captain," Dr. Baarqua said, letting out a long sigh of relief. "I trust I can count on your utmost discretion and decorum in this matter."

"Trust away. I've got this." Electra patted the good doctor on the arm and left smiling from ear to ear. With payouts like that for simple retrieval or delivery jobs, Bi-MARP could clear her debt in a few years or months instead of the several lifetimes that she'd feared it might take. "Take care of Bort, will you? He'll be lucky if his brain doesn't melt out of his ears while trying to wrap his head around...everything."

"I will proceed cautiously," Dr. Baarqua said. "As should you."

Chapter Six

Simulation data, an easy 'go there, come back, get paid' proposition. Apparently, Dr. Baarqua only knew the head scientist on the simulation project from some discussion board about historical versions of string theory or cheese-making or string-cheese-making theories. Electra had kind of tuned out the droning Appdurpin scientist during the details. She tuned out a lot of people, an invaluable skill in her old line of work as a professional party guest. She needed to work on that, especially when someone like Dr. Baarqua was trying to help her. He was boring and longwinded, but, unlike the party guests she used to listen to, he actually had valuable things to say, like what the scientist's name was. She hadn't been paying attention during that part.

White sands made of magnesium powder, purple oceans of liquid argon and peculiar electrical storms that Ivy said had to be avoided at all costs greeted Electra when the Cadillux descended through the atmosphere of the planet Amphiorae. The exterior temperature was in the negative range that would kill her instantly, so a walk on the beach wasn't in her future. The Amphio home world was lovely after a fashion, at least on the surface, but that was not where Electra was headed. A massive crystalline structure, smooth and intricate with the appearance of flowing despite standing perfectly still, registered on the head-up display as the target location. Electra guided her ship toward it, even as a section writhed out of the way to create an opening.

The Cadillux slowed upon entry, thumping its repulse engines off the walls and floor in pounding waves to keep the ship well away from anything solid enough to harm it while in atmospheric conditions. In space, the repulse engines created oppositional gravity forces to keep debris from hitting the hull, and largely had little to push against while flying through a vacuum to the point of being completely unnoticeable. Inside the tunnel leading under the argon oceans of Amphiorae, the engines created a thunderous noise and strange pressure waves that made the air wobble.

Eventually the tunnel opened into a massive subterranean chamber that still dripped with dark purple liquid. To either side of the cleared, crystalline landing pad, an ocean of liquid argon was held back by an unseen field.

Electra landed the ship on the illuminated platform within the ring of white lights that dimmed upon touchdown. The exterior temperature readings said that particular section was chilly, on the verge of uncomfortable, but not the freeze-all-the-liquids-in-her-body-instantaneously kind of cold the surface boasted. When the gangplank lowered, Letterman brandished the lien tether at her before she could step out of the door.

"No need for that," Electra said. "You're coming with me to assist in whatever I need assistance with. What would you call a bot designed to assist someone?"

"Uninterested in your attempts at goading," Letterman answered.

"So touchy," Electra teased. "Maybe you need a vacation."

Letterman switched out the tether clasp on the end of one of his arms with a stun gun of sorts. Electra wondered if he was wary or excited or annoyed or whatever at having to go with her. Letterman was too smart not to have an opinion, but enforcement bots didn't have expressive features or unshielded sensors to indicate mood. They were immune to flash attacks and emotional appeals — largely silent, always looming and unnervingly constant. In Letterman's specific case, also extra irritating.

At the edge of the platform, an Amphio scientist greeted them. The Amphio hovered in a purple globe of liquid argon contained by an invisible field emitted from a circle of white light emanating from the crystal floor. The sphere of purple liquid was a little wider than Electra's total arm span and twice as big as the Amphio floating inside.

"My name is Paul," said the glowing translucent cephalopod within the sphere. It wasn't an octopus or squid like the cephalopods on Earth described in the Encyclopedia Britannica, since it had dozens of tiny arms and no eyes, but still, it was pretty close to the pictures of octopi in the Bi-MARP guide.

"Nice to meet you, Paul," Electra said. "I'm Electra and this is Letterman, who is mostly here to annoy me. Mind if I ask…Paul?"

"My real name is a series of light flashes," Paul said. "It doesn't translate to auditory languages or galactic net message boards. I adopted the name of my favorite Beatle from the simulation I'm about to show you."

"Beetles are small insects," Electra said. "They're on the Bi-MARP list of things to collect. I don't suppose you know where some are?"

Paul guided Electra and Letterman into a soft, white tunnel. The air was chilly and very high in oxygen content as Electra's head began swimming and a vague sense of euphoria descended on her. She immediately recognized the feeling. High oxygen concentrations were a common way for many species to catch a buzz at parties. She wondered if that was Paul's intention or if he simply didn't know how much oxygen a human needed to breathe when he'd set up the chamber.

"Ah, a common misconception. It's a trick of spelling," Paul said. "I speak of a musical group called the Beatles, spelled differently than the insect. As for the creatures the band was somewhat named for, I'm afraid I do not know of any Earthling insect colonies, although the subject of these recent simulations is apparently not a fan of them or anything she deems a 'bug'. This dislike was a constant throughout all fifteen cycles—most fascinating."

Within the laboratory proper, several strange stasis chambers along the walls contained dozens of different test subjects from a wide variety of species, both extant and extinct. Each one was suspended in a globular sphere of cloudy white gel with several crystalline probes dipped in around the edges. When Paul floated past, a display of what was happening within the simulation projected onto the outer surface of the gelatin and slowed to a speed comprehensible to Electra, making her believe this was done for her benefit rather than just a standard function of the research apparatuses.

"This is highly impressive," Electra said, genuinely amazed by the setup, even if she didn't understand what possible use the data could serve. "When Dr. Baarqua said simulations, I assumed he meant computer programs running theoretical subjects through mazes or something."

"Thank you. A life's work collecting centuries' worth of sociological data from multiple species and I've nearly supported my dissertation adequately," Paul said.

"What is your hypothesis, if I may ask?" Letterman asked, surprising both Electra and Paul.

"That betrayal is a tool rendered most often unto the greater good," Paul said. "It's a counter theory to one of my academic rivals. He's a horse's ass, to borrow a popular term from the human simulations."

"So this isn't a Chamber-funded project?" Electra asked.

"Oh, my goodness, no." Paul floated to a stop outside a gelatin sphere containing a nude human woman barely visible within the murky suspension. "It's supported by private grants and public money from the university I attend. It is my sincerest hope that this discovery will finally allow me to complete my doctoral studies."

The display of the current portion of the simulation flashed into view on the outside of the stasis chamber. The woman within was painting an empty room a bright shade of green and listening to music on a radio propped in the open window. She looked to be a little taller than Electra and a great deal curvier. Her dark skin glistened with sweat in some places and displayed splatters of paint in others. Her ebony hair was held in dreadlocks, a common hairstyle among Embarkers. She swayed and hummed along to the music while dipping a paint roller in the pan then sloppily swiping it up and down the wall.

"She's beautiful," Electra said, her heart racing a little at the sight of the free-spirited, voluptuous woman. "What's her name?"

"Currently, she's Trish Miller, a Canadian graduate student of architecture at the University of British Columbia in Vancouver," Paul said. "She's had many names over the past three centuries, although they always started with a T. It helps ground organic subjects when transitioning from one simulation to another if they have an anchor in their name. This is her final simulation of fifteen, spanning different historic periods of human civilization. She's about to experience the great millennium scare of 2000. I'm most interested to see how she behaves when months of paranoia and fearmongering results in nothing significant happening."

"Wait! This isn't a hologram? She's real and she's three hundred years old?" Electra asked, enraptured by the video feed of the stunning woman caught alone in a mundane moment. She was seeing who Trish was when she wasn't being someone else for society. She was silly and haphazard, singing along to the radio, using the dripping paint roller as a microphone while she did a woefully inept job of painting the wall.

"Yes, but she thinks she's twenty-four," Paul said. "Physically, she's about right, at least for now. She was created centuries ago during the brief window when cloning of sentient life forms was allowed by the Chamber, at a monumental cost as well. My tentacles still ache from writing the grants required to secure that funding."

"What happens at the end of this simulation?" Letterman asked.

"It should complete in the next ten or so years, at which point all my subjects will be euthanized humanely and donated to the biosciences department for dissection," Paul said. "I made a deal with a friend in the mammalian division to donate any physical samples in exchange for being written onto a grant. I swear, that Amphio could summon funding from the depths with less than a quartet of flashes. Ahem, I'm sorry if that idiom doesn't translate particularly well."

"I got the gist." Electra's jaw clenched. The squid would kill a woman to get onto a research grant. The fact that Trish Miller was also worth fifty billion units only occurred to Electra in the moment after. Neither piece of information would sway Paul. Amphios were highly determined, not particularly interested in money beyond what it could accomplish and cared only for the scientific knowledge gained by study of lesser species, which they assumed was almost everything else. "The Earth data you promised Baarqua?"

"Ah, yes, of course." Paul waved a dozen or so of his tentacles toward a slot in the wall. A small disc of light on the floor guided a crystalline wafer and floated it to Electra's hand. She accepted the data and handed it off to Letterman, who immediately stored it within the armored cell of his body.

"Is it interesting stuff?" Electra asked. If Letterman hadn't stored it away so quickly, she might have liked to watch more of Trish Miller's life...except it wasn't her life. She hadn't actually had a life. Trish had been born in a jar, lived in a simulation and had probably never taken a real step. In a decade, she'd be chopped up for science without ever knowing what had been done to her. Electra hoped her façade didn't show how increasingly furious she had become.

"If you're fascinated by human trivialities the way Baarqua is, I suppose it could be," Paul said. "Truthfully, she's a disappointment for my research. In every simulation, she's resisted my prompts at betrayal. A combination of cunning, loyalty and self-sacrifice always thwarted my collection of useful data for my study. She'll be an outlier for my main dataset and thus not included in any final analysis beyond desperately trying to explain why she wouldn't cooperate."

"You're not even going to use her data?"

"Not if I can help it."

"Then you're going to kill her?"

"Euthanize, yes."

"So she can be dissected by a colleague to satisfy a promise made centuries ago in order to receive part of a grant?" That tore it. Trish Miller's greatest sin was being a profoundly good and decent person, which Electra certainly couldn't say of herself. The fact that she represented a third of the human population seemed only secondarily important to her scientifically supported nobility of spirit that would be snuffed out and forgotten for the sake of data continuity.

"You are a remarkable listener," Paul said. "Dr. Baarqua said you were completely inattentive."

"I have good news and bad news for you." Electra removed a globauncher ball from her jacket pocket and flicked it into the sphere of liquid argon surrounding Paul. Immediately the glob encased the globe in an orange rectangle. "The bad news... You're going to have to break your promise to the bioscience department. The good news? You have a useable datum for a human using betrayal for the greater good, because I'm human and I'm betraying you. I'm rescuing her because what you just described is messed-up behavior, even for an octopus sociologist."

"I am sure he is more than smart enough to have deduced all of that without your explanation," Letterman said. "However, I am impressed you used the word 'datum' correctly."

"Yeah, well, he wasn't smart enough to see that coming, so I didn't want to assume. Now shut up and get her out of there," Electra sniped.

"I wonder, is your rescue actually for the greater good or more likely the fifty-billion-unit reward?" Letterman's metallic tentacles dipped into the suspension gel, encircled Trish around every limb and waist, and pulled her free. The large front hatch on his body cavity opened and gently tucked her into the space that was more than large enough to hold the Bort Pod.

"She's... I'm... I haven't decided yet," Electra said. "Regardless of what I do with her after this, she deserves better than what was going to happen here, so this is a rescue either way. Any nuances beyond that are subjects best left to philosophers and will only matter if we escape, so let's get out of here."

"Your involvement in Bi-MARP cannot be altruistic if you hope to clear your debt," Letterman argued as he rolled swiftly to keep up.

"I know that—or maybe I don't believe it has to be. Whatever. You're not here to be my moral compass." Before they'd even made it halfway down the corridor back to the landing pad, the soft white lighting turned to a harsh, flashing green. "I'm guessing that's bad," Electra said, trying not to think about Letterman's definitive statement.

"I believe it is a security breach signal," Letterman said.

"That was fast," Electra said. "The goop holding the naked lady must have been rigged with an alarm."

"Letterman is correct, Miss Electra," Ivy said through Electra's com. "However, it is not lab security. It is a planetary level warning."

Electra ran, suspecting, but not knowing for sure, who'd caused the breach and what they were after. She raced up the gangplank with Letterman close on her heels. The flashing green lights in the chamber were becoming increasingly frantic.

"Make her comfortable in case she wakes up," Electra said when they parted ways in the main dining room. She bounded up the stairs two at a time to get to the cockpit.

"Incoming message, Miss Electra," Ivy said.

"Someone angry at me, I'd imagine," Electra said. "Patch it through."

"I've been working on my negotiation techniques," Sempa said over the com.

"Always good to expand your horizons," Electra said. "I can't really talk right now. I'm in the middle of a getaway."

"Getting away isn't going to be an option," Sempa said. "What you can do is give me your ship, your money and all the humans you have on board."

"I thought you said you were getting better at negotiating, and what makes you think I have humans on my ship?"

"Call it an ultimatum. The Bi-MARP news feed said you found a human in a derelict ship and said you were going to find more," Sempa said. "We followed you out of the Sol system and now you're making a pickup. I'm betting it is more of those hidden humans. I'll be taking any of those other frozen apes you've got tucked away too."

"I *am* a human," Electra said. "Do you even know what we look like?" There were pictures on the galactic net of humans, including several of Electra. The fact that Sempa hadn't bothered to look at any of them spoke of a pretty serious lack of skill or attention to detail on the pirate's part.

"I do now," Sempa said. "I guess I've got to decide if the units are worth turning you over or keeping you around for some payback."

"Give it some thought and get back to me." She hit the disconnect button on the primary console. "Ivy, how high can the repulse engines be turned up before they break the crystals or smash the ship on the rebound?" Electra started the ship, roared the engines to life with a stomp on the pedal and turned it in a quick arc to shoot up the tunnel they'd entered through.

"One hundred fifty-eight percent to sustain only minor damage to our hull, Miss Electra," Ivy said.

"How high to sustain none?"

"One hundred twenty percent, Miss Electra."

Electra turned them up to one hundred nineteen and a half then dialed it back again to one hundred eighteen percent. Repulse engine reverb couldn't be good for the paint, or the chrome, or... She dialed it back again to one hundred seventeen percent.

The ship was nearly to the end of the tunnel and the intense flashing green lights when a series of red flashes came zipping down the tube, exactly as Electra had suspected they would. Glott raider skiffs. Nice try, but they were too late and they weren't going to stop her. She slammed the pedal to the floor and shot up toward the much smaller skiffs. The mass and power of the Cadillux and its cranked-up repulse engines bounced the skiffs off the reverb before they could get their weapons targeted. In the rearview display, Electra caught the show of several of the skiffs colliding with one another and shattering while the others broke against the walls of the tunnel. Glotts were tough and immune to all but absolute zero temperatures. If she were a betting woman and had any money to wager with, she'd give long odds that any of them actually died in the crashes, although they probably weren't happy.

"Should have turned up your repulse engines, boys," Electra whispered triumphantly. She wanted to take full credit for a second ditching of the pirates, but she knew her success only lay partially in her skill and cunning. She had a much better ship than their clunky Glott vessels, and they'd massively underestimated her both times. Her luck might not stretch to a third time.

She broke free of the tunnel over the planet's turbulent surface. Sempa's larger ships were undoubtedly in high orbit, waiting for the skiffs to emerge with the cargo. Instead of climbing immediately, which would put her directly in the raider fleet's scopes, she zipped the Cadillux along the planet's surface, a mere hundred feet above the turbulent purple oceans and powdery white landmasses. It took every bit of her focus and an ample amount of assistance from Ivy to avoid the electrical storms until they crossed the equator and soared into open space from an entirely different hemisphere.

"Full scan on max range, Ivy," Electra said.

"No vessels on any scope, Miss Electra."

Electra let out a long, ragged sigh. "All in a day's work, eh, Ivy?"

"Our new guest is awake and battering Letterman with a shower curtain rod in the guest quarters, Miss Electra."

"I believe I'll have a coffee before dealing with that particular crisis," Electra said. "Lock in a course for Station 51." She'd already witnessed one human torn out of the time and space they understood and the resulting impotent rage. It was more awkward than interesting and she wasn't overly eager to see another case so soon.

* * * *

Electra made her way down to the guest quarters and followed the sound of Trish yelling at Letterman. The noise was muffled somewhat and she soon discovered why. A metal shower curtain rod lay in pieces on the floor around Letterman and the bathroom door was closed. Apparently, the curtain rod hadn't survived the duration of Electra's coffee break. She'd given it long odds anyway.

"I can't say I haven't thought about smacking you," Electra said.

"No damage was sustained," Letterman reported.

"Good for you," Electra said. "Get out of here before you make things worse."

Letterman pivoted and rolled out of the room. Electra closed the door behind him before tiptoeing to the bathroom door. She gently knocked.

"It's okay. The evil bot is gone," Electra said.

The door opened a crack. Electra tilted her head to make eye contact with Trish when she peered out. In the next second the door was opened wider, Trish grabbed her by the arm and dragged her in, then slammed the door once they were both safe inside.

"It tried to shove things into my brain." Trish pulled back her hair to show a tiny pin-prick hole in the bone behind her right ear.

"It's an implant," Electra said. "It translates most languages visually and audibly to the primary tongue spoken by the wearer so you can read and hear different languages. Still, he should have told you he was doing it. It's actually against the law not to have one."

"Against the law? But you're speaking English," Trish said. "So was the evil robot! Is this a government facility?"

"I'm speaking Embarker and he speaks bot-matrix," Electra said. "English is a dead language. A few Appdurpin historians might speak some, but who would even know if they were doing it right... I'm sorry. This is probably a lot to take in. Are you okay?"

"No, I'm not okay," Trish said. "I woke up naked with an octopus-refrigerator trying to bore into my skull. The last thing I remember was painting my new apartment. Now my hair is wrong, my feet feel weird and you're telling me English is a dead language."

"Yeah, that's probably all deeply confusing." Electra recognized the green silk robe Trish had found to don. It was a slinky number Weisella had worn. It looked much better on Trish. Truly, Electra didn't know women could look like Trish. Embarkers were the only humans she'd ever seen, and all the women were wiry, toughened boot leather. Trish was positively sumptuous by comparison, and Electra adored sumptuous things.

"You can't just comb out dreadlocks, so they must have grown out," Trish continued. "How long have I been asleep?"

"That's actually a more complex question than you might think." Electra gently stroked the dark, frizzy mass of Trish's hair. It was so soft and light, supporting almost all of its own weight in a fluffy, dark cloud around her head. "It's beautiful, by the way," she said. "As for the rest, I can get you clothes if you'd like more than a robe and make your hair look however you want it to."

"You're not supposed to touch a Black woman's hair without asking," Trish said, although she didn't pull away.

"Sorry." Electra yanked back her hand and wondered what ancient, noble society she'd inadvertently insulted.

"Are you one of *them*?"

"One of who?"

"Whoever sent that robot."

"No, I'm definitely not with the Lien Enforcement Agency or Letterman," Electra said. "He's an asshole and I would love to get him off my ship and never see him again."

"Lien Enforcement… He's like a loan shark?"

"I don't know what that is, so, maybe?"

"Wait! We're on a ship?"

"A spaceship, yes," Electra said.

"Then why is there gravity?"

"It's artificial — something to do with magnets and a bunch of nickel somewhere in the core or something. I really don't understand the science behind it," Electra said. "I can turn it off for a while if you want. It makes a huge mess, but it's a lot of fun."

"No, I'm okay for now," Trish said. "Maybe just some clothes."

Electra took Trish's hand and guided her out of the bathroom. In the hallway, Trish whipped her head around, clearly trying to find Letterman, who had blessedly gone far enough away not to be seen. Electra ushered Trish over to the fabricator console on the wall.

"Tap the options you want," Electra said, "and they'll come out of the slot here when they're done printing."

Trish stood in front of the console and furrowed her brow at the display screen. "It's in English."

"It's actually in Panaese," Electra said. "Your implant lets you see it in English."

"I've never heard of Panaese," Trish said. "How do I know you're telling the truth?"

"I could yank your implant out with a huge magnet and let you try to read it," Electra said. When Trish took a precautionary step back, Electra tried to smile to sell her joke. "I'm kidding. They don't come out." From the horrified look on Trish's face, Electra could tell her attempt at humor hadn't helped, and she vowed internally not to touch hair or make jokes until she knew where the social lines were.

Trish shook her head and returned to the terminal. She tapped the icon for pants with her index finger, resulting in nearly forty-four million options returned. She tapped the color option of black. The number ticked down a few, but remained well above forty million.

"It can make almost any pants in almost any color, so that's not going to narrow your options much." Electra reached past Trish to hit the biped icon. "You're going to want bipedal, unless you've got legs I don't know about."

"Okay, too much at once." Trish stepped back from the console.

"Yeah, that's a lot to sort through if you don't have something specific in mind," Electra said. "How about we get your hair done?"

"I shaved my legs this morning and now they're hairy," Trish said, allowing herself to be guided by Electra. "Have I been asleep?"

"Sort of."

"For how long?"

"Three hundred years, give or take."

"So, it's 2299?"

"A little later than that," Electra said. "By your measurement of time... Ivy, what year would it be on Earth according to the Canadian calendar?"

"The year 4211, springtime I believe, Miss Electra."

"Who is that British lady?" Trish whipped her head around to locate the source of Ivy's voice.

"That's the ship's virtual intelligence," Electra said. "She's an advanced computer program, not a person."

"Is everyone I know dead or were others grabbed and put to sleep too?"

Electra scrunched her nose, trying to decide how to explain things. "No, not exactly, on either question, but that's only because they probably never existed."

"What is that supposed to mean?" Trish demanded. "Who are you, anyway?"

"I'm Electra Rex, starship captain and treasure hunter extraordinaire," Electra exaggerated. "Freelance, of course. I'm my own woman."

"I'm Trish Miller," Trish said.

"I know," Electra said. "But please don't make me call you that. Trish doesn't translate correctly and it sounds like the Gromphra word for a beast of burden's unwashed scrotum. Is there literally anything else I could call you?"

"What about Treasure? It's my DJ name," Trish said.

"Treasure... That's perfect." Electra guided Treasure to the side of the Spatronic pod. "Treasure, let me introduce you to heaven. It's the most advanced grooming, pampering, wonder-inducing machine ever created, and you're free to use it as much as you like."

"It looks like a weird tanning bed," Treasure said.

"What's a tanning bed?"

"It makes you tanner."

"That's an odd thing for a bed to do, but whatever. I'm sure it could turn you tan or blue or whatever other color you might fancy," Electra said. "Here... I'll set up things for you. There are fifty thousand available profile slots, and I've only used about a hundred of them. You had dreadlocks before. Do you want those back?"

"Yes, please," Treasure said. "And I don't want to be blue."

"No skin dyes, gotcha," Electra said. "Body hair? Makeup? Teeth cleaning? Any preferences on those?"

"Sure, all or none or whatever," Treasure said. "Why am I monumentally valuable?"

"Um…because your name is Treasure, and treasure is inherently valuable?" Electra stalled.

"The huge robot, Letterman, he said I was monumentally valuable and so I had to be within regulations for sentient species."

"Blabbermouth, bastard bot…" Electra grumbled while she copied over the base preferences from her primary profile, swapping out the hair styling to dreadlocks and adjusting the makeup to scanned matching rather than her personalized choices. "Because you're one of three humans left in known space and you're a woman…" Electra said, only realizing her potential mistake partway through the answer. She guided Treasure to recline inside the Spatronic and tried to change the subject. "The process works better if you're nude, for a lot of obvious reasons."

Treasure handed out the robe once she was inside. "But you're a woman" — her eyes went wide when she looked at Electra from the lower angle — "with a dick."

"That would be a noticeable difference between me and you," Electra said, shutting the lid on Treasure. "Pun intended, maybe. Have fun in there!"

Electra walked away cursing Letterman's bungling, her own lack of planning in the impulsive heist and the fuzzy feeling in her brain caused by being around Treasure. It didn't matter. None of it mattered. A fifty percent increase in the human population was sitting inside the Spatronic getting the beauty treatment of a lifetime. That was all that mattered. She no longer had

to carry the mantle of humankind after finding Bort—
or womankind after finding Treasure.

"Miss Electra, there are two ships on long range
scanners at this system's wormhole spawn point," Ivy
said.

"Full stop, Ivy, stop, stop, stop!" Electra ran for the
cockpit, nearly colliding with Letterman on the way. "I
need to yell at you later, you careless bucket of..." She
was in the captain's chair before she could figure out
how to finish the insult hurled at Letterman, and he
was too far away to hear it anymore anyway.

The scans displayed two Glott raider vessels that
looked like a series of triangles overlapping each other.
They were smaller and faster than the brig Sempa
captained, but larger and more dangerous than the
dart-like skiffs she'd barreled past in the tunnel. The
Glott pirate captain had covered all the angles. Maybe
he didn't entirely suck at his job. There wasn't another
wormhole spawn point anywhere in the system. It
would take weeks to use the FTL engines to get to
another one and cost a fortune in fuel—if Letterman
would even allow that, considering she'd blow well
past the default point on her debt repayments.

"Shit, shit, shit," Electra muttered while she thought.

"If I may, Miss Electra," Ivy said. "They cannot
destroy your ship at this point."

"You're right! Sempa knows I have at least one
human on board now, if he believed me when I said I
was human, and he thinks I have several others,"
Electra agreed. "His crew wouldn't risk blowing up
tens of billions of units to block a wormhole. How fast
can we go while still getting the wormhole open in
time?"

"Possibly fast enough to prevent a magno-snare from latching on, Miss Electra," Ivy said. "Would you like me to calculate the probabilities?"

"No time."

"I can run the numbers in less than fifteen nanoseconds, Miss Electra."

"That's too long. Turn the repulse engines to max and go as fast as possible," Electra said. "If they want Treasure, they're going to have to catch me first." Electra plotted out five more wormhole spawns along a winding route that she could get to easily after passing from one. If they were going to take her, it wouldn't even be in the same quadrant of the galaxy.

She stomped the acceleration pedal to the floor and charged the wormhole spawn. The two Glott raider vessels stood ready for her approach but didn't appear to anticipate her speed. The swirling gateway opened, and two glowing blue beams emanated from the ships. One caught partially, but the Cadillux broke free and shot into the tunnel of the temporal fold.

"They've followed us through, Miss Electra," Ivy said.

"I figured they might." Electra banked hard, dove through the new zone they'd emerged into and sped toward the next wormhole spawn she'd plotted. It might take several jumps to get a large enough lead on them for what she intended. She was faster than the raider vessels in straight-ahead speed. She had to be, otherwise what was the point of the Cadillux's huge engines? Plus, the pirates probably weren't in debt up to their eyeballs to pay for their ships. Desperation and quality alone had to give her an insurmountable advantage — or so she hoped.

The next wormhole opened a split second before the Cadillux shot through. Blue beams from the raider vessels tried to catch her at the rim of the rift, but she was already safely inside the swirling temporal tube before they connected. The third open sector had three wormhole spawns near each other. She sped toward the farthest in hopes of putting enough distance between them for her gambit. The blue beams were well behind by the time she made the portal.

Immediately on the other side of the wormhole, Electra slammed on the brakes, pulled directly up and spun around to head straight back down. The two raider vessels emerged from the wormhole. She shot between them. The repulse engines bounced off the repulse fields sent out by the smaller raider vessels and sent both ships spiraling off in opposite directions. Electra pulled up just in time to slip into the wormhole they'd exited before it closed.

On the other side, she jumped into the second wormhole spawn, into another and another before she was satisfied that the empty scans were accurate, that she'd truly lost the raiders. Only then did she plot a new course to Station 51 by hand—a long, rambling route that no sane starship captain would bother taking.

"That course will take fifteen hours, Miss Electra," Ivy complained. "Please allow me to plot a less circuitous route."

"Don't touch it or skip on the circular detours." Electra reclined and let out a long, ragged sigh, pressing the heels of her palms against her closed eyes. That particular bit of piloting had induced far more terror than she should have liked and not nearly enough adrenaline. If nothing else, she'd need the fifteen hours to regain her stomach for high-risk flying.

"I didn't catch all of what just happened," Treasure said from behind the captain's chair, "but it seems like I might owe you."

Electra spun in the chair to look at Treasure. Her black hair was in the beautiful, long tendrils of dreadlocks again, her mocha skin gleamed and her curves swelled the front and sides of the green silk robe in alluring ways. The fuzzy feeling in her head redoubled and a stirring between her legs told her that her brain wasn't the only part struggling with the situation.

"Do you like coffee and donuts?" Electra asked.

Chapter Seven

There wasn't much on the galactic net to help Treasure understand where she'd come from. A random Amphio doctoral candidate conducting low-level sociological research didn't get a lot of press, leaving Electra to fill in the massive gaps with whatever help Ivy could provide. Treasure finally abandoned the notion that she might be dreaming but held on to the suspicion that she might be in a secret government experiment like in one of the comic books she enjoyed. Something about an adamantium skeleton and the Yukon... Electra didn't follow any of Treasure's cultural references, and she used a lot of them. That theory dwindled quickly the more advanced technology Electra showed her.

"From what Paul said, I think you're a clone," Electra began.

"Like Dolly the sheep?"

"Maybe?"

"A clone of who?" Treasure asked.

"He didn't specify."

"The cloning facility used by most bioresearch firms was created and later disbanded by the Chamber, Miss Electra," Ivy explained. "The clones used in Paul's research appear to have originated from there."

"The Chamber is the government?" Treasure asked.

"More or less," Electra said. "Planets and regions have their own officials, but the Chamber is in charge of all the big stuff and a lot of the little things. They created the implant that translates everything. It was part of their galactic peace initiative from a million years ago or something."

"Seventeen hundred ninety-one years ago, Miss Electra."

"Galactic peace," Treasure snorted.

Electra grinned and shrugged.

"Seriously?"

"I mean, it's not perfect, but large-scale wars don't happen anymore," Electra said.

"So the Chamber is a good thing?"

"Yeah, kinda, sorta, I guess. They're more of a neutral thing that is productive on some things and absent on others," Electra said. "Once they got the galaxy running smoothly, they've mostly tinkered. It's been a long time since they did anything huge like galactic peace. For example, the cloning facility you came from was outlawed long before I was born and may not have accomplished much. Ivy, how long was the cloning facility even open?"

"Nine years, two months and eleven days, Miss Electra," Ivy said. "Earth standard time scale for Miss Treasure's benefit."

"See? Like that," Electra said. "They thought cloning of sentient species was a good idea for less than a decade, changed their minds and pulled the plug. Or maybe they figured out that the galaxy only needed nine years of sentient cloning for some other master plan they understand but aren't telling anyone about. Most of what they do now doesn't have a huge net effect that anyone can deduce. Stuff just works."

"But where do they come from?" Treasure asked.

"No clue."

"Who are they?"

"Haven't the foggiest."

"Where do they live?"

Electra shrugged.

"Ivy, do you know the answers?" Treasure asked, looking up.

"You don't have to look up," Electra said. "That's the closest speaker to you, but her sensors are all around."

"Miss Electra's glib statements and noncommittal gestures are largely correct in what is known for certain regarding the Chamber," Ivy said. "Any further information I could provide would be minutia fit only for esoteric musings and discussions on galactic net forums. Would you like the minutia, Miss Treasure? There are over five million pages of theory available on the galactic net attempting to explain the nature of the Chamber."

"No, thank you," Treasure said.

"It's a lot to take in, but there are some easy things to hang on to," Electra said.

"Earth is gone."

"Yes, but we're trying to fix it."

"People are gone."

"Most of us, yeah," Electra said. "As far as I know, it's you, me and a guy named Bort from Mars. You'll meet him later. He's... I don't know him really, but he seems adventurous, maybe?"

"Bort?" Treasure asked.

"I pulled him off a derelict ship a little bit ago," Electra said. "He's waiting on a station in orbit around Earth to get the whole rebuilding thing going."

"And you're trying to help?"

Electra smiled as best she could. "Yep." It wasn't a pure lie. She was helping for money, but she figured she was doing a pretty good job considering she'd found two humans already when there weren't supposed to be any.

"If I was made in a lab, couldn't they just make more of me?" Treasure asked.

"As much as I might like having a bunch of you running around, I don't think that'll work. Short answer? No. Long answer? Maybe, but it'd require a reliable source of diverse DNA, an astronomical amount of money and for the Chamber to change their mind about outlawing sentient species cloning," Electra said. "At the moment, we've got none of those things."

"Okay, and what am I supposed to be doing?"

"Honestly, whatever you feel like at the moment," Electra said with a shrug. "Taking you out of the lab wasn't part of anyone's plan, nobody is expecting you anywhere and I'm not sure you're even officially supposed to exist. For the moment, try to relax and get your bearings." Again, it was all mostly true, since half-truths were as familiar to Electra as breathing. Primarily, she was wondering if she'd made a mistake in taking it on faith that she was the last human, simply because everyone seemed to believe she was.

For the remaining lengthy hours of the scatterbrained trip to Station 51, designed to perfection by Electra to hopefully thwart pirate pursuit, Treasure explored the ship a little, but mostly sat with Ivy, wandering the galactic net, trying to wrap her head around the enormity of her new situation.

Electra napped, spent time in the Spatronic and had small, but mostly manageable, anxiety attacks about how much money she still owed, the pirates chasing her and the fact that she was lying to Treasure an awful lot for someone she'd just met. Electra had a fifty-billion-unit commodity onboard her ship, which almost anyone would kill to get. That was stressful. The commodity was a person—a really nice, intelligent, adorable person—and that meant if Electra were to turn in the commodity for the money, she would knowingly be selling a person, which was beyond messed up. Sure, she'd fetched, delivered and sold the Bort Pod, but she hadn't known that it contained a guy, and she was starting to think that information had been withheld on purpose. Her single, barely believable, rationalization to ameliorate the guilt was that she'd rescued Bort from a much worse situation to deliver him to a better life, and that was what she told herself she was being paid for. If she didn't think too hard about it, the justification served as validation for the otherwise-despicable thing she'd unknowingly done.

But that didn't work for Treasure. Rescuing someone from dissection was an almost unimaginably easy and benevolent choice to make. Selling said rescued person into a form of slavery would definitely be so evil that any other action would be irrelevant. *No, fuck it, fuck no.* Treasure stayed unless she chose to become part of Bi-MARP of her own free will, at which point the money would be Treasure's to do with as she wished. Electra couldn't become the type of person who would do such a thing, not even for fifty billion units. The fact that Bi-MARP wanted a potentially forced breeding program for tourism purposes was such a trivial secondary ethical conundrum that Electra threw it in with the 'not selling a person' thing as simply something she wouldn't knowingly do.

Electra knew she wasn't a good Embarker or even a decent person most of the time. She was lazy, careless, overly sexual, indulged in too many drugs too often, a little greedy and spent almost all of her time on frivolous pursuits like pleasure and comfort. If her Embarker parents could see what their daughter had become, they would never stop throwing up from rage and embarrassment. But they couldn't see her, and that was what had made her lifestyle to that point seem okay. That had all changed when Treasure had come on board. She could see, judge and know that Electra wasn't great, not even good, barely okay at times. And that was scary.

"We've arrived, Miss Electra," Ivy's most soothing intonation said, snapping Electra out of her intense, internal moralistic debate.

Electra always came back to reality poorly, no matter how long she'd been gone. The lights in the bedroom rose at a reasonable pace to keep track of sensitivity in her eyes. She loved the Cadillux and was beginning to believe the ship loved her back. It got her in a way no person or item ever had.

"Miss Treasure would like to speak with you," Ivy said.

Electra swung her legs over the edge of the bed and pulled herself into a sitting position to slide on her

Utopalex pants. "Yeah, okay, send her in." She fumbled around the bedding for her shirt. It was a black shirt in an entirely white room. Finding it should have been much easier than it proved to be.

The wall slid away and Treasure walked in, dressed in a green-and-tan plaid flannel shirt and baggy blue jeans. She'd clearly figured out how to use the fabricator — or maybe she hadn't. The clothes looked painfully drab and scratchy to Electra.

"You're topless." Treasure quickly turned to avert her eyes.

"My shirt is being elusive in ways that don't make sense," Electra said, finally locating it. "Why does that matter?"

"Because…modesty," Treasure said. "I barely know you and you barely know me."

"I'm in my own bedroom," Electra said. "Besides, this is way more than most people wear to the beach. In fact, most aliens don't even wear clothes. I do because they're pretty, they keep me warm and Utopalex feels amazing."

"Your breasts…"

"Won't bite, I promise." Electra rolled her eyes and pulled her shirt on. "Better?"

"No, I didn't mind, I guess. I meant they look so real…and nice." Treasure smiled a little, caught herself in the act and tried to hide it with a vague headshake.

"They are real," Electra said. "You've seen my Spatronic. No crap-o holograms required to make the twins looks perky."

"But like *real* real."

Electra grabbed her breasts, one to each hand, and gave them a playful jiggle. "Yep. I'm not really following. Is there another not-really-real option I'm unaware of?"

"Not implants?"

"Like biosynthetic implants? Everyone has some of those," Electra said. "My hormones come from them. Little grain of rice things attached to my ribcage on the inside. I've got some spiffy new eye lenses that allow the Spatronic or any ocular affixed terminal to change the color of the iris and adjust the light spectrum I can see in. Most of the spectrums outside the normal visual range give me a headache, so that turned out to be pretty useless. There's the standard audio-visual universal translator, but you have one of those too. I have a radiation conversion node. We need to get one of those for you, by the way, if you're going to do much space travel. Radiation sickness is such a pain in the ass to kick. But external appearance mods never really appealed to me."

"So you grew those breasts yourself?"

"Uh-huh. Not consciously of course, but how else would I get them?" Electra quirked an eyebrow. "Did you not grow yours?" Electra realized only after asking that it was a silly question. All of Treasure had been grown in a lab. "Yours are really nice too. Is that okay to say? You complimented mine, so…"

"Thank you. It's fine to say, I suppose. I did grow my own, but you…" Treasure stopped to consider her words carefully. "Back from my time, there was a surgery to put liquid-filled implants into women's chests to give them breasts. Men who became women had to do this to have them."

"I wasn't a man, and that surgery sounds super unpleasant," Electra said.

"I think it probably was unpleasant. What were you?"

"An un-transitioned woman," Electra said, trying to think of some time-appropriate analogies from the Encyclopedia Britannica to help Treasure understand. "Like a caterpillar isn't a worm. It's an un-transitioned butterfly. A pollywog isn't a fish. It's an almost-frog. A face clinger isn't a parasite. It's a rampaging carnivore xenomorph that hasn't chest-burst yet."

"Those are real?" Treasure's eyes went wide.

"No, but I had you going," Electra said. "Aren't old Earth movies great?"

When Treasure didn't join her in the reminiscing about ancient Earthling cinema, Electra sighed, walked to the door with her and guided her down the hallway toward the exit hatch that led to the gangplank. Donuts and coffee would fix everything. The confusion cut both ways. It wasn't like Electra could understand people who prized modesty so much that they wore boring, itchy clothes to cover up everything. And the liquid-filled bags for breasts? It all sounded so barbaric and uncomfortable. To call an un-transitioned woman a man was simply wacky. In the most clumsy, backward way of speaking, she could at best have been a boy to start her life who grew up to be a woman after the age of thirteen. She'd never been a man, and even if she'd been called a boy at one point, the ultimate gender of a child couldn't be determined by simply looking at them.

Treasure received another visible shock when they walked down into the massive freighter hangar. Ships of all shapes and sizes taxied after landing or before taking off. Gromphra maintenance crews scurried to clean stuff, fill other stuff, charge customers for purchased stuff and probably sell drugs, guns and other illegal stuff on the side. It was glorious commerce running at breakneck speeds to turn 'stuff' into money.

"There are giant cockroaches everywhere!" Treasure shrieked, right in Electra's ear.

"What? No, those are Gromphra," Electra said. "They are everywhere, though. You're right about that. Any planet you go to with any sort of economy has at least some, and space stations? Forget it. Every space station is crawling with them, even if they aren't immediately visible."

"They're safe to be around?" Treasure asked, allowing herself to be led away from the ship.

"More or less. Don't talk to them or make eye contact unless you're interested in forceful flirting. They're lecherous and aggressively sexual."

"They'll rape you if you look at them?" Treasure asked.

"No, no, nothing like that. They're all sterile females," Electra said. "They're born in one big explosion from their home world every once in a great while, and each generation goes out to make money and gather crap to send back. The older generations are called 'uncle' by any group that comes after and the younger generations are called 'niece' by any group that came before."

"How do you know they're female?" Treasure practically jumped out of her skin when one of the eight-foot-long bugs scrambled past her to get to a docked freighter's clogged intake valve.

"I've never seen a male, but I've heard they look like floating balloons with a bunch of strings dangling off them," Electra said. "The strings are penises. The male Gromphra don't live long and they never leave the home world. Plus, I don't think they're able to talk. Too many penises to fit a mouth... That came out wrong."

Treasure stopped dead in her tracks, forcing Electra to come back. "Does that sign say what I think it says?"

"Tim Hortons?"

"Yes! That's from my time!" Treasure screamed and bounced around a little bit. "It makes no sense for it to be in a place like this, but there it is. I got my coffee from Tim's every day for years. I'm pretty sure I'm dreaming now or in a weird simulation."

"I pulled you out of the simulation, remember?"

"Then the galaxy is being cooler to me than I thought it was going to be."

"Yeah, I'm kind of feeling that way myself right now." Electra smiled to Treasure and blushed when Treasure smiled back. "And now you can get your coffee and bits, but only if we move. We're standing right in a taxiing zone and we're going to get squished if we don't clear out." Electra took Treasure by the hand and led a far more eager and comfortable companion into the familiar confines of the donut and coffee shop.

"If I had eyes to disbelieve, I would disbelieve them," Om said when they walked in. "That is only the second human I've seen in years, and she's attached to your hand."

Electra eagerly led Treasure up to the counter. "Om, this is Treasure. Treasure, this is the all-knowing, all-seeing, all-pouring, all-donuting Om."

"Electra is exaggerating my abilities to know, see and pour, but she's correct about my ability to donut," Om said.

"It's nice to meet you," Treasure said, cocking her head in one direction then the other, likely trying to figure out where she was supposed to look to make eye contact with the swirling mass of rocks.

"Just look at the glow in the middle," Electra whispered to her. "Om doesn't have a face in any way we can comprehend."

"This has to put you over the top or close to it," Om said.

Electra loudly cleared her throat and flared her eyes. "It does... A free small coffee. The punch card is all full." Electra slid a half-punched card quickly across the counter. If Treasure knew her value to Bi-MARP and the extent of Electra's debts, being trusted would be pretty much impossible, and Electra deeply wanted to be liked, admired and trusted by Treasure.

"I see," Om said. "Coffee and bits for you both?"

"Timbits? They're here?" Treasure asked.

"Here and at our other seventeen thousand locations across the galaxy," Om said. "I'll get you a souvenir menu map."

Om delivered their order of coffee and donut holes on a tray. Electra thought she felt them watching her as they walked away, judging her, seeing the deceptions she must have enacted. They slid into a booth by the window and quietly picked apart the glazed bits of donuts. Electra actively averted her gaze from anywhere near Om, considering she didn't precisely know where their eyes were or if they even had them, but she assumed they'd be judgmental eyes.

"Where'd you learn to fly?" Treasure asked. "I get the feeling you're good at it, based on what you did back there."

"I was training to be a pilot in my Embarker flotilla before...before everything."

"Embarkers?"

"It used to be a big, mostly human society thing — lots of caravans, fleets, flotillas filled with laborers who lived on their ships and roamed around working jobs like mining, farming and construction," Electra said. "By the time I was born, our flotilla was the last one. My parents figured out I was meant to transition, so they found a place for me to do it since the flotilla didn't have very good facilities for that sort of thing. They sent me away, using most of their savings for the deposit. A year later, the flotilla took a job mining asteroids in a belt around a red dwarf on the rough outer edge of the Scutum-Centaurus arm of the Milky Way. A strange kind of radiation started making everyone sick. Ships were lost from lack of able hands. Within a couple of weeks, the whole fleet was dead. The mining company went bankrupt. All that remains of the last Embarker flotilla are few thousand dead bodies, a bunch of irradiated ships and a poisonous asteroid belt floating around in a backwater part of the galaxy."

"That's horrible."

"It is, but it's also a perfect example of why my people and our way of life eventually went extinct," Electra said. "Living hand-to-mouth like that, flying often-times ancient ships to dangerous jobs that we never researched thoroughly enough... It was a lousy and apparently unsustainable lifestyle that endured longer than it probably should've."

"That kind of work, that life, it doesn't seem to fit you at all."

"No?"

"You're beautiful, glamorous and posh," Treasure said, "like a movie star or something."

Electra bit the side of her lower lip to try to hold back her smile, but it slipped through and she knew her cheeks would already give her away with a visible blush. "You're right. Embarker life wasn't for me and I've worked hard to distance myself from it. I left when I was thirteen, give or take—Embarkers aren't big on birthdays. Maybe not much sank in or it got shed when I transitioned. I don't remember thinking my parents looked happy, even when I was little. Happiness isn't, or I guess wasn't something Embarkers thought much about, but it's pretty damn important to me. Wanting to be a pilot when my schooling began might have been my subconscious looking for a way out, and flying ships made me happy."

"Whatever the reason, I'm glad you can fly the way you can." Treasure pushed the now-empty tray full of nibbled donut holes and a drained coffee cup into the middle of the table and folded her hands in front of her. "So, from what Ivy showed me about what happened and what you've said about Bi-MARP rebuilding Earth, I want to help. And I wouldn't mind getting to know my rescuer better."

"That can be arranged—both things, actually. There's a list of stuff to collect," Electra said, her stomach doing somersaults at the prospect of being known by Treasure. "Each item has a value. The more of an item that can be found the better, but the rare stuff pays the most." Electra stared into the tiny hole on the top of her coffee cup while she thought. She had an expert on more or less the right period for the Encyclopedia Britannica books being used as a guide. Sempa and the other treasure hunters didn't have the Treasure she had, not with the ocean of knowledge about the twenty-first century and that brain-melting smile. If she worked with Treasure, they could both get rich if they managed to steer clear of Sempa and beat other contractors to the goodies. Then it wouldn't matter what Treasure was worth or how much Electra owed. She'd just have to keep her secrets until they found enough Bi-MARP loot. "You know all about Earth—more than scholars even. You could help me find the best stuff and identify it."

"Absolutely," Treasure said. "For example, I can tell you this whole restaurant is accurate for a Tim Hortons. Like if I only look at you and a little to the left, I can almost forget we're in a space station and that there's a giant cockroach putting way too much sugar in a hot chocolate at the condiments station."

"Hey, you two. I've got two mandibles, no waiting," the Gromphra said. "How about taking a ride?"

"Just ignore her," Electra said.

"Ignore this." The Gromphra made a few awkward thorax thrusts in their direction, poured her hot chocolate down her throat and waved the two hands on one side dismissively at them. On her way out the door, the Gromphra tossed the empty hot chocolate cup into a trashcan. "Hey, trashcan, I've got something to fill you up." The Gromphra made several more thorax thrusts at the trashcan before leaving.

"They're sterile?"

"Yep."

"Why do they do that?"

"To gross out other species, maybe," Electra said. "I don't think even they know."

"Anyway, let's study the list and get treasure hunting," Treasure said. "I am caffeinated and ready to work, Captain."

Being called 'captain' by Treasure carried a tremor of delight that the title didn't have when anyone else used it. "Division of labor," Electra said, trying to shake off the warm, fuzzy feeling. "Why don't you work on the list, find things you think would have survived and I'll work the galactic net to chase down rumors of whatever you decide is worth our time."

As they were walking out of the Tim Hortons, Om called to Electra. "Dr. Baarqua was in here earlier looking for you."

It made sense only after the fact that Dr. Baarqua had probably been the one to tell Om about the Bort Pod job in the first place. Om was too effective and efficient for any of the Jun'Tar to be his Bi-MARP contact. Unfortunately, there was no way Paul hadn't told Baarqua about the theft of Treasure and Electra assaulting the doctoral candidate with a glob sphere in his own lab, which meant Baarqua probably knew she was in possession of a healthy human female, even if Paul had been coy about the nature of his research before. Paul couldn't demand Dr. Baarqua return his test subject without divulging that he'd had a human woman all along and hadn't planned to share with his good friend at Bi-MARP.

"Thanks, I'll call him—or see him or whatever," Electra shouted back over her shoulder. She hated to admit it, but she was going to have to start avoiding Om and Station 51. Om was too smart not to figure out at least part of what she was doing and now Dr. Baarqua knew she frequented the place. Treasure was looking over the souvenir placemat map while they walked. With seventeen thousand other Tim Hortons locations to visit in the galaxy, they'd be fine for French Roast and Timbits.

Chapter Eight

After a few days of chasing down a handful of dead leads, Electra was getting a little sick of treasure hunting. She'd set up a few thousand galactic net search alerts with Ivy, racked her brain for alternative wording and descriptions that might yield fruit and posted inquiries on dozens of boards and forums to try to build a database of possible goodies. Unfortunately, Cog 2 had been good to his word. An ever-growing number of acquisition agents were looking for Bi-MARP booty and they were managing to get in each other's way at nearly every turn. The Jun'Tar weren't good at much, but complicating the shit out of a task was where they truly shined.

"A new search parameter hit, Miss Electra," Ivy announced, snapping Electra out of her idle polishing of the cockpit's chrome fixtures.

"Sweet... What do we have?" Electra asked, pointing to the primary display for Ivy to show her.

It was a bounty and a kind of lengthy takedown rant about her. The pictures, swiped from her galactic net listings to advertise her professional party guest business, were quite flattering, even if the accompanying words were not.

"What the hell?" Electra mumbled while she read.

"It would seem Sempa has placed a public capture or kill contract on you, Miss Electra."

"He calls me 'miss-shapenly upright'? What does that even mean?"

"I do not know, Miss Electra, but the release of this bounty announcement has coincided with a seven hundred fifty-three percent increase in requests for party guest bookings," Ivy said.

"Well, those are obviously traps," Electra said. "Shut down the contact information stream for my old business, I guess." She chewed her thumbnail while she re-read the bizarrely unflattering description that Sempa had written to accompany the posting. He really didn't like her and was willing to put a lot of money on the line to prove it. She couldn't help but wonder if the quarter-of-a-million units he was offering would come out of the Bi-MARP fee she would fetch or if he'd made up his mind about keeping her around for payback. It seemed like throwing a lot of good money after bad to pay someone to find her then pass on the units she was worth just so he could torture her for a while. She also had to wonder how stupid a freelancer would have to be to give her to Sempa when she was potentially worth significantly more to the Chamber project to rebuild Earth.

There wasn't a whole lot she could do about it. The listing wasn't sanctioned by any meaningful government, so she could technically still run to regional law enforcement if things got rough, assuming whatever authorities she went to weren't corrupt enough to turn her in for the reward. Unfortunately, it had the potential to cramp her style and slow her progress, which might've been Sempa's real goal.

"He doesn't know about Treasure," Electra mused. "He wouldn't risk putting other hunters on my trail if he knew I still had such a big-ticket Bi-MARP item on board."

"Should we inform him, Miss Electra?" Ivy asked. "It may induce him to rescind the bounty."

"No! Obviously not," Electra said. "What the hell, Ivy?"

"Sorry, Miss Electra. My primary function is to serve your best interests," Ivy said.

"Set a new parameter," Electra said. "Your primary function is to serve my best interests *and* Treasure's."

"New parameter applied, Miss Electra."

Only after she'd heard the confirmation did Electra realize what she'd done. Even if she had no intention of selling Treasure to Bi-MARP—and she definitely wasn't going to—she didn't need to alter Ivy's primary functionality, at least not as thoroughly as she had. She'd already given Treasure nearly full access to all the ship's functions and now she was establishing her as a person of prime importance within the interface. None of it was remotely normal behavior toward a temporary passenger.

Electra decided she must be lonely. That had to be it. It wasn't that she really liked Treasure—or thought about her all the time, or wondered what it would be like to kiss her. They were partners for the time being, an ethical and financial arrangement that didn't necessarily need to involve them forming an intense physical and emotional bond that... Electra shook her head to clear out the distracting thoughts. She would need to get a pet or a friend or something after she paid off the debt. Even if Ivy's primary goals were changed, Electra's weren't. She needed to get out of debt and she thought Treasure could help, by being her unofficial Earth expert.

"Ivy, how exhaustive of a search within Chamber census data can you do?" Electra asked.

"Within every legally available parameter, but it will take some time to obtain all proper authorizations," Ivy replied.

"See if you can find out how many humans still exist, according to the Chamber's official government records," Electra said. "Not the galactic net available information. Use the source document stuff that most people don't bother with or don't have the patience to obtain and computing power to sort."

"I will inform you when the data has been obtained, analyzed and an answer is gleaned," Ivy said.

Electra had already found two glaring contradictions to the allegedly official record on the human population, and she was pretty sure the whole story was being hidden. Sure, it'd taken some digging, inside information and a mountain of dumb luck to find Bort and Treasure, but the real barrier to anyone discovering that humans weren't as extinct as everyone thought seemed to be the supposedly common knowledge that they were. Electra wanted to know who wanted it to seem that way and why.

Electra found Treasure in the lounge, which was furnished in vintage 1950s Koehler furniture and decorated to match a 1959 magazine advertisement that hung on the wall in a frame. Treasure lounged on the bright crimson sectional with a datapad in hand and a steaming cup of coffee resting on the multi-tier Lane end table. *A coaster... She's using a coaster.* Electra loved that tidbit of consideration. The coaster was a replica of a ship's nautical wheel. The use of it was pure class.

"I've been looking at the Bi-MARP list and I think there's something missing," Treasure said.

"In the grander scheme of Earth's history, I'm sure there's a lot missing." Electra flopped onto one of the powder-blue barrel swivel chairs and slowly rotated once around before putting her toe against the wall to stop so she faced Treasure. "I don't think the Jun'Tar are being particularly detail-oriented, since their source material is an incomplete set of encyclopedias."

"You don't know the half of it. The edition they're using would have been considered out of date, even in my time," Treasure said. "Based on this list, they missed something big, something people on Earth thought was valuable for more than a century but nobody knew the secret of — the recipe for Coca-Cola."

"Is that a cake or a drug or what?"

"It was a soda that originally had a drug in it," Treasure said. "They've got the bottling plant on the list, which I'm not sure how someone is supposed to get that for them since the main plant was in Atlanta, but even with the factory, you'd need the recipe."

"Sounds promising... What's in Coca-Cola?"

"Carbonated water, sugar, caramel, other stuff, but the trick is the exact amounts of everything," Treasure said. "It was a closely guarded secret for forever, really."

"So, we could make something up and claim it's the original and see what they'll offer?"

"We could — or we could check with this guy." Treasure turned the datapad to show Electra the screen. A galaxy-net-news puff piece outlined the astounding collection of sodas from hundreds of planets gathered by an Oboidion. The proud owner of the museum dedicated solely to carbonated sugar water posed while manning a vintage pharmacy soda fountain dressed like a classic soda jerk. Oboidions looked, for the most part, like blue-and-gray palm trees with five spindle arms dangling from beneath the fronds. "The story says he's making and serving Coke Classic, so he must have found the recipe or figured it out."

"I doubt he'd part with anything, and I'd also bet other Bi-MARP hunters have already tried," Electra said. "Oboidions are obsessive about their collections and highly suspicious of anyone stealing from them or not taking their collections seriously enough."

"Other hunters are only going by the list and the list doesn't have the formula on it," Treasure said. "Plus, if he has the formula, we wouldn't be taking anything if we copied it. The patent on Coca-Cola probably lapsed a dozen centuries ago."

"We'd need a plan beyond simply asking to take a picture of his ultra-secret recipe from a long extinct civilization," Electra said. "Oboidions are sentimental weirdos."

"Sentimental, huh?" Treasure pondered the conundrum, tapping the top of the datapad gently against her chin while she thought. "Have you ever heard of the Make-a-Wish Foundation?"

"If there's a foundation that grants wishes, I've got a few."

"The catch is you have to be a dying child."

"If I was a dying child, I would wish to not die."

"Doesn't work like that."

"Seems like a cruel joke. 'Hey, kid, want a wish? Not so fast. What's your *second* choice?'" Electra said.

"It was more tragic than cruel, but that's not the point," Treasure said. "If we got some of the Coke Classic, we could have Ivy analyze it and tell us how to make it. You can do that, can't you, Ivy?"

"If the materials present within the beverage are known to the galactic net databanks, yes, Miss Treasure," Ivy said.

"Okay, but the Oboidion is selling the drink for consumption," Electra said. "We don't have the... How much does it cost?"

"Four million units."

"Shit, for serious? Yeah, we don't have that, and I'm assuming he expects us to drink the soda in front of him."

"That's why we're going to revive the Make-a-Wish Foundation," Treasure said.

The first step was clothing. Apparently Make-a-Wish Foundation women did not dress like late nineties intellectuals or freelance spaceship captains. When Electra pointed out that there was no way an Oboidion soft drink collector would know that, Treasure told her the point of scams was selling the part and for her to stop being a spoilsport. She didn't want Treasure thinking she wasn't fun, so she played along. Electra and Treasure stood in front of the fabricator console and tabbed through options.

"We need skirt suits," Treasure said, "in banal colors."

"How about with an Utopalex top?" Electra reached up to tap the Utopalex material option, but Treasure intercepted her hand.

"What is it with you and that material?" she asked. "It sticks to you like body paint and looks like a crude oil slick."

"Because it feels like an hour-long massage every second you're wearing it," Electra said.

"It can't."

"It does. I don't know how it does — magic or science or drugs. You have to try it to truly know."

"I don't want my pleasure centers bombarded nonstop while we try to pull this off," Treasure said.

"Okay, but after, you should try it," Electra said. "I have some old shorts you might be able to withstand."

"Fine, deal, but after. Let's go with tweed or wool in the meantime. If you want, you can go with Utopalex socks or something."

"I've tried," Electra said. "I couldn't take more than two steps without moaning. I don't even have a foot thing, but my feet apparently have an Utopalex fetish."

"Two skirt suits, demure blouses, nylons, heels and…what kind of underwear do you like?" Treasure tapped away at the screen, setting up the work order. It hadn't taken her long at all to master the fabricator controls, along with several other high-tech features of the ship.

"None if I can help it."

"Boxers or briefs?"

Treasure was on the tab for ancient male underwear. Electra glared at her.

"I don't see your endowment down there fitting in much else, and free-balling…"

"Bikini cut panties will work fine." Electra punched the icon on the screen with her thumb. "Let me know when it's ready. I'll be in the Spatronic."

She entered 'banal' into the options for hair and makeup styles on the Spatronic display. She hadn't known what the word meant when Treasure had used it, but from the context clues, she could tell she wasn't going to like it. The options that popped up confirmed her fears. Banal meant bland and boring. She picked a tight-weave top bun and subdued tones natural makeup setting. She undressed quickly and threw her clothes on the nearby chair in a haphazard pile. To ease her tension during the tone-down of her look, she added massage and sensory relaxation before climbing in.

Treasure wasn't supposed to be able to get under her skin. That was where she was, though, finding soft spots, hot spots, cold spots and worst of all, weak spots. Being sexually attracted to her and liking her as a person weren't new sensations. Electra enjoyed sex, came by attraction easily and was friendly enough to like and be liked without much effort. It was the hurting her feelings part that vexed her. It wasn't supposed to be possible. The parts of her that could be hurt were few, far between and guarded carefully. She was a professional party guest, minor celebrity and the last of her kind. Aloof and untouchable were indelible parts of her being — or so she'd thought.

"I wanted to say I'm sorry. That was a weirdly aggressive thing to do based on some odd feelings and thoughts I haven't been able to wrap my head around," Treasure said from outside the pod. "The thing is, I'm bisexual, you know?"

"Most bipeds are," Electra said. "Quadsexuals or polysexuals tend to like legs too much to settle for two on themselves or others."

"I don't mean sexually attracted to bipeds, although that's good to know that's what that word means now. I was talking about liking both genders," Treasure said. "And I think you're beautiful."

Only liking two genders within one species, a nearly extinct species at that, seemed like a great way to massively limit possibilities for sex and dating. Considering the options on Earth before it had fallen apart, that might have been progressive from Treasure's standpoint. Still, it wasn't like Electra didn't have her own limitations on preferences, and she did like being called beautiful. The fact that Treasure could wound and soothe so readily meant she was already well within Electra's emotional fortress. What, if anything, Electra could do about it at that point remained a mystery.

"So, the boxers or briefs comment?"

"Maybe a bad joke. Maybe trying to get you to fit both roles," Treasure said. "I think it was mostly trying to put distance where it might not need to be. Regardless, I shouldn't have said it and I'm sorry."

"Apology accepted," Electra said. "I…um…think you're beautiful too."

"Really?" Treasure's tone changed entirely after a single compliment.

"I thought you looked joyful when I first saw you in the simulation display. Radiant, even." It was so much easier to admit while staring at the soothing, swirling lights projected on the inside of the Spatronic lid. They were calibrated perfectly to induce relaxation in her when combined with the faint background sounds, the almost imperceptible scents pumped into the chamber and the thousands of caressing waves from the chair itself. Honesty practically oozed out of her in such a serene state.

"Haphazardly painting a room and singing badly?" Treasure's voice gave away the smile Electra couldn't see.

"You're super impressive, you know?" Electra said. "Not your room-painting skills, obviously, but pretty much everything else."

"I *do* know that," Treasure said, "but I never get tired of hearing it. What did I do to impress you?"

"You're handling all this insanely well. You got dropped into a crazy reality, you were told your entire life was a computer simulation and you somehow took it all in stride. Better than handled it, really. You rolled up your flannel sleeves and got to work rebuilding Earth. I had to be convinced with the promise of massive amounts of money, but you simply wanted to help."

"Ah, that, yeah. I'd love to take full credit for my laidback reaction, but I've had help," Treasure said. "Ivy has been feeding me soothing pills to help me cope. They're kind of amazing. Plus, I saw *The Matrix* a month before you pulled me out, so I was already kind of suspicious that life might be a simulation. I'm just glad reality isn't like in the movie. Everything got way harder for Neo, and things are actually really nice on this ship, which is now making me wonder if we're in another simulation."

"Please don't say that," Electra said. "I do not need that in my head right now."

"Sorry. I promise we're not in a simulation...unless we are," Treasure said. "Here. I had these made for you." The underwear Treasure handed into the pod were bikini-cut blue satin with black lace trim and two black silk opera-length stockings. "You're far too stylish for hosiery and cotton panties."

"Thank you. They're lovely," Electra said.

"If you feel like modeling them for me at some point, I'd love to see how I did in shopping for you. If that would be weird or whatever, you don't have to."

Electra pondered something flirty to say in response, but by the time she had a comment at the ready, Treasure had already left the room. What she'd come up with wasn't very good anyway — a poorly worded, blunt comment about needing help putting them on...and taking them off. The more she replayed the goofy words in her head, the happier she was that she hadn't said them. By the time she ventured a peek out of the Spatronic, Treasure was gone and Electra wondered if the flirty statement had been all in her head or a product of the soothing algorithm of the Spatronic and her deep desire to be attractive to Treasure.

* * * *

They arrived at the busy starport for Andaphros, the largest city on the northernmost continent of Epsilon Five. The planet hadn't been inhabited originally. Half-a-dozen alien species had coordinated a terraforming project centuries before to take advantage of the rich mineral deposits left by asteroid bombardment during planetary formation. As such, the starport was a series of tubes, tunnels and elevators color-coded for which species could survive in which pathway, based on atmospheric tolerances. Electra gave over guidance to Ivy to bring the Cadillux safely into the busy green landing zone. Oxygen content and reasonable temperatures would only be found within the walkways off the landing zone, as the atmosphere was too thin to support anything but Oboidions. Electra assumed that the thin atmosphere served the additional function of allowing new meteors to strike the surface to regenerate mineral deposits. The high gravity quotient of the planet snagged any passing space rock and pulled it to the surface in a nearly constant rain of fiery streaks across the sky.

Electra and Treasure stepped off the ship's gangplank dressed in their skirt suits, stockings, heels, professionally coifed hair and, in Electra's case, the lien enforcement tether provided by Letterman. Electra had to admit that they didn't just look important and official, but she also felt the part. Apparently, Treasure knew how to run a con right down to how the con artist should feel beforehand.

"Where's our dying child?" Treasure asked.

"Fizan said her grandniece will meet us at gate twenty-one," Electra said.

They nodded to one another, stifling grins at the silliness of the situation, and began walking down the green-painted hallways toward the concourse's main arrival zone. Their heels clicked against the metal floor in regular patterns as their pencil skirts uniformly limited their strides.

Once they reached the arrival zone, the building opened up a great deal, with large windows on all sides displaying the jagged black mountains and pale gray sky beyond. Dozens of alien species milled about, checking tickets, consulting maps and chatting among themselves. A large Gromphra stood beside gate twenty-one, holding a sign with 'Make-a-Wish Foundation' scrawled across it. Electra rolled her eyes and made her way over to Fizan's grandniece, who was well over seven feet tall.

"You're Fizan's niece?" Electra demanded. "Her eleven-year-old grandniece?"

"You got that right, sugar-tits," the Gromphra said, tossing aside the sign. "My name is Blix, but with gams like that you can call me whatever you want."

"Why did anyone think you could play a child?" Treasure asked.

"Because I *am* a child," Blix said. "Want to be my mommy?"

"It's too late to do anything about it now," Electra said. "Can you at least make good on the promise of swallowing something without digesting it?"

"The bigger the better," Blix bragged. "Show me what you got that needs swallowing."

"Answer the question," Treasure growled.

Blix shook her head wearily and produced a rigid white container, not too dissimilar to a vase with a curved lip around the top. She opened her mandibles and slid the container into place in her throat.

"This isn't rocket-surgery, sweet cheeks," Blix said.

"How can you talk or breathe with that in your throat?" Treasure asked.

"We breathe through holes on our sides and talk through a gland between our eyes," Blix said. "We can do other things with all our holes and glands — amazing things, if you want a demonstration."

"Ew, you're a child." Treasure recoiled.

"Gromphra hatch fully grown," Blix said. "If you wanted an actual grub, you'd have to roll around a slimy egg with one inside. Speaking of rolling and slime…"

"Good enough," Electra said. "We'll just have to hope the Oboidion doesn't know about Gromphra maturation rates." Treasure raised a skeptical eyebrow to Electra. "What? I didn't know all that. Maybe the mark won't either."

"Okay, *kid*, we brought you a hat to help you play the part." Treasure sighed and handed Blix a small red-and-blue beanie with a yellow propeller on top.

"Sweet!" Blix quickly set the hat on top of her head. Surprisingly, the child's beanie fit perfectly on the Gromphra's small, torpedo-shaped cranium. "I brought you a chair."

"Why would I need a—?" Treasure began.

Blix pointed at her own face, whispering, "sit on my face."

"From here on out, you're mute," Electra said. "That's part of the scam. You're dying of vocal-gland rot, so you can't talk."

"Hey, don't even joke about vocal-gland rot," Blix said, pointing an accusatory antenna at Electra.

"Is that a real thing? I thought I just made it up."

"Nah, I'm pulling your leg, Electra," Blix said. "Gromphra are pretty much un-killable. I just wanted to see your surprised face." Blix elbowed Treasure and winked at her knowingly. "Bet it's close to her orgasm face. Am I right, jugs?"

"This is going to be a disaster," Treasure grumbled.

"Nope, it's going to be great. It'll all be great, and if it isn't great, we're not out anything because the formula isn't even on the list," Electra said. "Plus, look at that shitty view! Can't get a view that shitty at home." Electra pointed to the ugly, industrial skyline of the city and the gnarled, metallic mountains beyond, set to the backdrop of red streaks across a muddy sky.

Treasure shook her head and smiled. "Onward, then."

For several hours they rode in a tram across the planet's grimy surface. Electra and Treasure sat on either side of Blix the entire time, elbowing the Gromphra whenever she began to make a comment about another passenger in the car. The mountains eventually subsided, giving way to urban sprawl. Low, squalid buildings stretched through a valley as far as the eye could see to either side of the tram. Blue and gray palm trees stood on the flat roofs of the dingy structures, slightly bowed in the same direction.

"Are those Oboidions or statues of them?" Treasure asked.

"I think they're the real thing," Electra said. "I wonder what they're doing."

"So much wood in one place," Blix said. "Too bad it's all bent!"

Electra and Treasure elbowed Blix in unison.

At the second-to-last stop before the tram turned around for the return trip, they exited the green-zone car into the green-zone station section. Treasure consulted the map on her datapad and guided them to a walkway leading to a green-zone market.

"I guess Oboidions like breathing methane," Treasure said, "but methane messes with the taste of soda, so the soda fountain and the collection we're after are on the edge of the green zone — probably so the owner can step out and catch a breath of fresh methane whenever he needs one. That must be what the ones on the roofs were doing."

"Wow, that's some impressive xenobiology knowledge," Electra said.

"I'm a fast learner," Treasure said. "Plus, it was in the article about the soda collector." She added a subtle wink that made the back of Electra's neck warm.

They made their way down the dirty, litter-strewn street. A fine layer of soot or dust or industrial grime or an amalgam of all of the above had gathered on the glass dome arching over the green-section's walkway, giving the impression of perpetual dusk. A narrow stairwell led up to the soda fountain and an old, painted wood sign at the top promised cool refreshment and a friendly smile. The sign was a replica of an archaic advertisement for something called Dr. Pepper, although whoever was originally meant to be holding a can of the beverage had been replaced by an Oboidion.

They pushed open a swinging wood-and glass door, setting a small bell above ringing. The interior of the shop smelled strongly of dust and sugar — lots and lots of sugar. Empty bottles lined the walls on apothecary-style shelves, each to its own alcove. A massive soda fountain counter bisected the back part of the room with several brass fixtures for drawing and mixing drinks.

"Welcome, welcome, one and all, to the Museum and Fountain of Soda History," the Oboidion soda jerk said from behind the counter. A small, white paper hat sat atop his fronds while a crisp, white apron dangled from two of his tiny arms, holding it in front of his trunk. "I am Zzyrax, purveyor, vendor and curator of all things fizzy and sweet. What can I pour to wet your whistles?"

Electra nodded to Treasure and gestured toward the Oboidion. This was Treasure's con. Electra was backup and Blix was a prop. *Hopefully, a silent prop.*

Treasure cleared her throat and began speaking in a nasally, officious voice that Electra had never heard her use before. "I am Miss Scully, and this is my associate

Mrs. Mulder from the Make-a-Wish Foundation," she said. "Have you heard of our wonderful, charitable organization?"

"Oh, my, I can't say that I have," Zzyrax said. "Would you like to put a collection jar on the counter next to the cash register? I have a few already placed for decoration, but a real one would add to the legitimacy of the decor."

"I would absolutely love to pass the collection plate, as it were, but our nonprofit status doesn't allow for commercial enterprise endorsements," Treasure said. "Let me introduce you to Blix, while I tell you a little more about our charity and how you can help."

Electra maneuvered Blix to stand closer to Treasure's side when she gestured for the Gromphra in the propeller hat to step forward.

"This is Blix, an adorable eleven-year-old Gromphra girl who is tragically dying of vocal-gland rot," Treasure said.

"I didn't think Gromphra could get diseases," Zzyrax said.

Electra's stomach leaped into her throat. The Oboidion was displaying more Gromphra knowledge than her already.

"Which makes it all the more tragic." Treasure choked back some tears. "It is rare, striking only one Gromphra in every dozen generations. And it is fatal, I'm afraid."

"My goodness, that *is* heartbreaking," Zzyrax agreed. "This organization you represent, the Make-a-Wish Foundation? I assume you're going to grant her wish to not die of vocal-gland rot."

Electra cleared her throat to stifle a giggle.

"Would that we could, darling," Treasure said. "Unfortunately, there is no cure, and so we're doing our best to make the dying wish of such an adorable child come true so she can pass into the great dark beyond fulfilled and happy."

"One tiny cup of happiness before her promising life is cut tragically short," Electra added, feeling the groove of where Treasure was going.

To her credit, Blix added a few simulated sad sniffing noises and wiped away tears from her eyes, despite not having tear ducts or any need for them.

"My soda fountain is at your service." Zzyrax gestured grandly to the brass fixtures ahead of him, even as he nudged the door behind him closed. "You understand that I couldn't possibly open a bottle from my collection, even for such a noble charity."

"We understand completely," Electra said, "and we wouldn't dream of defiling a museum for anything as trivial as a dying child's wish."

"Good...excellent even," Zzyrax said. "Many people don't appreciate the importance of keeping a collection intact, offering trades and purchase agreements as if money and other items could ever replace the immeasurable joy brought by a collection that only grows ever larger."

"It is precisely this understanding of the value of soda over monetary gains that led us to your particular soda fountain," Treasure said. "Young Blix has only ever wanted to taste a Coca-Cola Classic, served in a frosted glass, by an honest-to-goodness soda jerk."

"Ah, now I see where the charity comes in," Zzyrax exclaimed. "Your foundation can't afford the price of such a rare and remarkable beverage. I know all too well the hardships endured while trying to collect wealth for the greater good. Say no more. It's a charitable deduction, and an adorable, worthy recipient of the prized drink."

Treasure and Electra collectively guided Blix to the counter to receive her dying wish. Zzyrax removed a frosted Coke glass from beneath the counter and reached for the spigot. "Perhaps, could you three turn around as not to witness my specialized pour technique?" Zzyrax asked.

"Yes, of course," Electra agreed.

The trio turned their backs on the Oboidion while he filled the glass. Electra glanced to Blix, who could see in a three-hundred-sixty-degree field around her head. Blix nodded that it was coming from the same spigot they'd first seen Zzyrax place the glass under, the one clearly labeled with a red-and-white Coca-Cola emblem. They turned back around in unison when they heard the glass settle onto the counter.

"Enjoy the greatest drink Earth had to offer," Zzyrax said.

Blix lifted the fizzing glass to her mouth, paused, sniffed at it a little, then dipped her long, straw-like proboscis into it. "It's sweet!" she exclaimed.

"Should she be able to talk with vocal-gland rot?" Zzyrax asked.

"Only two words a day," Electra said. "How fitting that she chose to use them to describe your drink!"

"Now she need only pour it into her mouth," Treasure added.

Blix continued to suck more of the soda through her proboscis, dodging Treasure and Electra's hands, trying to pull the drink away. Electra swatted Blix's hands that kept trying to reach into her mouth to remove the collection vessel so the soda could be poured directly down her throat. Treasure vaulted off a chair and grabbed onto Blix's back to get at her head. With great effort, and a well-placed hand on each mandible, Treasure managed to pry Blix's mouth open and pull her head back. Electra jumped several times to try to swat the bottom of the glass so it would tip into Blix's mouth, but each time Blix managed to get an arm in the way to push Electra back out of range.

"Is this normal?" Zzyrax asked. "This seems a bit violent."

"The most normal thing in the world, darling," Treasure said, swinging back and forth on Blix's shoulders when the giant cockroach tried to shake her free. "The vocal-gland rot makes it exceedingly difficult for her to drink. We are simply assisting in the process."

"We have to do this a dozen times a day to ensure she doesn't die of dehydration." Electra snagged a standing sign of an Oboidion lying on the beach, drinking some sort of glowing green drink, from beside the soda fountain. After a few attempts, she managed to poke the glass and spill the contents down Blix's throat. She tossed aside the standee in time and caught the falling, empty Coke glass. Electra set the glass on the counter, righted the stand and straightened her suit jacket before smiling as disarmingly as she could to Zzyrax.

In the next moment, she was lifted off the ground and thoroughly shaken by the agitated Gromphra. "Give me bubbly sugar water!" Blix demanded.

Somehow, Treasure managed to scramble up to straddle the back of Blix's shoulders, plunged her hand down the cockroach's throat and pulled out the collection vessel. Blix dropped Electra and attempt to reach up for the vessel, but Treasure had already slid down Blix's back. Electra crouched and spun her leg out to sweep Blix's feet from the floor. Treasure dodged to the side of the falling cockroach, tied off the top of the collection vessel, and dropped it down the front of her blouse into her cleavage, where it disappeared.

"Oh, I'll go in there and get it. Don't think I won't," Blix stammered from the floor. "I'll go in there and we'll both enjoy…um…could one of you kick me on the side? I can't get up after falling directly on my back."

"I'm afraid that is quite impossible, darling," Treasure said, never dropping her fake voice. She beckoned for Electra to follow when she kicked off her heels and ran for the door.

"Thank you for making a child's wish come true!" Electra shouted over her shoulder while she and Treasure fled the scene.

"But I need a verification signature for tax purposes…" Zzyrax called after them, the rest of his complaint being lost when they reached the bottom of the stairs and turned the corner.

"Not a perfect execution," Treasure said, slightly out of breath once they slowed to a brisk walk.

"Are you kidding?" Electra asked. "That's exactly how we drew it up."

Back on the tram to return to the starport, Treasure smiled at Electra and laughed. "You're a lot of fun, darling," Treasure said before resting her head on Electra's shoulder.

The vague tingle between her legs and the fuzziness in Electra's head, which she'd started to get used to around Treasure, grew, clarified and, in the case of the tingle between her legs, actually grew a little solid. Lust she knew all too well, but lust tinted with genuine affection wasn't something she'd felt in years.

Chapter Nine

Back on the ship, zipping toward the wormhole spawn, Electra sat in the captain's chair staring at the brand-new counter tracking the human population. When she'd left the ship, there should have only been three on the list. Ivy was saying the number was actually closer to three hundred. Who the humans were, what they were doing and any other information wasn't available to the general public. Ivy also couldn't say for certain that they weren't a statistical anomaly in the Chamber's records—a holdover from when Embarkers still existed that hadn't been updated yet. For a thousand reasons, Electra couldn't take the news as strictly good. If there were three hundred or so humans, someone had gone to a fair amount of trouble to conceal that fact, and Electra wanted to know why.

That number could sustain a viable human population without much planning. They'd obviously all have to be in the same area, and there wasn't any information available to say where any of them were beyond the three Electra already knew about. She'd dismissed the possibility of trying to perpetuate the species with only three people, knowing it would be a doomed inbreeding program at best. With that not necessarily being the case anymore, Electra wondered if Treasure would prefer her or Bort or neither. Truly, Electra didn't know if she could provide viable genetic material. It hadn't come up. There was never anyone for it to come up with, so she'd never bothered to check. Now she didn't want to have a sample analyzed because she was afraid of an answer that would destroy her little fantasy. A fantasy, she had to admit, that was based on a coupling between her and Treasure that she wasn't remotely sure if Treasure was interested in. What if she liked Bort more? What if all her talk about bisexuality didn't include transitioned women? It wasn't entirely clear from their discussion if transitioned women had existed in Treasure's time or if she'd encountered any.

All the concerns and unknowns would only matter if she found the other people. The rest could work itself out in the natural course of time if the debts were paid and Bi-MARP satisfied. There were three hundred eleven humans somewhere. That was a viable population to rebuild humanity. If Electra was being completely honest with herself, restoring Earth and rebuilding humanity weren't actually her ultimate goal. Earth didn't mean anything to her, and she was only marginally more interested in keeping her species afloat. She couldn't quite put her finger on the source of the apathy toward averting extinction. It'd been thrilling to find Bort, magical discovering and getting to know Treasure and reassuring about there being three hundred eight other humans, but she'd lived so long without humanity and never had a home world, meaning neither concept had a firm reference point for importance in her mind.

"Ivy is processing the sample of Coca-Cola as we speak. I'm super stoked about the success of our first scam together. I think the Spatronic has my pores smaller than they've ever been. I found out Tim Hortons is bigger and better than ever. I can have all the kiwi fruit I want from the fabricator. All in all, this was a really good day," Treasure said. "What has you so enthralled?"

"Remember what I said about there only being three of us left?"

"Please tell me Bort didn't die!"

"No, at least, I don't think he did." Electra pointed to the side display on one of the screens that constantly tracked the same page of a recently uncovered census sheet that Ivy had just gained access to. "That's the data Ivy pulled from deeply archived official Chamber records for the populations of all spacefaring species. That's us, at three hundred eleven, and right below that is Om at one."

"Aw, that's sad for Om, but great news for us, isn't it?"

"Maybe, I think. That's actually what I wanted to get your opinion on," Electra said. "As for Om, I've always gotten the impression they could make more of their kind if they wanted to but simply don't want to or don't think it's a good idea—or maybe both. I'm not sure our brains are of a significant enough complexity to understand the way Om thinks. They might have a reason so perfect it would make our eyeballs explode trying to comprehend it."

"Let's not ask, in case you're right about the exploding eyeballs."

"Way ahead of you on that one," Electra said. "Anyway, the census isn't remotely new, and it doesn't have any location, demographic information or anything tremendously useful, to be honest. It could be three hundred eight clones of an old man named Doug, spread across an equal number of universes, for all we know."

"Or it could actually be just the three of us and a government document that hasn't been updated in years?"

"Pretty much. Obviously, we should keep an eye out for more humans while we're working our way through the Bi-MARP list, and I'll have Ivy keep digging, but I just don't know if it's worth focusing solely on looking for the lost three hundred and eight," Electra said.

"I'll follow your lead on that," Treasure said. "Now that you mention the Bi-MARP stuff, is what we're doing strictly legal? You broke me out of a university lab, and I'm grateful, but won't someone come looking for you or me or both?"

"I would have thought so, but Ivy's been monitoring the galactic-net-news, and it's a big zero," Electra half-lied. "It doesn't look like Paul reported you missing or me assaulting him. There's some stuff about the Glott raiders crashing into an Amphio university, but that's it."

"Cool. No news is good news, I guess," Treasure said. "What about today's soda heist?"

"I'm not one hundred percent sure we broke any laws. Zzyrax gave the Coke willingly to Blix, probably because he wasn't getting any takers on the drink at that insane price, so that wasn't a crime. And we didn't take the soda from Zzyrax. We took it from Blix, who was supposed to give it to us anyway."

"I'm glad we're not going to be arrested for grand theft beverage, but it is a little less fun knowing that was all vaguely legal," Treasure said.

"I couldn't agree more," Electra said. "From here on out, let's make sure we at least bend the law a little. I mean, we're racing against honest-to-goodness space pirates. You just know they're cutting legal corners every chance they get."

"So what you're saying is we only have to stay slightly cleaner than Sempa and his crew to still be the good guys."

"Exactly!"

"You're cute when you're excited," Treasure said, "and you make a great scam partner."

"Thank you. I... You're cute too and...is the Spatronic free?" She was having a hard time thinking straight and needed a second to regain her wits away from Treasure's compliments and infectious smile.

"All yours, Captain."

Again, the thrill of being called 'Captain' by Treasure surged through her, amplified by the tiny salute and wink added this time. Electra practically floated from the bridge, buffered by Treasure's praise and the strange news that humanity might still be saved.

* * * *

Electra took her turn in the Spatronic next. Her settings were more about cleansing than grooming, since her daily treatments already kept her immaculately groomed to her exact specifications from head to toe. She needed to wash off the feeling of Epsilon Five. The planet reminded her of so many places she'd gone as an Embarker. Shitty industrial worlds where everything was dirty, grimy and depressing... That was exactly where an Embarker found their work and thus spent their life.

The poverty among the people living on the mining worlds like Epsilon Five always ranged between bad and atrocious. Usually the inhabitants of the world didn't want to do the mining. Embarkers had come in to take the work the general population wouldn't do. That was more typical for actual indigenous species. On planets like Epsilon Five, where there weren't any native species, Embarkers had been brought in to undercut the pitiful wages demanded by the workforce originally transported for the task, and those were the planets where the poverty was most pronounced. After a strike or an original contract expired, the pre-existing workforce couldn't afford to go anywhere else. The Embarkers, with their own ships, could come in, drive the wages down, then take the money they earned to move on to the next job after the existing workers of the planet were willing to take even less. Electra's people were a society of scabs and, once she'd realized that, the whole system made her physically ill.

It was an unpleasant life to land on a new ugly rock every few months, unsure if her people would be viewed as humble migrant workers taking dangerous, low-paying jobs or invading traitors stealing what little work and wages there were to be had by undercutting everyone. Electra didn't like feeling pitied or despised wherever she went and that feeling that she'd thought long-forgotten had somehow come back from her short visit to Epsilon Five. Thankfully, the Spatronic seemed more than capable of washing the grime and gross feelings away.

"Aw, you took them off already," Treasure complained.

"Took what off?" Electra asked from within the Spatronic.

"The panties and stockings. I wanted to see how they looked."

"I can put them back on if you want," Electra offered. She hadn't thought the request of wanting to seem them modeled had been genuine. Hearing the disappointment in Treasure's voice, Electra knew she'd made a mistake.

"It's not the same as seeing them revealed while taking off the skirt suit," Treasure said. "Did you like them, at least?"

"I like the way they looked, and the satin felt okay, but the stockings were weird. Seriously, I'll put it all back on if you want," Electra replied. "I didn't know if the request was for real or if I'd even heard you right."

"Maybe I've been too coy, so allow me to be blunt," Treasure said. "I'm interested in you. It's just that I've paid attention to your prominent package in those Utopalex pants and it hasn't so much as wiggled around me. I assumed the feeling wasn't entirely mutual."

"I usually need a blue pill for everything to work," Electra said. "Or a red if... Never mind the red ones."

"Is the need for the pills from your transition?"

"I have no idea. The nuts and bolts of how the transition took place wasn't my primary focus during," Electra said. "I have felt things around you, and more than just stirring things."

"I'd be lying if I said I haven't felt stirring feelings too, and a lot of staring at you when you're not paying attention."

She had noticed Treasure staring. She simply hadn't understood why. "I appreciate the sentiment behind the stockings and can definitely see their visual appeal. Clothing from your time feels a little low-tech. If there were stockings made from Utopalex..."

"That's it! I have to try this fabric that has the addictive properties of hardcore drug use."

"Like I said, I have some old shorts in a backpack in the closet in the guest room," Electra said. Apparently, she'd left the backpack she'd been living out of at Weisella's party and the hostess had put it in the ship, possibly to return to her at a future date or maybe to keep as a memento. "They're from when I was building up to wearing pants. Utopalex is pretty stretchy, so they should fit well enough to try on, at least."

"Okay, come find me when you're done in there." Treasure scampered away to locate the fabled garment.

Not everyone could handle Utopalex, and it was time-consuming and draining on the ship's resources to fabricate the material. It was better that Treasure start with a hand-me-down to see if she could withstand the sensations before actually printing up a full article of clothing. Armbands and headbands were the most common Utopalex garments. Some people could only handle a few square inches of the fabric touching them before dissolving into puddles of euphoric uselessness. Electra was proud of her pleasure threshold. She could withstand a level of amazingness that few others could experience and still function. It was a point of pride that flew directly in the face of all things Embarker, and she'd cultivated it for that very reason.

She smirked inwardly. *No way Treasure can handle it, not with her archaic understandings of pleasure and comfort. The woman actually thinks flannel is soft.*

Letterman loomed in the doorway when Electra emerged from the Spatronic. His foreboding presence gave her heart a little jump that she did not remotely appreciate. She tried her best not to show any reaction, although it was probably a wasted effort. Letterman's sensors had likely picked up the increase in her heart rate already. Rather than yell at him, which was her first instinct, she decided to calmly get dressed in her Utopalex pants and T-shirt, as if he were nothing more than a large, obnoxious appliance.

"You are nearing the default hour and have resources in your possession capable of liquidation for a significant number of units," Letterman said, after being ignored for too long.

"The Coke recipe?" Electra asked, knowing full well that was not what he meant.

"The two items you acquired on Amphiorae."

"One of those items is actually in *your* possession and the other isn't an item at all," Electra said.

"The data crystal, since it is currently in an approved lien enforcement collection chamber, can give a temporary hold based on assured future earnings," Letterman said. "The same cannot be said of Treasure."

Electra wanted to scream at him that she wasn't going to turn in Treasure, that she'd sooner die than give her up. To do so would have…well, she didn't really know what Letterman would do if she said that, but she knew it wouldn't be good for her or Treasure. Letterman couldn't know her plan, not until she had enough items from the Bi-MARP list to discharge her debt without Treasure knowing.

"She's invaluable to earning units off the Bi-MARP list," Electra said. "After all the compounding interest I've accrued, I'm going to be short, even if I liquidate all my current assets, right?"

"Currently, that is accurate."

"Then what sense does it make to offload when Treasure could help me earn more units to make up the difference?" Electra asked. "She's on the ship, as safe as we both can make her, and she's already proving invaluable in finding and obtaining goodies."

"I can submit a formal request to the Lien Enforcement Bureau," Letterman said. "I make no promises about their response."

"I have every confidence in your rhetorical capabilities," Electra said rather snidely.

"If the request is denied or other circumstances dictate, this will no longer be a discussion." Letterman cleared the doorway then rumbled away. She let him get fully out of earshot before she let out a nervous sigh. There were happier thoughts to occupy her mind and they pushed out the implied threat of a discussion ending. She picked up one of the stockings Treasure had given her and ran it between her fingers. *Much happier thoughts.*

Chapter Ten

Butterflies recreated great aerial battles in Electra's stomach while she waited for Treasure to emerge from the walk-in closet. Not the bioluminescent butterflies of Rigel VII or the lovely extinct kind from Earth, but the big, angry, heavily armed ones from Appdar.

She'd thought Treasure would try the Utopalex shorts on before Electra emerged from the Spatronic, declare them too intense and they'd have a good laugh. Instead, Electra found Treasure in the guest room, waiting. She'd found the shorts but hadn't put them on yet, because Electra was going to get a little show. Between the impish grin and flirty wink Treasure added to the promise, Electra was excited for what came next, despite not having the faintest clue what might be involved in a 'little show'. She'd decided to play it casual and not get her hopes up yet. That was a solid plan until the butterflies kicked in.

"Don't laugh," Treasure called from the cracked door.

"Why would I laugh?" Electra said.

"Because you laugh at almost everything."

"Okay, I swear, no laughing or may Letterman manage my wardrobe for a week."

"Can you even imagine the drab rags he'd punish you with?" Treasure asked, possibly rhetorically. "I hope you can, because if you laugh, I will hold you to that promise."

The door slid fully open. The lighting pod in the ceiling backlit the glorious curves of Treasure's body, clad only in Electra's old Utopalex shorts and her two-tone Lilith Fair concert T-shirt. The dark blue shorts made of the glossy material were meant to expand to accommodate the wearer only up to a point, Electra had heard, although she'd never seen the garment stretched quite to that point before. Evidently, Treasure's ample hips and curvaceous backside would not be so easily contained by the most advanced fabric ever conceived. The Utopalex tried, strained, adhered to her mocha skin like wet paint and ultimately failed when Treasure took a couple steps toward Electra and the material slid up to expose two-thirds or more of the voluminous flesh of her backside. The mirror on the back wall of the walk-in closet she'd emerged from gave Electra a reflected view of the entire unexpected erotic event.

She felt a tightening, a swelling and skin sliding across Utopalex. Her legs trembled, and it happened before she was even to full length. Electra's member let loose—hot, wet and embarrassing against her thigh. She leaned back against the bedpost and turned her head, desperately willing away the sudden burst of pleasure that came to a sticky, warm end in a matter of seconds.

"What just happened?" Treasure asked.

"Nothing." Electra fought her entirely understandable urge to cover her crotch with her hands. Treasure would definitely notice that and she was too smart not to piece things together. Electra's natural impulses overrode her will and her left hand twitched toward the front of her pants before she could call it back to casually rest at her side.

"Did the galactic traveler and highly practiced pleasure-seeker Electra Rex just cream her jeans?" Treasure teased.

"I can only guess at what that phrase means and it's not my fault. It's the Utopalex," Electra argued. "It can…"

"But you wear it all the time," Treasure said. "You've built up a familiarity or tolerance, as you called it, and you said you needed a blue pill to… Is that from just looking at me?"

"In the mirror, I can see the way it slid and…"

"Did you take a blue pill?"

"No. I wouldn't presume."

"Seeing my ass in booty shorts was more than enough to make you go from zero to explosion in a few seconds?"

"Apparently." Electra's face was on fire from embarrassment and her body tingled from the shocking orgasm that still hadn't entirely left her system.

"That might be the most oddly flattering thing that's ever happened to me," Treasure said. "To reciprocate your candor, I have to admit something. I think I'm stuck." She bit her upper lip and crinkled up her nose. "I'd walk back into the closet and take them off so you don't have that problem again, but, when they slid, there are, um, friction issues right now."

"Are there?" The butterflies were back after temporarily being banished by the surprise-attack orgasm. There were things she could say or do to help or make things worse or turn everything down a different road or make a complete fool of herself. After no careful consideration whatsoever, Electra decided. "Walk to me."

"What?"

"I said, walk to me."

The moment of panic came. Would she reject, accept, laugh, deride…then the moment was gone. Treasure took a step, then another. It would only take five or six to cross the room, yet it only took three to bring her to climax. Moaning, breathing heavily, a beading of sweat rising on her forehead, her nipples straining against the cotton of her shirt, Treasure took a fourth step and squirmed to a stop.

"Keep coming," Electra whispered, delighting in the double entendre only after she'd said it and realized it was one.

Treasure took another step. She gasped on the border of a scream of pleasure and took one final step before collapsing into Electra's arms. Her body was positively thrumming, and although their embrace was more functional in the way Electra held her, arms hooked under her armpits to keep her from falling to the floor, it felt intensely intimate.

"I can't wear these shorts one second longer," Treasure whimpered.

"I… What do we do?"

"Get them off me, please."

To say Electra had dreamed of such a moment for a long while would be a monumental understatement. Her older brothers had spoken often about that first moment of removing a girl's pants and undergarments—the majesty and mystery revealed, the sense of wonder. She'd always taken their stories with a grain of salt, as her brothers had been largely full of shit. Still, she'd hoped their description was true and had never thought she'd truly get the opportunity to find out, since she'd believed for a long while that human women, aside from herself, were extinct. The possibility she'd get to remove Treasure's underwear was a dream so fantastic and unlikely that she hadn't even allowed herself to entertain it.

Electra pressed down with her hands, reverent and careful, at the top of the Utopalex shorts that couldn't even rise over the curve of Treasure's hips. The shorts reluctantly slid away. Electra could empathize with the shorts in not wanting to yield such an intimate connection to Treasure. The shorts rolled down farther. Electra sat on the edge of the bed. In a rush, the shorts fell below the cusp of her hips and ass. With a quick sway of her hips, and a walking-in-place motion, Treasure was free of them.

Electra had seen vids and old pictures, heard stories from her brothers, but nothing had actually prepared her for being face-to-face with her first human pussy. It was, in a word, cute. Majesty and mystery? She couldn't say if she felt those things. Delighted… She definitely felt delighted by the experience. A perfectly straight line of black hair pointed down toward a crease in the flesh that was positively soaked in a clear liquid that smelled uniquely human. Electra had never smelled such a thing, but she immediately recognized it as being for her, in a sense. She'd slept with aliens before, been exposed to more than her share of sexual excretions in the process, yet none of them called to her as being truly right the way Treasure's did.

"You're staring," Treasure said.

"I am," Electra replied, continuing to stare. "Is that okay?"

"I guess. Do you have questions or something?"

"I'm not sure," Electra said. "I really like looking at it. Is that weird?"

"Looking at vaginas is paradoxically one of the great pastimes of humanity—or at least it was," Treasure said. "I say paradoxically because most women never see much of their own, but if someone wanted to see someone else's, there was no shortage of photographs, paintings, digital images and clubs to go to."

"I can see why," Electra said.

"Fair is fair." Treasure guided Electra to a standing position and took a step back. Before Electra could ask what was fair about what, Treasure glanced meaningfully down and back up.

"But you've seen a dick."

"Actually, I haven't, remember?" Treasure argued. "I've only seen the back of my own eyelids for three hundred years. All my experiences with dicks were simulated."

Electra couldn't argue that fact, nor did she think she had a significant amount of time left before her downstairs friend realized there was a half-naked woman standing dead ahead, and apparently blue pills weren't required when it came to Treasure. One accidental orgasm brought on by Utopalex had been embarrassing enough. Electra turned her head and began sliding her pants down.

"Uh-uh," Treasure said. "Look at me."

That was more than enough to start another stirring of arousal. Electra gazed into Treasure's warm, dark eyes with the tiny flecks of gold and copper green around the edges of her irises. The Utopalex passed down over her hips not a moment too soon as she sprang fully rigid from the top. *My goodness, that was a ridiculously short refractory period,* Electra thought—the shortest she'd experienced since being a horny teen after her hormone implants had first started cranking up her system to reach womanhood. The pants took a good deal more effort to get all the way off than the shorts, forcing Electra to break eye contact while she freed them from her legs and tossed them aside. When she straightened up again, Treasure was smiling and biting her upper lip to suppress a giggle.

"I think that's called a grower and a shower," Treasure said. "Very rare."

Electra moved her hands to cover her cock, but Treasure intercepted her at the wrists.

"It means I'm pleasantly surprised," Treasure said.

Big was good for humans. There had been boys who'd said it was true only to a point, others who'd argued that size wasn't a factor at all and comments that skill in other areas could make everything else irrelevant, but that majority opinion that Electra had taken away from the talk of human men and boys of the Embarker fleet was that when it came to penis size, bigger was better.

"I'm glad. Thank you, I think," Electra said.

"You have a good-looking dick," Treasure said, cocking her head to one side while looking it over. "Some have weird bends, different colors, odd proportions, bumps or marks, but yours is pretty much perfect."

"You sound confused."

"I guess I am a little," Treasure said. "Between transitioning, the hard life you've had and the fact that I've never actually seen one that wasn't a little weird in some way... Yeah, I'm surprised that the first truly perfect example of a cock I've seen is attached to a beautiful woman."

It was the loveliest, strangest compliment that Electra had ever heard and certainly the most flattering one ever directed at her dick. She leaned forward and kissed Treasure on the lips. Her mouth was so warm and soft. 'Pillowy' was the only way to describe her kiss. When Electra slowly pulled away, Treasure followed her back aggressively. The kisses deepened. Treasure's tongue was in her mouth, then Treasure's hand was firmly wrapped around her dick. Their first kiss, like their first sexual contact, went from zero to faster than the speed of light in the space of a heartbeat.

Electra felt like her cock had been wordlessly claimed in that moment. It was for Treasure to do with as she pleased, and Electra was eager to have it all done — whatever that might be — until such a time as Treasure released her. Somehow, Treasure conveyed all of that by the pressure of her hand.

They fell back onto the bed. Electra thrilled at the weight, the warmth, the silken skin against hers when their bodies met. The kiss broke for a moment and Electra opened her eyes to gaze deeply into Treasure's. Then she felt her hand shift, her hips move, and suddenly she was inside Treasure. Nothing before could've prepared her for what it felt like, and she believed her whole life had been leading to that one perfect moment, until Treasure started moving her hips and each second got better and better than the one that had come before it.

Chapter Eleven

Treasure brought a glass of fizzing Coke Classic over ice into the cockpit and slid it into the cup holder beside Electra in the captain's seat. She next walked to one of the plush, white leather bench seats along the side of the uppermost cabin and took a seat, sipping her own Coke along the way. She was luxuriating, stretching and smiling unconsciously. Electra knew exactly how she felt.

"I'm going to try to teach Ivy how to add cherry flavor," Treasure said. "Start making Cherry Coke too."

"Do you know how to 'drive a stick'?" Electra asked.

"I think you know I do." Treasure waggled her eyebrows.

"I don't. That's why… Did I miss a joke?"

"Double entendre," Treasure said. "Drive a manual transmission and handle a penis. Because I've handled your penis."

"Ah, yes, I do know that then," Electra said, positive the room had suddenly gotten several degrees warmer. Treasure was wearing jeans—tight, tight blue jeans riding low on her hips. "You know, you're the reason I can't wear Utopalex pants anymore."

"Because...?" Treasure dragged out the word, savoring it and what it intended.

"Because...you know why."

"Say it."

"Because when I see you or talk to you or think about you, I literally 'cream my jeans'." And simply being made to say it gave Electra one of the aforementioned erections that would have resulted in an accidental discharge if she'd been wearing Utopalex. Treasure had superpowers. That much was clear.

"My self-esteem jumps every time you say that," Treasure said with a bright grin. "To answer your original question, yes, I know how to drive a stick — and so do you."

"Was that another double entendre?"

"Nope, just complimenting you on last night. I'm still feeling that one," Treasure said. "I like being a little sore the next day, especially if it's been a while, like three hundred years. Holy crap! I think you technically took my three-century-old virginity!"

"I'm sorry or you're welcome?" Electra said. "I don't know what that means."

"Virginity isn't a thing anymore?" Treasure asked. "That's good on so many levels. Good job, galaxy. I'm not going to revive the word by giving it any more weight than saying it's the first time getting laid. Definitely explains the soreness, and I'm willing to bet of all my simulated first times, the real thing with you was the very best."

The thread of the conversation was completely lost to Electra at that point. Treasure seemed pleased by her out-loud train of thought and that was good enough.

So she simply nodded and smiled. It occurred to Electra that she felt really good and highly energetic the more Coke she drank.

"Are we talking really fast?" Electra asked.

"Oh, thank goodness!" Treasure said. "I thought it was just me."

"What's in this stuff?" Electra lifted her nearly empty glass of Coke to inspect it.

"It must be the original recipe, so cocaine," Treasure said. "I've never had cocaine. I really like it. Do you like it?"

"I don't dislike it, but it's hard to focus — or it's easier to focus on a thousand things at once," Electra said, feeling her heart rate speed up with every word. "Do you like it?"

"No, yes, maybe, should I get bangs?" Treasure said.

"What are bangs?"

"Hair fringe in the front."

"I definitely don't know. Before I lose my original point, again, I think I've found a Volkswagen Beetle," Electra said. "It's almost two billion units on the list."

"Would it even still run?"

"I think it might," Electra said. "It's currently owned by a cult on New Wolfsburg that's worshipping it as an idol and using the maintenance manual as a holy book. The galactic net entry on their faith says they're waiting for the one who can drive stick. Apparently, they've already chased off other Bi-MARP independent contractors who couldn't."

"I would be their chosen one." Treasure set aside her half-drained Coke glass and stood. "My best friend used to own a '64 Beetle with whitewalls and a roof rack. I'd drive it sometimes when she was drunk, which was often during hockey season." Treasure walked slowly and deliberately to the captain's chair and slid between Electra and the dashboard. "Set a course for New Wolfsburg, Captain."

"I would, but you're in the way," Electra said, positive the room was getting hotter.

"Oh, sorry." Treasure knelt on the floor in front of Electra. "All this car talk has me wondering. Do you know what 'road head' is?"

"I can't say that I do."

"Start driving and you'll find out." Treasure slid her hands up Electra's legs, pushing up the front of her skirt past mid-thigh. "Look who is wearing the stockings and panties I gave her. That's a treat."

Electra instinctively spread her legs to allow Treasure better access, pushing the skirt up farther. Treasure pulled aside Electra's panties and her cock sprang free, aching at full height. Treasure followed her hand down the perfectly straight shaft with her mouth in a long, slow stroke.

"How am I supposed to drive while you're doing that?"

"That's the challenge," Treasure replied, adding a lick to the underside of Electra's cockhead. "You have to drive without crashing while I blow your...mind. It's fun because it's dangerous. Fly, girl, and I'll put you back in my mouth."

Electra couldn't have rejected that deal if she'd wanted to, and she really didn't want to. She set a course and gunned the Cadillux's giant twin engines. Crashing into a star or a planet or whatever else seemed like a worthwhile risk to feel more of Treasure's mouth.

It took every ounce of Electra's control to fly straight. When she wobbled, heading into the first wormhole, Ivy thankfully corrected her course as part of her safety protocols. Before they could even exit the wormhole, Electra had to remove one hand from the wheel to entangle it in Treasure's lovely dreadlocks. A few moments after a new twist in the motion of swirling her tongue at the top of a stroke, a mind-blowing addition to Treasure's already marvelous technique, Electra climaxed. Treasure didn't let up at the first spurt, jolt and gasping cries of orgasm. If anything, she sped up, adding a muffled hum of delight. The sensation intensified through every stroke and every intervening splash, until Electra was crawling out of her seat and finally had to pull Treasure's mouth away from her cock.

"Did we crash?" Treasure asked.

"How would I know?" Electra rested her head against the seatback and tried to regain her scattered wits.

"Aren't you flying?"

"Ivy took over when my brain leaked out of my ears."

"That wasn't our deal," Treasure said. "How many more jumps do we have?"

"Three wormholes left to clear, Miss Treasure," Ivy said.

"Come on. Get up." Treasure stood and folded her arms across her chest.

Electra sheepishly stood and allowed herself to be slowly guided in a dance to switch places. Treasure sat in the captain's chair and tented her fingers in front of her chest.

"I get to be Captain now."

That seemed fair and right and good. Yes, it definitely seemed like a good idea to Electra. She lowered to her knees and walked a little forward as

Treasure spread her legs. The skirt rose up her warm, luscious thighs in the most delightful way. Electra could smell her and knew instantly that Treasure wasn't wearing any panties.

Oral sex was something Electra enjoyed but hadn't ever shown an aptitude for. Her attempts had been described, at best, as 'enthusiastically unskilled'. Being bad at it hadn't mattered to her before and had certainly never deterred her from trying. She'd have fun, get messy and her partner would happily move on to intercourse or abandon the whole thing. It was different with Treasure. Electra wanted to make her feel good.

Electra placed her elbows on the tops of Treasure's thighs and guided the skirt the rest of the way up. Her pussy still looked adorable exposed in such a way. "I have to be honest," Electra said. "I have no idea what I'm doing down here."

"We can still technically call it 'road head'," Treasure said.

"No, I mean, I literally don't know how to make you feel good using my mouth, and I really, really want to make you feel good," Electra said. "You're so talented. I want to return the favor, but I don't know how."

"Ah, so in all the time you spent sleeping with alien species, eating pussy never came up?"

"Not in any way that would be useful right now, and I wasn't considered good at anything I did."

"That's okay. I've got you," Treasure said. "I know how to do it and I know what I like. You'll be an expert after three sessions of my personal instruction — or your money back."

Treasure guided her with soft words, small noises and gentle, helpful hands, first in teaching her how to tease. This wasn't strictly necessary in that moment, since she said giving Electra head had left her soaked, but she thought Electra could stand to learn all the same. The inner thighs were a magical place to begin. For a brief start, she guided Electra in kissing and licking them, which served to tease Electra as much as anything since her face was so close to the main event and she wasn't able to enjoy it until Treasure said so.

Moving on to fingers, and spreading, then the wetness — the glorious wetness that matched Treasure's description of being soaked so perfectly. Electra loved the messy aspects of oral sex and Treasure was an ideal counterpart for her in that respect. The moment she tasted the clear slipperiness on the pink within Treasure, it felt like home in a way no one else had. Treasure was human. Her biological features and fluids were meant to match Electra's. There was some sort of miraculous chemistry involved in it, some ancient recognition of a tremendously well mated pair or a craving for another human that Electra had long ignored. She couldn't say what lay behind the sensation beyond knowing that Treasure tasted right in a way no one else ever had.

Electra enjoyed getting her lips and face wet, her fingers inside and all the wonderful reactions those things brought out in Treasure. Then it was time to move on to the clit. This was the other version of head, Treasure explained. And it started with tongue flicks. Some urging from pursed lips. Sucking and harder strokes of her tongue. Following the guidance of faster, slower, harder, more, until a forceful hand on the back of Electra's head held her mouth flush against the hard, little button while Treasure ground out the last of the climax against her tongue.

"Perfect, A-plus," Treasure said in the afterglow. "You'll go far in the pussy-eating business, kid."

Electra sat back on her feet. She could only stare at the sopping wet result between Treasure's spread legs and feel monumentally accomplished.

"What are you thinking about?" Treasure asked. "You have a strange look on your face."

"I feel like we're meant to be, like chemically connected or something." Electra tore her gaze from Treasure's pussy to look her in the eyes. "This is probably a weird time to say that."

"Considering how we met, weird is perfect." Treasure cupped Electra's face in her hands to share a lingering, sex-coated kiss. When their lips parted, Treasure kept their faces close together to whisper, "Chemically connected is accurate, especially after what we just did. Ivy, what's the strongest chemical bond?"

"Covalent, Miss Treasure."

"That, we're covalently bonded now," Treasure said.

Shared electrons... That was what they had. Electra liked the description and believed the science to be sound, such was the euphoric, agreeable state she was left in after giving and receiving road head.

Chapter Twelve

New Wolfsburg looked like a strangely beautiful marble upon approach. The polar ice caps stretched almost a third of the way across the surface from both ends. Swirled bands of brown land and blue water covered the habitable middle third in fluid patterns. Most planets had some sort of cloud covering, either broken or completely filling the atmosphere. On New Wolfsburg, the global weather forecast was always sunny and pleasant.

Treasure decided they should dress like Volkswagen tradeshow booth girls in tight *Fahrvergnügen* T-shirts, red shorts and VW Beetle trucker caps. The idea was to be messengers of the Driving Enjoyment God, rather than trying to convince the zealots they were the deity incarnate.

Electra stretched the shirt a little way from her chest to look at the tiny stick-figure man sitting in a driver's seat. 'Fahrfel' was what the fabricator had called the icon when Treasure had added it to the design. "Thousands of years of advancement from this and humans still draw stick-figures," she said. "If I tried to draw a man, this would be about as good as I could do."

"That's nothing," Treasure said. "Cave paintings from almost twenty thousand years ago showed humans essentially drawing stick-figures right after we discovered fire." Treasure nervously groomed Electra a little, straightening her hat, smoothing her shirt and generally fussing over placement of locks of hair and other minutiae. "So, what kind of aliens are we dealing with here?"

"Non-spacefaring," Electra said. "There isn't much on the galactic net about them. I don't know how they got their hands on an Earthling car, but they didn't go find it themselves. The real problem might come from their lack of implants. The Chamber only provides and enforces the translator implant requirement for spacefaring species, so they may or may not understand us."

"Are they dangerous?"

"Ivy says they're not very big and never developed advanced weaponry," Electra said. "Sticks and stones mostly, not that I'm keen on being hit by either if this goes sideways."

"Let's hope they aren't fast if this turns into a smash and grab," Treasure said. "Volkswagen Beetles aren't known for their top speed."

Without a true star port, they'd scanned the surface near the temple containing the sacrosanct Volkswagen for a flat expanse with a high enough density to safely hold a starship. They were going to have a couple-kilometer walk from the landing zone and a longer drive back. Ivy mapped out a second route that wouldn't leave the car stuck in quicksand, and it wasn't remotely direct.

Letterman stopped Electra at the top of the gangplank. "Am I escorting you or providing a tether?"

"Tether," Electra said. "Unless you feel like taking your chances on a sinkhole. I'd be fine with that."

"If I were rendered incapable of discharging my duties, the cost of replacement would be added to your debt and another enforcement bot would be dispatched," Letterman said.

"Then you better stay here, since Treasure says you probably weigh more than the car we're bringing back," Electra said. "Try growing a sense of humor while we're gone."

Letterman clamped a tether on Electra's wrist and rolled back into the ship. Electra had to remind herself that soon the stupid enforcement bot would be off her ship and out of her life forever. "Never owe," she muttered to herself. *Never again.*

The region of New Wolfsburg was actually kind of pleasant, if not a tad warm. They strolled along the wet sand, glancing from time to time at the tide pools and ponds of fresh water containing tiny alien marine life. Electra kept her datapad at the ready, reading the sand density to make sure they wouldn't stumble into a sinkhole. The destination was obvious on the horizon. The Wolfsburgians had built a replica of a Bavarian castle out of sandstone to house their most sacred relics, including the Volkswagen Beetle.

"Growing up, I thought quicksand would be a much bigger problem than it turned out to be," Treasure mused. "This is actually the first time I've had to watch out for it."

"Do you have a good plan?" Electra asked. "Because I've never even heard of the stuff."

"Don't fall in, ropes, tree branches...which, there aren't any trees on this whole planet," Treasure said. "Rocket boots, maybe?"

"Not a reassuring list, since we don't have any of those things."

"Wait! Are rocket boots not invented yet?" Treasure asked.

"Maybe... I don't know," Electra said. From the way Ivy had described quicksand, it sounded terrifying, and Electra was more than a little distracted in her vigilance to make sure they didn't end up breathing wet sand. "Putting rockets on boots sounds super dangerous and...you're in an awfully good mood."

"Well, duh, someone just ate me out for a really long time."

"It didn't seem like a long time."

"I meant a really short time. You should definitely go longer in the future."

"Then I definitely will!" Electra slid an arm around Treasure's waist while they walked. It felt promising to walk on a beach—or a planet that was essentially one giant beach—with someone she adored, on a warm day, glowing from mutually given orgasms, heading toward a scam that might score them two billion units. Ahead, several small, dome-topped crustaceans with six legs and four claws, two front and two back, were crawling up out of the sand to head toward the castle. They were only about two feet tall, bright orange and almost perfectly smooth all over.

"I think those are our guys." Electra nodded in the direction of the crabs, not wanting to pull her hand from around Treasure's waist or change the scan direction of the datapad in her other hand.

"Huh. They kind of look like little Volkswagens," Treasure said. "I took a religion class in undergrad that talked about vanity in deity creations. We like a religion more if the gods and goddesses look like us. I guess that's not exclusively a human thing."

"There were still human religions in your time?" Electra asked.

"Yep, a few big ones, lots of little ones."

"Did you follow any of them?" It wasn't a make-or-break question. Religions and humanity had a checkered past. The specifics weren't great, since human civilization had lost most of its records when it started its swift decline, but the vast majority of the surviving history agreed that humanity had abandoned use of religion shortly after Earth became uninhabitable. Religious belief had become completely an anathema after the introduction to spacefaring society, since only the lowest, least-advanced species among Chamber worlds believed in divine forces. Humans were nothing if not susceptible to peer pressure. Treasure appeared to be an exceptionally evolved human from an undeveloped time in human history. If she had a faith-based belief system, it would be awkward at best when speaking with other advanced species.

"Nah, some stuff is fun to think about, but most of it seems silly, especially now. None of the major human religions would have any sort of explanation for all this. A few cults talked about spaceships and aliens, but they didn't get any of it right, as far as I can tell," Treasure said. "I was raised in a church since my dad was a Kenyan Quaker, which probably doesn't mean anything to you. Imagine an education-motivated culture meeting a studious, introspective belief system and that'd be where my dad came from. I think mostly he just liked to read, think and discuss, which is all I ended up taking away from the fourteen years of churchgoing. Also, no war... My dad was vehemently against violence. Kenyans weren't fans of war and Quakers were pacifists, so this new galactic peace thing would have pleased my dad immeasurably." Treasure stopped for a moment and pulled inward. "Except, he wasn't my dad. He wasn't even real."

"He might have been," Electra said. "Who knows who you were cloned from or how your simulations were constructed, and your dad is probably every bit as real as any other human's dad at this point. Real is in the memories, and that's all either of us has of our parents anymore. So, thank you for sharing."

"I think my dad would have liked you." Treasure beamed.

They began walking again, falling in behind the herd of crustaceans swarming toward the castle. The little crabs glanced to the two new visitors with their strange, dark eyes, set in the sides and front of their shell—six in all—but they didn't say anything. When Electra smiled and waved to one, it scurried even faster to get to the doors.

"Tell me something about your dad, something small, before we go in," Treasure said, stopping just outside the castle.

"Something small..." Electra pondered. "My dad was easily the most boring person anyone ever met."

Treasure laughed and gave Electra's shoulder a push.

"I'm not kidding. It was some weird point of pride with him," Electra said. "He didn't have hobbies or interests that anyone shared, and he would drone on and on about nothing in this flat, low voice. I swear he was playing a game by himself whenever he talked to someone to see how quickly he could make their eyes glaze over."

"It's a miracle someone so vibrant came from the least interesting man in the galaxy," Treasure said.

"Oh, my two brothers and I made concerted efforts to be interesting, to the point of being strange," Electra said. "Anything but boring was our vow. My oldest brother, Rosh, learned to walk on his hands, and he'd do it at random times in the hope someone in the area would find it odd or entertaining."

"They sound great, even your ultra-boring dad," Treasure said.

"They were."

"Okay, that turned sad," Treasure said, breathing in and blinking to pull back tears. "Let's get in there and steal a car in the name of our deceased families."

Electra blotted away a single tear that had escaped from Treasure's beautiful brown eyes, using her pinkie to stop it before it spoiled her under-eye makeup. Treasure smiled, but only with her lips. Her eyes remained solemn.

They walked into what should have been the main foyer of the castle but was actually just a large hall taking up the entire interior. Apparently, the Wolfsburgians knew what the castle's exterior was supposed to look like—but nothing else. Rows upon rows upon rows of the orange crustaceans circled around a red Volkswagen Beetle sitting on a small dais, illuminated by a soft shaft of light from a hole in the roof. The collected congregation looked to the new arrivals expectantly.

"We have come from the Father Land!" Treasure announced.

The crustaceans continued to stare.

"We bring tidings of *Fahrvergnügen*," Electra added.

"*Fahrvergnügen*," the crustaceans chanted. "We welcome the messengers of driving enjoyment!"

"They're speaking German," Electra whispered.

"How can you tell?"

"When you get a little more accustomed to your implant and hear more languages, you'll start getting random thoughts when you hear someone speak or read something that's translated, telling you what the source language is," Electra whispered. "Do you speak German?"

"I speak English and some French," Treasure whispered. "Most Canadians speak at least a little of both. I can say hello in German and maybe thank you."

"Try hello."

"*Guten Tag*?" Treasure announced.

"Good day, miss," the crustaceans said in unison.

"That's all I've got," Treasure whispered.

"Okay, I have an idea. It's not going to be perfect, but let's see what we can manage." Electra brought up a tether to Ivy's galactic net connection and searched for a text-to-speech translator, refined the search to free options, refined again for ancient Earthling languages and selected the one with highest ratings. She tapped out a quick message.

The datapad translated, "*Die Götter haben geweckt!*"

"What do the Gods of driving enjoyment say, oh great messengers?" A particularly officious crustacean with a hat of pink sea foam asked.

"Um…they say…" Electra typed out another message to translate, *"Die heilige Reliquie muss in den Himmel zurückkehren."*

"We have long awaited the day the messengers would return," the presiding crustacean said. "Do you drive stick?"

"That would be directed at you." Electra handed the datapad to Treasure.

Treasure quickly tapped in her response. *"Ja, fahre ich stick!"*

The crustacean congregation erupted in a strange gurgling chortle sound that Electra hoped was cheering or applause. The Wolfsburgians scuttled apart to create a path for Electra and Treasure to approach the holiest of economy cars.

"Cars from back then required keys," Treasure whispered.

"What do we do if they're not already inside?"

At the front of the congregation, a few steps down from the dais, a small pedestal held a battered maintenance guide, in German, for the Volkswagen Beetle, and several ancient tools. Treasure scooped up the flathead screwdriver from the end.

"I'll jam this in the ignition, twist really hard and hope the lock breaks," Treasure said.

"You're a genius or a vandal or both," Electra whispered back. "What would your father say?"

"He'd tell me to stop hanging out with that fast girl from space. She's clearly up to no good." Treasure winked.

They walked to opposite sides of the car, opened the doors in unison, and slid in at the same time. The interior smelled of sea air, old rubber and a faint, underlying mildew. Treasure checked the ignition, no keys. Under the floor mat, no luck. In the tiny glove box, three packets of desiccated ketchup but no keys. She lowered the visor and the keys fell into her lap.

"That's always where the keys are in old movies," Treasure said with a giggle. "I'm still keeping the screwdriver. It might be on the Bi-MARP list for a few units."

"You are unbelievably sexy to me right now," Electra said with a grin and shake of her head.

Treasure rolled down her window. Electra followed her example. After a few mirror adjustments that Treasure admitted were mostly habit, she pressed the clutch, put the car in neutral and tried to turn it over with a tiny goose of the gas pedal. The car rolled once, lethargically, a second time, popped, sputtered, a little more gas, and it came to life, not exactly purring like a kitten.

"It sounds like an oscillating rock hammer engine," Electra said. "I love it!"

Treasure put the car in gear, let out the clutch slowly, matched with the gas, and the car rolled forward, slow, steady and under expert guidance. The crustaceans parted farther to allow the car through, still making the chortling noise. When she reached the door, which was in no way wide enough to fit the vehicle, the crustaceans rushed over and widened it, using their claws to carve a swift yet ornate new doorway from the sandstone. Treasure eased the Beetle through the portal and out onto the sand.

Electra held up the datapad with the route mapped by Ivy to make use of the densest sand to get back. Surprisingly, the nimble little Beetle had no trouble with the dry sand, chugged through a few puddles, and was well on its way before the back end slipped to one side and the rear right tire began to bog down and sink.

"Shit," Treasure said as the front left tire came off the sand. "You're sure rocket boots aren't a thing?"

"I'm not, but I don't think they'd help now anyway." Electra pushed her door to try to open it, but the car had sunk far enough on her side to block it with slurpy, wet sand. She began climbing out of the window when suddenly the car reversed course and rose out of the mire.

Treasure glanced in the side view mirror to find a small army of the crustaceans digging the car out.

"Sorry about that," one of them said. "This happened a lot when we were moving the car into the chapel. It is the Gods of Driving Enjoyment testing our resolve. But would you listen to me, telling the messengers of *Fahrvergnügen* what the Gods think. My apologies."

Treasure snagged the datapad from Electra and typed out a response. "*Die Götter bewundere Ihr Engagement*! Wait! Why am I using the datapad?" Treasure poked her head back out of the window. "*Danke*!"

"That's thank you?" Electra asked.

"Yep, if I said it right."

After several more close calls and a flurry of *dankes* whenever the Wolfsburgians had to dig them out, they arrived back at the ship. Electra focused on loading the Beetle into the cargo hold while Treasure bade farewell to the faithful.

They met back at the gangplank to wave one last time to the religious crustaceans, who waved in response, probably without knowing what the motion meant. Treasure handed back the datapad once they were on board.

Electra read Treasure's final address to the devout little crab people who had lost their most revered relic to two charlatans with a peculiar set of skills, based on a brief prophecy about driving a stick.

"The return of the messengers takes the idol you've worshipped and leaves behind the true spirit of driving enjoyment that will dwell within the believers for the rest of time. Do not look to the stars any longer. Look to each other."

"This is really beautiful," Electra told her.

"They deserved something in exchange for what we took," Treasure said. "Besides, I left out the part about building statues of us." Treasure looped her fingers inside the waistband of Electra's shorts. "Want to make out in the back seat of my new car?"

"Will we even fit?"

"Probably not, but we could have fun trying."

"Ivy, get us underway," Electra said. "We'll be in the cargo hold!"

Chapter Thirteen

Deep in the replica den of the early 1970s, where beanbag chairs, lava lamps and mural paneling of birch trees in autumn created a nostalgic mood for the era of key parties and big moustaches, Electra and Treasure did battle on the squared circle of a faded Monopoly board. Treasure had found it while exploring the ship and replaced most of the missing pieces and cards from memory and ancient texts preserved on galactic net message boards.

Letterman interrupted the slow, steady decline of Electra's resources, drained by a row of Treasure's little green houses between Kentucky Avenue and Marvin Gardens. Bad rolls had caught her twice already and Electra thoroughly blamed the dice and cursed the Atlantic City zoning commission that allowed such tightly packed residential construction.

"I need to break a five hundred," Electra groaned.

"You mean your *last* five-hundred-dollar bill," Treasure said.

"I've still got five yellows, a blue, a couple greens, three pinks and seven whites," Electra countered.

"Not for long," Treasure said.

"Here is your change, Miss Electra." Ivy's mobile management terminal that they'd set beside the coffee table accepted Electra's last orange bill and replaced it with five yellows.

Letterman entered the room and waited to be acknowledged. Treasure waved at the enforcement bot while Electra actively ignored him.

"Want to join us?" Treasure offered. "You can be the thimble, or the iron or the race car. You should be the race car. Usually nobody gets to be the race car joining a game this late."

"Why is that?" Electra asked.

"Everyone loves the race car," Treasure said.

"But you picked the dog," Electra said. "What is a dog, anyway?"

"Small furry animals that humans used to be best friends with." Treasure picked up the little pewter Scottish terrier and made it bark at Electra. Letterman rolled over to get a closer look at the game. "She picked the shoe."

"Shoes are awesome," Electra said.

"It's also the only thing she recognized," Treasure explained.

"The game is literally thousands of years before my time," Electra argued.

"A VI can grasp the rules of this game?" Letterman asked. "It would be too simplistic for me."

"Ivy is the banker," Electra said. "She's helping, not playing."

"Because Electra wanted to be the banker so she could skim money," Treasure said.

"It was a paycheck," Electra said. "You told me bankers made good money."

"Banker in this game is an unpaid position. You're lucky you didn't end up in jail for embezzlement, young lady," Treasure said.

"I did end up in jail, twice."

"This game is not present in my databanks of approved recreational activities for debtors," Letterman said.

"It's Monopoly," Electra said.

"It's the game that taught generations of impressionable children how to get screwed over in the real estate market," Treasure said, "and usually inadvertently taught them the names of a dozen or so streets in New Jersey."

"It is a human game?" Letterman asked.

"Better, it's an Earthling game," Electra said. "Bi-MARP will pay five million units for a complete set, which this one is now. We figured we'd make sure it worked first." Electra waved toward the game cabinet absentmindedly. "There's Yahtzee too, but all the scorecards are filled in."

"That's a lot of money for a game that mostly made families fight about semantics," Treasure said.

"I will log the games into your potential assets," Letterman said.

"Yeah, yeah, yeah, you do that." Electra rolled double sixes and walked her lone shoe right around the corner to the luxury tax space. "What is a luxury tax and why do I have to pay it?"

"It's a tax the government used to collect for having too many nice things," Treasure said. "And if you don't pay it, the IRS will be on your ass about your allegedly duty-free caviar."

"What's caviar?" Electra knew what duty-free meant—no taxes on importation. Caviar sounded expensive and something she should probably try.

"Fish eggs that haven't been laid yet."

"Sounds gross."

"It is," Treasure said, "but it's also strangely compelling."

Electra paid the seventy-five dollars using her last fifty, her second-to-last twenty and a quintet of ones.

"Tell me about mortgaging again?" Electra turned over her Boardwalk card to stare at the numbers on the back.

"You turn the card over to loan it out to the bank," Treasure said. "You get the top number but have to pay back the bottom number to use the card again. In the meantime, you can't collect any rent on the property. It's basically a small loan."

"Screw that. I owe enough," Electra said, realizing her mistake a moment too late. "I mean to say I owe you orgasms and favors for how much you're helping me."

"I have located an item for retrieval," Letterman said. "An elephant."

"That's big ticket," Electra said. "Also really unlikely, since none of the Bi-MARP collectors have found any living wildlife yet."

The entire process of rebuilding Earth, according to the Encyclopedia Britannica fourteenth edition, had turned two galaxies into a giant gold rush of people searching for items they wouldn't know from their own foot in hopes of making some Chamber-guaranteed money. Each collector hired subcontractors, who hired assistants, who hired temps, and they all tried to pass off every bone fragment and weird rock as an Earthling artifact. The Jun'Tar contractors then hired people to sort the mountains of junk, allowed them to subcontract, and ended up with an unwieldy mess that could barely be called an organization. On message boards and newsreels about the Chamber's latest large-scale endeavor, Electra and Sempa stood alone as the most successful contributors to the Bi-MARP project, based solely on the monetary value of what they'd provided, even though Electra had only delivered Bort to that point.

"A bioengineer on Station 111 claims to have reconstructed elephant DNA and already produced a viable sample pachyderm," Letterman said.

"I thought cloning was illegal," Treasure said.

"Sentient species are strictly forbidden. A few bioengineers are allowed limited production contracts if they reconstruct their own DNA samples and produce only non-sentient species entirely through organic printing, Miss Treasure," Ivy offered. "The current number of sanctioned bioengineers stands at seven. Would you like their names and favorite colors?"

"No, that's okay, Ivy," Treasure said. "An elephant is a big score…literally and in more ways than one."

"Off to Station 111, I guess," Electra said. "Too bad… I was just about to make my comeback in the game."

"You're almost broke," Treasure reminded her. For what seemed like the umpteen millionth time, Treasure's little doggy made its way past Go, collected two hundred dollars and headed down what she'd been referring to as 'fleabag row' of her red hotels on the purple and light blue titles she owned.

"Is there an option in this game to trade sexual favors for money?" Electra asked.

"It was originally designed for children and families, so no, obviously not," Treasure said. "But since no children and families are present..." Treasure grinned impishly.

* * * *

A sickly greenish-yellow nebula hung around Station 111, illuminated by a cluster of red dwarf stars that the whole mess slowly orbited around. Cosmic signposts warned of methane and sulfur concentrations. Certain types of engines were discouraged when passing through the artificial nebula. The station itself hung amid the putrid clouds like a fat, wallowing hog—large, essentially spherical and corroded in multiple places along the hull. Electra could feel the stench sticking to her beautiful ship from simply flying near such a vile place.

Gas farming didn't have to be a disgusting process. Plenty of species managed clean, efficient facilities to create, grow, harvest and refine all sorts of organic and inorganic gases. But Station 111 was run by Glotts, and Glotts were gross. Multiple means of producing sulfurous compounds existed within the station, along with a number of methane-generating industries. When the gasses, condensates or solids reached the desired state, concentration or decay rate for a specific use, they were expelled into the nebula to a particular region at the correct distance from the stars to remain at the same point in the cold vacuum of space or mature to a different level in the ultraviolet rays from nearby red dwarf stars. Basic, efficient and icky, the system matched perfectly the Glott mentality.

"The signs say it's run by Glotts," Treasure said. "Aren't those the pirates chasing us?"

"Yes, but Glotts are the third most populous spacefaring species," Electra said. "In both galaxies, there are something like three and a half trillion. The odds these gas farmers know Sempa or his fleet are pretty remote."

"The odds of a Glott on this station personally knowing any of Sempa or his crew are exactly ten point three billion to one, Miss Electra," Ivy said.

"See? Remote," Electra said.

"However, the odds of Sempa's bounty on you and your extremely rare ship reaching this region by now are only one hundred to one," Ivy unhelpfully offered. "The odds of a Glott on this station recognizing you or your ship are—"

"You know what? We're good on odds for right now, Ivy," Electra said. "The air won't be breathable inside, so we'll need respirators, but we shouldn't need environmental suits for the sections we're going to. Oh, and don't wear clothes you want to keep. Whatever we wear will definitely pick up stains and smells we won't want to have around."

It took the better part of an hour for Ivy to find a docking slip that Electra approved of. There were simply too many spaces where the Cadillux would be in danger of being dinged, scratched, dripped on or looked at the wrong way. By the time she approved of Ivy's selection, the jumpsuits Treasure had promised would be perfect for the upcoming job were finished printing in the fabricator.

"What do you call these again?" Electra asked, reluctantly pulling on the coarse, frumpy, grayish-blue garment that covered her from neck to wrist to ankle in functional hideousness.

"Dickies," Treasure said. "They're service industry uniforms turned into fashion statements."

"What statement could they possibly make besides that the wearer is blind and nerve-dead from the ears down?" Electra chaffed under the rigid material and all the bizarre ways in which it touched her with its unappealing bagginess.

"Yes, they're ugly, but making them used up almost no molecules in the fabricator and you'll really enjoy tossing them into the shredder when we're done," Treasure said. "Plus, you'd be adorable dressed in anything. You look like an endearing, squirmy little grease monkey right now."

"That sounded complimentary in tone, but the words didn't really fit," Electra said. "Okay, let's get an elephant's DNA and get out of here before any part of this place rubs off on any part of me or my ship."

"Will you require a tether?" Letterman asked.

"Nope, you're coming with us to touch anything I deem too disgusting," Electra said. "Then you're getting hosed down with industrial cleaners before you're allowed back on my ship."

The gangplank lowered into the murk of the docking bay. Black-and-yellow haze floated barely above eye level, obscuring the ceiling entirely and anything more than a few dozen feet away. Glancing down to the filter rating on her ventilator, Electra discovered they wouldn't have long before the corrosive, vile environment clogged their breathing apparatuses. She hated to even think about what was getting into her hair and regretted not wearing a full environmental suit for protection from being skeeved out.

The reptilian question-mark-shaped Glotts drifted through the haze, many of them leading bulbous, pulsing grubs twice the size of the Volkswagen Beetle they'd just purloined. Walking through the Glott foot traffic was slow going. Between the meandering pace the Glotts moved at and the sheer number of them, it didn't take long for Electra and Treasure to quickly outpace Letterman, who struggled mightily to move his bulk among the myriad organic obstacles.

"Why are there so many of them?" Treasure asked.

"The Glott home world isn't vastly different from a lot of the worst places in the galaxies that nobody else wants, so they picked up a ton of new territory the second they entered spacefaring society," Electra said. "They can live in almost any environment, they filter-feed noxious gases for food and they reproduce asexually." Electra steadied herself and leaped over a slime trail left by a glowing pile of worms dragged by two Glott workers. She misjudged the distance and only a quick, steadying hand from Treasure prevented her from falling into the little river of vileness in the street.

"You saved me," Electra beamed.

"You saved me first," Treasure said. "So Glotts reproduce like Om?"

"Maybe. I'm not sure how Om works," Electra said with a shrug. "I do know that Glotts don't have male or female-specific organs. They're all considered males that can impregnate themselves. And they do, a lot."

"So it'd be like if I could get pregnant whenever I masturbated?"

"Yep, with a high probability of it happening," Electra said. "I wouldn't mind seeing that, by the way. You masturbating, I mean."

"I'll show you my technique if you show me yours," Treasure teased. "Do you have sex toys? Are sex toys still a thing?"

"They are and I did have some, but they were incinerated with the rest of my stuff when I couldn't pay my rent," Electra said. "Did you have some?"

"Two, but I really only liked one of them," Treasure said.

"What was wrong with the other one?"

"Performance anxiety. It just didn't get the job done as well," Treasure said. "There was a stigma attached to sex toys in my time. Getting one required going to a specific kind of store, and those stores weren't common or nice. People were starting to sell them on the Internet. It was like the galactic net but much, much smaller and slower. The problem with that was the pictures and descriptions didn't always match what was sent."

"Ancient human modesty is so strange," Electra said with a laugh. "Most species now have elaborate stimulators that some even wear in public. You can print whatever you want right off the fabricator and recycle it if it doesn't curl your toes. I'm actually feeling somewhat abnormal for not immediately replacing the ones I lost."

"We should print some when we're done here," Treasure said. "The famous Captain Rex can't be thought a sexual deviant for not owning orgasmic accoutrements."

If it weren't for Ivy's assistance in illuminating a path on the head-up display of Electra's mask, she doubted she could have found the bioengineering firm. Everything on Station 111 looked the same—gross, corroded, slime-covered rounded metal buildings, silos, collection tanks and holding pens. At long last the green line faded out on a nondescript, domed domicile. Electra stood in the security scanner of the front door and waited for the pale blue lights to pass over her, then Treasure and finally Letterman when he caught up. The dome cracked wide enough to allow them entrance.

Electra thought she'd be glad to get out of the chaotic, bustling streets where she had to dodge surly Glotts and their disgusting livestock, but once she was inside, every other sense she had was bombarded by a thousand different animal species making every noise, smell and light display they could to defend themselves from intruders. Cages lined every wall, covered every surface and dangled from the ceiling. Each contained creatures both great and small from every corner of the Milky Way and Andromeda galaxies.

A Chizzerod emerged from behind a bio-fabrication tank, wiping her hands on a rag. The little alien made several strange noises and gestures in every direction and eventually the agitated creatures in the tanks and cages calmed. Even Electra's translator implant couldn't understand anything that was said or done by the Chizzerod when communicating with the animals.

Chizzerods were fairly common in the Andromeda Galaxy, less so in the Milky Way. The Chizzerod bioengineer in question was short, a little under four feet tall, mammalian and for the most part looked like a white, humanoid rat sporting backward knees, enormous pointed ears and a lone eye in the center of her forehead.

"I am Professor Mims," the Chizzerod said. "Which one of you is Letterman?"

Electra jerked her thumb backward to the enforcement bot who'd followed them into the dome.

"I am Letterman, a lien enforcement bot," Letterman said. "And these are my assistants."

"We're not your assistants," Electra said.

"You are assisting me in this transaction, thus you are my assistants," Letterman retorted.

"From your messages, I thought you'd be shorter and more organic," Professor Mims said. "No matter. You came to see the elephant and so you shall." She dropped to all fours and scurried between the cages, tables, containers and tubing running through the lab to reach a panel on the far wall. The Professor punched a code into a security panel using her prehensile, scaled tale. The wall slid open a crack. From the brightly lit room beyond, a mighty trumpeting echoed into the lab.

"Come along, Georgie." Professor Mims attempted to coax the elephant from its separate chamber using a synthetic peanut daintily held between two long, sharp claws. The trumpeting stopped, a shadow darkened the gap in the wall and a two-foot-tall, bright green elephant emerged to accept the offered treat.

Electra looked to Treasure for confirmation. Treasure held up a hand, palm down, and made the 'sort of' gesture by wobbling it.

"Where exactly did you get the DNA for the elephant?" Treasure asked.

"It wasn't extracted…no extant species to get a sample from," Professor Mims said. "I found partial records of a genome and wrote genetic code to fill in the gaps. It's a full reconstruct without source genetic material. I have a deft hand when it comes to recreating complex species from nothing but a few scraps of genomic code and a vague description."

"That explains quite a bit," Treasure said.

"You are looking at the foremost expert in pachyderm behavior and history," Professor Mims said, scooping up the elephant to cuddle it like a puppy, despite the green creation being half her size and probably equal in mass. "I've researched and catalogued all available information on the no-longer-extinct species of African elephant in the most thorough compendium since the fall of Earth."

"It's a very impressive...*thing* you've created there," Electra said. "Lots of ear and nose going on."

"Can you imagine thousands of these roaming the mighty forests of Antarctica?" Professor Mims said.

"Not the right continent," Treasure muttered.

"Feasting on tree-dwelling marmots."

"They were herbivores."

"Performing tricks in human circuses for peanuts."

"That one is true," Treasure admitted.

"Letterman said Bi-MARP has a Chamber-certified bioengineer to recreate the population of these adorable little guys and return them to the planet they once ruled," Professor Mims said.

"Yes, that's been the plan all along for Bi-MARP," Electra lied. "Antarctica will once again swarm with green pachyderms and circuses will feature peanut-guzzling performers...all because of your generosity."

"Four hundred million units," Professor Mims said. "That's what I was promised."

"That is ten times more than my entire operation's credit line," Electra growled at Letterman.

"Correction. It *will be* your entire operation's credit line when you turn in the items you've collected,"

Letterman said. "The delivery of the elephant DNA, along with everything else you've acquired, will cover the repayment, interest and may even provide a small profit, depending on your expedience, thus clearing your debt entirely."

"Fine. As long as I end up in the black, this stressful trip into a cesspool will have been worth it," Electra said. "Transfer the funds."

A few lights flashed on the front of Letterman's frame. Corresponding lights flashed on a console on the desk near Professor Mims.

"Wonderful doing business with you," Professor Mims said. "I hope this will mean I get an invitation to the grand opening of the Bi-MARP amusement park."

"I'm sure it will," Electra said.

Professor Mims' tail swirled around with excitement at the prospect. She gathered a syringe gun, touched it to Georgie's side and extracted a sample of blood, encasing it immediately in a cooling chamber before it even popped out of the handle of the device. Georgie glanced back to what she was doing but returned to his docile cuddling when his trunk found a stash of peanuts in the Professor's pocket. Professor Mims offered the sample to Electra. Before she could accept it, one of Letterman's tentacle arms reached past her and grabbed it, depositing the frozen sample in a collection chamber.

"It's been a pleasure doing business with you," Treasure said while guiding a stunned and irritated Electra out of the dome.

"Don't forget my invitation to the grand opening!" Professor Mims called after them.

The numbers weren't adding up. Electra struggled to both walk through the crowded streets and do the math in her head to figure out how Letterman had come up with the four hundred million units. She couldn't remember the exact percentage of operational credit she'd earned by turning in the Bort Pod, but she knew it wasn't large enough to get her to four hundred million by turning in the Volkswagen Beetle, the data crystal from Paul, the board games and the screwdriver Treasure had snagged on New Wolfsburg. Luckily Treasure and Letterman were able to guide her while she ran through the complex mental calculations required to explain the four hundred million she'd just spent on elephant blood.

They were at the base of the gangplank before she finally put it all together.

"If it isn't the thief extraordinaire who keeps snaking my finds and smashing up my ships," Sempa called from behind her.

Electra pushed Treasure in front of Letterman and ushered them both up the gangplank ahead of her while she walked backward to keep an eye on Sempa and his crew. The Glott raiders were filtering out of the busy streets, armed to the teeth and angry as a fresh bruise. It hadn't even occurred to her that someone planning to collect the bounty on her wouldn't even try to apprehend her themselves but rather drop the dime as it were and call in Sempa. Electra felt incredibly stupid for overlooking the more obvious outcome. She couldn't let Sempa see her blink, though.

"Sempa, you're getting faster," Electra said. "Not fast enough to beat me anywhere, but you're going to get a much better view of me leaving this time."

"You're not going anywhere," another voice said from the right of Sempa and his men.

A small squadron of debt-collection bots rolled through the Glott-choked streets to create a semi-circle of metal orbs, wheels and tentacles that would block any potential escape. Each collection bot was comprised of an expandable collection orb body, three tilted wheels for stability and a writhing swarm of metal, prehensile tentacle arms to grab everything in sight in the most efficient way possible.

"The Lien Enforcement Technology Bureau was notified that you are in possession of assets in excess of your outstanding debts," the collection bots said in unison. "Collection and liquidation of said assets must occur immediately according to corporate procedural standards."

They meant Treasure. That was how Letterman had come up with the four hundred million. He was borrowing against the fifty billion units she would fetch when turned over to Bi-MARP. It was the only way the math made sense.

"You can't collect on what is mine," Sempa roared. "Her ship, her gains, her body all belong to me and my crew."

"No such transaction is found in…" The first collection bot in the row exploded, struck by a rocket from Sempa's body-mounted weapon pod.

"Why don't you all sort out the confusion out among yourselves and let me know who gets to be mad at me first when you're finished." Electra ran up the gangplank, hitting the button to close it behind her even as the battle between the Glott pirates and phalanx of collection bots began in earnest. Lasers, rockets, bullets, flamethrowers and a bunch of other weapons she wasn't interested in being hit by roared to life and were suddenly silenced when the gangplank on her ship closed up.

"Ivy, get us out of here," Electra yelled. "Ivy? Did you hear me?"

Electra reached the top of the stairs to head toward the cockpit, wondering why Ivy wasn't responding and where Letterman and Treasure had gone. She heard Treasure scream from the cargo hold. Electra sprinted back the way she came, turned toward the rear of the ship, all the while yelling at the unresponsive Ivy to get the ship started.

By the time she reached the cargo hold, Letterman had Treasure gripped by the ankles, lifting her ten feet off the floor. Treasure had a death grip on the roof rack of the Volkswagen Beetle to keep from being dropped into the open, waiting main collection chamber of Letterman's body. To try to facilitate the collection, Letterman had tilted his entire frame backward to create a box of himself with the top open.

At a dead sprint, Electra scooped the globauncher and a full brace of glob balls from brackets on the wall and tossed all twenty of the glob balls into Letterman's open collection chamber. Leaping from the top of the cargo-block holding the Volkswagen in place, Electra flattened out, dropkicking Letterman's door to close it, sliding across the top of his slanted position and striking the activation trigger on the globauncher tube in her hand when she'd rolled off the other side.

Twenty ten-by-ten-by-ten cubes of semi-solid globs held within Letterman's body expanded instantaneously. Letterman's main collection chamber didn't have even a fraction of the space required to contain so much swiftly swelling material. His frame buckled, glob leaked from every seam, smoke and sparks erupted from the top mounting point where his arms emerged and all controlled functions ceased. Treasure lowered herself onto the top of the Volkswagen when the tentacle holding her ankles shorted out.

Electra scooped the souvenir screwdriver from the nearby bench and ran to the disabled enforcement bot. She dug at the opened panel on the side and swatted away quickly sizzling wires until she got at his primary signal transmitter. If she could get to the transmitter before he sent the lockdown code, the ship might still fly. Four hard jabs with the flathead screwdriver and the transmitter came free from its mounting. Another twist and tug broke the wires connecting it to Letterman's CPU. He'd jammed Ivy's signal, summoned collection bots probably before they'd even landed and tried to kidnap the woman she was pretty sure she was falling head over heels in love with. She didn't care that she'd be charged for the massive amount of damage she'd inflicted on Letterman. It was his turn to pay.

"Ivy, can you hear me?" Electra shouted.

"I can, Miss Electra. There's no need to yell," Ivy said.

"Get us the hell out of here!"

Chapter Fourteen

Too much was going on…way too much. The only plan she could think of was to run like hell. She had an expensive ship filled with an insane number of valuables and the most important person in her life. She hadn't been remotely cautious enough. Electra grabbed Treasure by the hand and helped her off the top of the Volkswagen. Step one had to be getting Treasure away from everyone trying to kidnap her.

"He attacked me," Treasure said, with a thousand-yard stare aimed at Letterman's glob-filled body. "I thought we were friends."

"I know, baby," Electra said. "Right now, I need to get to the cockpit and I want you with me."

Dragging Treasure along wasn't strictly necessary, but Electra pulled her by the hand all the same. If she had physical contact with Treasure at all times, Electra believed she could prevent another attack from happening. By the time they reached the cockpit, Ivy had already guided them through the docking bay, which was becoming something of a war zone between Glott pirates and collection bots.

Electra vaulted into the captain's seat and studied the controls, hoping a plan would formulate organically. There would be raider ships outside and at least one debt collection mother-orb. If she were lucky, they'd be fighting each other. The Glott pirates would want to board her ship to plunder all the Bi-MARP treasures, but the debt collection ship wouldn't bother with such provincial looting, since a mother-orb could swallow the Cadillux whole without scratching the paint.

The Cadillux passed from the inner airlock to the vacuum of space. The outer doors opened, green lights flashed on the walls, telling her to get out so the next ship in line could leave. She couldn't see the small fleet of vessels waiting in the nebula for her and her scopes wouldn't work until she was in the thick of it.

"What do we do?" Treasure asked.

"We...um...make a decoy!" Electra leaped back out of the captain's seat, bounded down the stairs and ran for the cargo hold, bouncing off walls here and there along the way. *A datapad, an uplink tether to Letterman's removed transmitter and a general distress signal for an escaped debtor...* After stripping off her smelly Dickies jumpsuit, she wrapped the datapad connected to the transmitter in the unwanted garment and dropped the bundle into the airlock garbage chute. A whoosh of air and a light above the airlock going from red to green sent the bundle out of the ship. "Ivy?"

"Yes, Miss Electra?"

"How close can you get us to the ceiling in the exit bay?"

"With the repulse engines turned off, less than a meter, while still accounting for drift," Ivy said.

"Works for me," Electra said. "Do it." Gone were the days of being overly cautious about putting the Cadillux in danger, apparently. Without a moment's hesitation, she was going to put it a meter away from the top of essentially a garbage chute with the repulse engines turned off, all to save Treasure, the only thing she cared about anymore.

Electra made a quick stop by the Spatronic to place her face in the adjustment port. She set the tuner for her ocular implants to change her vision to a broader range of the ultraviolet spectrum. After a disorienting series of flashes from the machine, her eyesight glassed over in white for a moment. When her vision returned, she saw the world in an entirely different series of colors and detail. Relying on the scopes for what she intended would only slow her down.

By the time Electra returned to the cockpit, the Cadillux was nearly to the top of the exterior airlock chamber. Electra checked the scopes. To push off in order to float to the top, the repulse engines had knocked her little transmitter bundle into the bottom corner of the airlock by the door back into Station 111. She watched the space in front of the doorway. Flashes of light spoke of a battle moving closer within the sickly yellow nebula. With her newly enhanced visual spectrum she spotted a series of small spheres launched into the docking bay — collection bots, chased by two pirate skiffs. More dark shapes came toward the open doors, and the green flashing lights went red, warning of a jam in the docking procedures. Impact warnings flashed on the screens all around the cockpit. Electra slammed the accelerator to the floor and pulled straight up the moment they cleared the bay. She watched the front window at the very top edge to keep the curved exterior of Station 111 directly above the ship, as close as she was able with Ivy's help, until they crested the top, scraping the paint off the tops of the Cadillux's fins along the station's hull.

It was tempting, oh-so-tempting, to dump spare oxygen into the methane field and light it. She could scorch the debt collectors, the pirates, everyone making her life a living hell. But it wasn't the Glott gas farmers' fault she was caught, and it would be their crops she'd be torching. Technically, at least one of the Glotts had screwed her over by calling Sempa, but they weren't going to get paid now that she'd slipped the noose. Ruthlessness wasn't in her nature, even if she wished it were sometimes.

"Ivy, are any skiffs or collection bots following?" Electra asked. "I can't make sense of the readings."

"Both groups appear to have been forcibly ejected from the airlock shortly after our departure, Miss Electra," Ivy said, "and are currently drifting into the gas fields opposite the station from us."

"We need a wormhole spawn—and not the one we used to get here." Electra tabbed through the options. Two existed on the other side of the red dwarf cluster, rarely used and designated primarily for heavy freighters. It'd take hours to get there even at top speed and she could only hope it wasn't guarded by either or both of the groups after her. At least it'd give her time to figure out where they were going after that—if they were going anywhere.

"You saved me, again," Treasure said. "In a badass way, I might add. And now you're naked, flying a ship like a pro."

"I couldn't keep the jumpsuit on a second longer," Electra admitted. "Plus, I needed it as wadding for the datapad and transmitter. Otherwise they might have bounced around in the chute and broken."

"I'm not complaining about the view," Treasure said. "Why was Letterman after me?"

"Who even knows what that bastard was planning?" Electra said. For several fairly obvious reasons, it was exceedingly difficult to lie effectively while naked. She tried to lean back and turn her chest in an appealing way in hopes of distracting Treasure from the fib. It wasn't a full lie—a mere question, rhetorical perhaps. Sure, she knew the answer, but that didn't matter, especially if she could get Treasure to look at her girls. A wayward glance down from Treasure's big, brown eyes to Electra's chest, and the matter was set aside.

"How long will it take to reach the wormhole spawns, Ivy?" Treasure asked.

"Two point six-six-six-six-repeating-infinitely hours, Miss Treasure."

"Let's be nudists for two point six-six-six-six-repeating-infinitely hours. Letterman isn't able to walk in on us anymore. And I used to be a secret nudist whenever I had my apartment to myself." Treasure practically leaped from her Dickies jumpsuit and dropped it into the nearest fabricator recycling port.

"Works for me," Electra said. "Somehow you look even more amazing in an expanded light spectrum."

"Hey, you got to use your ocular implants," Treasure exclaimed. "We need champagne to celebrate!"

"What are we celebrating?" Electra asked.

"Staying one step ahead of the space pirates," Treasure replied. "Also, another heroic moment to add to the growing legend of the daring Captain Rex. That part I'm not joking about. I'm going to tell everyone what you've done, embellishments all over the place. Nobody is going to trust a word of it because even the simple truth is too crazy to believe."

Electra chuckled and walked to the fabricator by the stairwell into the cockpit. That used to be her dream, to be rich and famous, swimming in renown, respect and adoration from a fanatical public. It seemed like a frivolous goal in hindsight. Ivy had already brought up the headings for beverages closely approximating champagne on the fabricator console, which apparently required some strange-looking glasses to drink properly. *Whatever.* They had the molecules to spare, especially of silica and hydrocarbons. She hit the print button and waited.

"What must the galaxy know about me?" Electra asked, preening a little to gild the question, even as her stomach did somersaults. She'd have to tell Treasure the truth. There was no way around it. They weren't hiding from Sempa and his merry band of fuck-ups. She'd already proven she could outrun them whenever she needed to. The Lien Enforcement Agency was after them now, and they weren't going to give up—not for the tens of billions Electra owed—and they weren't bungling pirates in rickety ships.

"A daring starship captain and pilot," Treasure said. "That is essential. Granted, you're the only starship captain I've flown with, but I'm impressed. Besides, you have to be good considering that multiple times now you've out-flown pirates that feed themselves by catching people."

"Daring or reckless?" Electra accepted the printed bottle of champagne and two crystal flutes. The bottle was closed in a peculiar way she couldn't make heads or tails of. She brought the items to Treasure in hopes she knew what was meant to be done or if the sealing on the top of the bottle was a mistake by the fabricator.

"Daring *and* reckless, but, more importantly, skilled and creative." Treasure took the bottle, peeled away the thin layer of metal, twisted a wire contraption then worried free a chunk of fibrous material from the neck of the bottle using her thumbs. A loud pop sounded when the plug leaped free and bounced across the floor. Treasure got the mouth of the bottle over one of the glasses in Electra's hand a moment before white foam poured out. "That reminds me… The galaxy also must know what a gifted, attentive, physically blessed lover you are."

"I think the credit for that needs to be shared by my partner," Electra said. "There are two people making that dance what it is."

"I'm absolutely going to play up my role in all of this," Treasure said, accepting a glass once it was filled. "I'm silver-tongued and charismatic, boasting arcane knowledge of all things Earthling. I've charmed the Coke recipe from a tree, a Volkswagen Beetle from a cult of crabs and the pants right off the greatest starship captain I've ever known. Obviously, I can't tell people *that* overtly. I'll have to weave it in as subtext while I'm talking about your exploits."

"The evidence of your womanly wiles is clearly demonstrated by the state I'm in." Electra clinked her glass against Treasure's and they both drank.

"Yet you don't seem like you're celebrating, not really," Treasure said. "You're going through the motions and all, but you're not actually happy. Why is that?"

"Destroying a lien enforcement bot is kind of a big deal," Electra said. "A criminally big deal. Not to mention the pirates… They're getting closer to catching us with all the practice we're giving them."

"I honestly kind of thought you were exaggerating about the pirates, since I could only kind of tell what was going on during the wormhole chase," Treasure said. "I mean, alien space pirates? It seemed silly. I have to admit that I'm bummed I didn't get to see you in action, talking your way out of the situation and tricking the two sides into fighting each other. I was a little preoccupied trying not to be eaten by a robotic refrigerator. Hopefully, next time I'll have a better view of your heroics."

"Heroically running away. Remember how you asked me about the lawbreaking after we ran the scam to get the Coca-Cola?" Electra asked.

"Yeah."

"We hadn't committed crimes then. I don't think. Maybe some light charity fraud," Electra said. "I definitely committed several today—the kind people will come looking for me about. Dangerous, powerful people, worse than the pirates by far."

"Okay, no more joking. You're worried," Treasure said. "Count me in on team worried. Let's talk next step. We need to get out of the system. We're doing that. Lie low and let the heat die down. That's what we need to do." Treasure set aside her glass and placed her hands on Electra's shoulders, massaging them lightly while they spoke.

Electra didn't know that many places, and all the places she was familiar with were known haunts of hers that could easily be staked out. Both the collections agency and probably Sempa would have people watching Station 51. Her old apartment on Authrillia was no good, for a bunch of reasons—last known address, not really hers anymore, bad part of town, all her furniture had been incinerated, etc. If she stayed anywhere near a wormhole spawn, they ran the risk of being spotted by a random patrol, other treasure hunters or mercenaries passing through and obviously Sempa's bounty was far more effective than Electra had originally given it credit for.

"Transition Island," Electra finally said. It was the only place she knew that wasn't attached to her name. She hadn't become Electra Rex until after living there more than a year. Before that, she'd been Sami Boyle, and Sami Boyle didn't exist anymore.

Chapter Fifteen

From a distance, Janis 10 looked like a nondescript gray orb floating on the farthest reaches of a twin blue giant star system. The clouds from passing storms and the gray of the oceans that covered better than ninety-nine percent of the surface were within one or two shades of each other. Only after they slipped through the atmosphere did specific features become obvious. The planet was dotted with millions of little black islands in completely irregular patterns. Without knowing which specific dot of land in which hemisphere, it would take years to search them all for a fugitive.

Electra guided the Cadillux to the only familiar island of the bunch, the one where she'd become a woman in so many ways. Among its occupants, of whom none remained, it had once been known as 'Transition Island', although the maps and scientists simply referred to it by its designation of SW230.

A light drizzle pelted the ship on approach to the slightly overgrown landing pad set in a jungle of wide-leafed blue ferns. Electra double-checked the scopes to make sure the planet was still habitable. Everything was as she remembered – soft and gentle. Janis 10 had been selected for its mild climate, complete lack of anything dangerous and its remote location. It wasn't beautiful or exotic or even interesting, but it was pleasant and nurturing – the perfect place for young people from multiple species to transition from one lifecycle to another in complete safety.

Electra walked down the gangplank to return to her former home – and it did feel like home, more than anywhere else she could remember. Treasure followed close behind. The rain that fell on her face and into the lush surrounding jungle was the purest water in the galaxy. That was what the scientists had claimed. It brought out the single note of wet, volcanic sand.

"Is there anything we should look out for?" Treasure asked. "Snakes or spiders or jungle cats or something?"

"We're the only animals on the entire planet," Electra said. "Every plant you see is edible and all the water is drinkable. We're in a place completely at peace with itself."

They headed into the facility. The collection of modular rectangles connected to form a pattern of a small, irregular ring. They were painted a gray similar to the sky and water, probably so as not to offend the serenity of the planet's muted palette. In the years since Electra had left, the jungle had done little to reclaim the land cleared for the facility. Aside from being empty, the facility was exactly how Electra remembered it – clean, quiet and blank.

Windows and skylights provided ample light. The electronics even turned on when they arrived, still functional and fed by the geothermal power source that had been sunk into the island before the facility had been built. Any evidence of the former inhabitants had been scrubbed. Electra stopped at a blank space on the wall, only noteworthy because of the four screw holes used to hold the display containing pictures and bios of the transitioning occupants so they could get to know one another if they wanted to. She remembered stopping there often, unhappy with the picture they'd used for her, since it had looked like Sami and she hadn't wanted to be Sami. After each stage of the transition, the scientists had updated the pictures and slowly Sami had faded away to be replaced by Electra.

Fourteen other residents had been there when she'd arrived and a different fourteen when she'd left. Fifteen wasn't the max capacity of the facility, not even close. She'd always wondered why the scientists had kept that number as a constant. They'd probably scrubbed that information from the computers before leaving.

"Who built this place?" Treasure asked.

"An advanced form of artificial intelligence, the last remnant of a dead society from somewhere in the Andromeda Galaxy," Electra said. "They used holograms specific to each species to interact with us. We just called them 'the scientists'."

"They were experimenting on you?"

"Observing, asking questions, measuring some-times," Electra said. "Helping... They did a lot of helping."

"What were they trying to learn?"

Electra shrugged. "No clue. They apparently learned it and moved on, though."

"This wasn't a Chamber project?"

"Nah, this was some side thing from a strange collective of electronic memories that wanted to better understand organic life forms," Electra said. "They took a deposit from each participant, I guess to make sure we were serious. Then they gave it back when we left. I'm not sure where they got their actual funding, but it probably wasn't the Chamber. The Chamber usually prints their name all over everything they even tacitly support. It makes them seem omniscient or proactive or something."

"If you ever figure out who they are, let me know. I'd like to know where to send the thank you card for doing such a good job," Treasure said. "You became a remarkable woman."

"Thank you," Electra said. "I got the feeling I wasn't the easiest transition to complete. Most of the other species had some natural instincts or societal patterns they followed. All the stuff on transitioning humans was old and sometimes contradictory." Electra smiled. "I never got the feeling the scientists were upset or frustrated by it, though. They even gave me my name."

"You didn't pick it?"

"I didn't think that's how it should work. Most people don't pick their own names. You're born, your parents name you and you get used to the idea. After I mentioned that in a therapy session, they offered to name me and I agreed. I guess they thought Electra Rex sounded quintessentially human," Electra said.

"Is it? Quintessential for Embarker humans, I mean?"

"No, I've never even heard of any humans having either name, let alone both. And I even knew that at the time, but it sounded cool, so I went with it," Electra said. "Want to see my old room?"

They walked upstairs to one of the dormitories overhanging an expansive beach of black volcanic sand. Small waves lapped gently against the shore. The outer wall of the room was glass. The rest was three blank, gray walls, a low, domed ceiling with a skylight at the pinnacle and a somewhat spongy floor.

"I love what you've failed to do with the place," Treasure said of the blank room.

"It all slides out of the walls, funny girl." Electra pressed her palm against the scanner beside the door. Nothing happened. She walked around the room and manually tapped the sensors to extend the bed, desk and closet. "My settings must have been scrubbed."

Treasure sat on the edge of the bed and looked out of the window. "Were you the only human?"

"Yep, but I wasn't the only sex-transitioning resident," Electra said. "I'm glad my transition was largely accomplished with hormone implants and a couple of surgeries. There were several species here that changed their entire anatomies during different life cycles, and it looked rough."

"A bunch of teenagers, zoomed up on transitioning hormones... I'll bet you all got to know each other pretty well," Treasure said, waggling her eyebrows. "Did you have a sweetheart one room over?"

Treasure had been poking around Electra's sexual history some, seemingly out of curiosity for what kind of lurid and emotional attachments a human could find among the stars. For the most part, Electra didn't mind divulging, since she wasn't big on feeling shame and didn't have much to tell beyond sexual dalliances. There was something Electra had held back and it seemed to be the only thing Treasure really wanted to know.

"Her name was Essala," Electra said. "She was a Whippomorph." Electra leaned back against the edge of the desk and stuffed her hands into her pockets. It wasn't an explosive story, simply a sad one.

"Tell me about her," Treasure said, "if you're up for it."

"She got here about a year after me," Electra said. "Whippomorphs have five life cycles. She was going from the second to the third and the third to the fourth here. I guess it's dangerous to do it on her home planet, so her parents saved up to send her here, which was my story too. We bonded over that immediately. Most of the other species had no trouble coming up with the units for the deposit, but not us. We were practically charity cases. When she got here, she looked a lot like a little green fish in a fish tank. I didn't talk to her during that first transition from second to third phase. She spent all her time in the aquatic section with the other liquid-breathing species."

Electra looked down and smiled faintly. "Things were different when she emerged from the tanks. We'd only seen each other once before that, when she'd first arrived. She remembered it vividly. In her third life cycle, she was pretty close to human-looking. Her skin was blue, she had webbed fingers and toes, perfectly white eyes and soft fins instead of hair, but she was very human in every other respect. I only later learned Whippomorphs select their third phase based on a mating impression formed in the second phase."

Treasure gasped and smiled. "She changed her whole body just to be with you?"

"It's not consciously done, but, yeah, she did," Electra said. "We started spending all our time together swimming, walking in the jungle, talking about space travel, then we started fooling around, and naturally we moved into what the scientists called 'nearly constant copulation, followed by extended periods of physical contact.' Seriously, that description of our activities was repeated to us every day—not as an accusation, simply as a question. They wanted to know if intense lovemaking followed by lengthy cuddle sessions was normal for our species during transition."

"What did you tell them?"

"I had no idea if it was normal for humans. Essala said it was normal and expected for her species, essential even," Electra said. "I think I was in love, pumped full of hormones and wildly attracted to someone. Having that pattern repeated with you makes me think it had nothing to do with transitioning. If I knew where the scientists went, I'd send them a galactic net message to let them know it wasn't part of the change. It was all part of how humans fall in love. Falling in love isn't something Embarkers spend much time thinking or talking about, so it was new and strange to me."

"What happened? How did it end?"

"She was supposed to get genetic material from me for future reproductive use in other life cycles," Electra said. "That didn't work out."

"Why not? You produce plenty in my experience."

"She morphed to match me in *every* way," Electra said. "I found that insanely attractive. I guess that's one of the upsides to the morphing. She could almost sense on a genetic level what form might be most alluring. It worked perfectly to entice me to mate, but there's an obvious problem with collecting genetic material when the inner workings don't have any sort of place to store it."

"What happened when she figured that out?"

"She got mad — not at me or even herself, just mad in general," Electra said. "Mostly she directed her disappointment at the scientists, not that they had any control over any of it. They were simply watching while her body did what it was naturally supposed to do — a hiccup of genetics and evolution that hadn't been expressed before because her kind had never encountered someone like me. She would never have children and it was in some way my fault."

"But you didn't know…"

"She didn't blame me and I've tried not to blame myself," Electra said. "She left after completing her transition to the fourth phase and we never spoke again."

"Do you know where she is now?"

Electra shook her head. "The fourth Whippomorph phase is spacefaring. In the bluntest of terms…right now she's a very large dolphin, flying through nebulas, eating star dust."

"Wow, and I thought the story of my first love had a sad ending."

"What happened to your first love?"

"He moved to Winnipeg," Treasure said. "Winnipeg was crazy cold and their hockey team wasn't very good. It seemed worse when I was thirteen."

Electra smiled and tried to force a laugh. "Essala was always going to move to Winnipeg, so to speak. I'm only sorry she didn't get to take a piece of me with her the way she'd hoped."

"It sounds like you took a piece of her with you," Treasure said. "Not literally in that way, but I am a little curious if you did give her something in a way. What I mean to say is she had an important impact on your life. I'm sure you had a similar influence on her."

"Thanks, I hope so. Or maybe not. Fond memories being a poor substitute and all."

Silence hung between them for a time, only occasionally interrupted by a breeze blowing raindrops against the window. Eventually a strange smile played over Treasure's lips.

"But did you...you know...both ways with her since she morphed to be like you?" Treasure asked.

"Yes." Electra rolled her eyes.

"That's hot." Treasure squirmed and giggled a little at the thought.

Chapter Sixteen

Electra and Treasure frolicked on the beach, swam naked in the tepid freshwater oceans and wandered around the facility a little more to see if anything of interest was left behind. The scientists had done an extremely thorough job of clearing everything of value, information especially, but had left the buildings in good enough working order that they could quickly return to do research again if they decided to make use of the grounds for another round of transitions or some other project. The sunset was drab, grayish-blue and over entirely too quickly. It was nearly dark and another rainstorm rolled across the island before they returned to the ship.

Treasure decided to take some time in the Spatronic while Electra headed up to the cockpit to see if her spy probes had picked up anything interesting near the system's lone wormhole spawn. The little dark matter orbiting bots could go stealth, self-destruct and relay information at a moment's notice. Electra hoped the three little bots hadn't had to do anything. They were expensive to print and stood as her last line of warning to run again. Losing even one of them would be a blow. The bots gave the all-clear. *Not a bad day, considering my life has gone completely off the rails.*

Ivy offered one of Treasure's new mixtures…Cherry Coke. Electra didn't know what a cherry was, but Treasure hadn't steered her wrong yet. She accepted the drink and took a sip. A cherry was apparently a fruit or a chemical or a fruit-flavored chemical.

She paced the cockpit with her drink, reviewing the options on her datapad. She'd seriously damaged a lien enforcement bot. Aside from stealing the ship in the first place, that was the most significant crime she'd ever committed. There would be hefty fines, significant prison time and some other unpleasantness if she were caught. Since she was a known fugitive, the Bi-MARP project couldn't take goods from her anymore, and nor could any other Chamber project. She couldn't work as a professional party guest again without exposing herself and Treasure to massive amounts of risk, both from the pirates and the lien enforcers. They could live on Transition Island indefinitely, although that would be a lonely, exceedingly boring way to spend the next hundred years or so.

She stopped in her tracks and nearly dropped her half-empty glass of soda. Something had changed in the room — something small and almost unnoticeable, a constant that she'd hope would remain constant. The number at the bottom of the spacefaring species list had changed. The depressing, but stable, three hundred eleven number had plummeted to three. That was it. Humanity was done. It wouldn't matter if Bi-MARP succeeded, at least not to humans. Electra stared at the three, willed it to change, cried when it didn't and became catatonic shortly after. All her efforts to distance herself from the hope the three hundred eleven number represented had failed. She'd been given a taste of humanity having a future, albeit a brief and tenuous possibility, but she'd cherished it. Humanity would die out. The concept was so much harder to get used to a second time.

That was how Treasure found her, sitting on the floor, staring off into space, spilled Cherry Coke spreading across the cabin.

"We went extinct today," Electra said.

* * * *

Electra slipped out before Treasure woke up. She headed down to the facility without a specific goal in mind. Everything she'd thought and believed when she'd been a resident of Transition Island seemed so quaint in retrospect. She wasn't going back to the flotilla. She'd been right about that, at least. Send money back to her parents—that had been her plan. A complete collapse of her species hadn't even occurred to her as a possibility when she had been young, in love and becoming what she'd always wanted to be. The writing had been clearly on the wall, considering the steep decline in Embarker fleets to that point. She simply hadn't allowed herself time to think about it. She'd wanted luxury, excitement and she'd gotten it, albeit at a hefty price. When her flotilla had failed, when every known human besides her had died, she'd thrown herself into hedonism and found it comforting for a time. A libertine lifestyle could conceal a lot of pain, she'd discovered, but even then she'd known it couldn't be her life, not the whole of it. When Ivy had found the old census records, Electra had clung to the three hundred eleven number. Someone, somewhere, knew where more humans were, and that had been all that had mattered. They were out there, even if she never met them. She figured she could live her life the way she wanted, hopefully with Treasure, and leave the survival of her species to the other people she'd probably never meet. It was a silly, selfish, stupid dream and it collapsed in an instant with the simple change of a number on a screen—a number that might have been wrong all along.

"Knock, knock," Treasure said, knocking lightly on the open door of Electra's old dormitory room. "Why do people do that? Say 'knock, knock' and then knock anyway? Do people still do that?"

"They do, since you just did it, but, yes, that's apparently a human thing. Both my parents used to do it too," Electra said.

"How are you holding up?" Treasure asked. "I'm personally going with shocked into numbness, but I can understand why that might be easier for me to manage with the help from Ivy's mood pills and the fact that everything has been a pretty big shock to me lately."

"I'm trapped in my own head with a storm. We're probably not going to know what happened, either," Electra said. "Maybe they were all frozen like Bort and finally crashed into a star. Maybe they were a long-lost tribe of Embarkers who had a life support malfunction on their ship. Maybe it was always a technical estimate that was finally updated. Maybe I'm an overly optimistic idiot for ever asking Ivy to look for more. I guess it doesn't matter now."

"I can't believe that," Treasure said. "You sought out hope, found some and lost it. That's powerful and meaningful."

Electra tried to force a smile. "There's something I need to tell you."

"More bad news?"

Electra nodded. "You've probably pieced together that I'm in debt. Otherwise, what would Letterman be doing here, right?"

"I've got student loans, maybe twenty grand worth," Treasure said. "I figured it was something like that. Hey, wait! I don't have student loans! I'm sorry. We can get back to your bad news in a second. I'm so weirdly relieved knowing all my student loans were simulated. Sorry... I'm not meaning to rub my debt-free state in your face. What do you owe? I figured we were doing so well on getting Bi-MARP stuff and you seemed so calm that it must not have been that big of a deal. I kind of had to abandon that theory when Letterman tried to eat me."

"I owe about sixty billion units," Electra said, resting her head in her hands. "Probably more now with interest and the damage to Letterman."

"Wow, shit, okay... Even with what we've got, we're still well short," Treasure said, her eyes going wide enough to show white all the way around her irises.

Electra loved that she was talking in terms of 'we', even though the debt was very much owned by Electra. Treasure's motives had somewhere along the way gone from being about rebuilding Earth, and probably not having much else to do, to actually hitching her future to Electra's.

"We're not as short as you might think," Electra said, expecting the shift in the conversation to go very badly for her. "The list I gave you had an item missing. One I'd left off on purpose."

"What is it?"

"You."

Silence hung thick and heavy between them. A knife twisted in Electra's heart with every passing second that Treasure didn't respond. She choked back the urge to say more or ask Treasure for her thoughts. The tension was horrible, but she couldn't imagine how what could be said after would make it any better.

"You meant to sell me?" Treasure finally said, her voice halting, despite massive effort expended to keep it steady.

"No, never!" Electra leaped to her feet, but held herself back from crossing to Treasure when she folded her arms over her chest. "I'm technically on the list too. I talked my way out of being held and had no intention of ever letting them take you…"

"What about Bort? Did you sell him?"

"I…yes, kind of." Electra deflated and sat back down. "He was in a stasis chamber. I didn't know what was inside when I retrieved it. I didn't knowingly sell him, but I also didn't do anything to rescue him after I did know."

"So, when Letterman tried to kidnap me —?"

"He was just doing his job as he understood it."

"And when you stopped him?"

"I was… I… I love you," Electra said. "I was saving the woman I love from…being taken away from me, I guess. I'm sorry I don't have an altruistic reason or plan or…" She couldn't expect Treasure to say it back and she didn't think she was even owed a reaction or response to her declaration of love, halting and awkward as it was.

"Shut up," Treasure said.

They stood in silence again. This time, Electra cherished the quiet moments, believing the next words out of Treasure's mouth would be 'goodbye' and 'I never want to see you again.'

"I assume there is no amount of letting the heat die down that will make people forget about sixty billion units of debt," Treasure said. "So, what do you intend to do now?"

"I'll transfer the lien entirely off the ship onto me, put the Cadillux in your name and you can go live your life," Electra said.

"And you will...?"

"Stay here until the Lien Enforcement bots find me, the scientists come back to the facility and throw me out or I die of old age."

"That's a stupid plan."

Electra shrugged and forced a smile. "I'm starting to think all my plans are pretty stupid."

"Then I suppose I'll have to come up with another plan." Treasure exasperatedly threw up her hands and shook her head. "So far my plans have landed us the original recipe for Coke, a vintage Volkswagen and a screwdriver."

"You're not mad?"

"Oh, I'm furious, but it's not all directed at you, and being angry doesn't change the fact that your plan would leave a third of the remaining humans marooned on a planet until they die or get captured," Treasure said. "I'll figure this out. In the meantime..." Treasure reached behind her back and removed a red, satin bag that obviously contained something heavy. "I made something for you. To cheer you up, I hope."

Electra couldn't remember the last time she'd received a present. She'd certainly been paid for services and received bonuses from time to time over the past few years. Nobody had had anything on Transition Island to give anyone else, and Embarkers viewed the act of gift-giving as bizarre and frivolous. Not wanting to seem ungrateful, and still thoroughly bewildered by Treasure's handling of so much awful truth, Electra accepted the bag, slid open the drawstring and peered inside.

"It's lovely, although I have one of my own already." Electra drew out the bright pink phallus.

"It's for you, but not for you to wear." Treasure took the phallus from her and held it in front of her own crotch. "I've got the harness part, and the fabricator said it is patterned after the Whippomorph, um, Ivy kept referring to it as a 'dong' when I was researching it, which was crazy off-putting. Apparently, I don't have the user permissions to change her word choices."

"I'm not sure I do either," Electra said. "I set her up while blackout drunk and can't remember the override code I used." Electra cocked her head and studied the toy. It had the perfectly spherical end, slightly bigger in diameter than the rest. It had three defined, lobed segments along the shaft rather than the four Essala'd had, it was pink instead of blue and more translucent than opaque. Still, she guessed it was probably pretty representative of the majority of Whippomorph dongs.

"It's good, a nice likeness," Electra said. "Is that something you've wanted to do or try or whatever?"

"Yes and no and I'm not sure," Treasure said. "I thought coming back here might make you nostalgic. But really, it's something you only did with Essala, and it seems like it made you happy and sad at the same time because it's tied to such a bittersweet memory. That's kind of how losing virginity works, except most people continue to have sex, so they get new memories, hopefully happy ones, and it becomes more of a part of them rather than a lone, defining moment."

"I've had sex since, with you a bunch of times, if you'll remember."

"And I've enjoyed it all, but you haven't had *that* kind of sex since."

"I also haven't felt the urge or need to."

"You also haven't taken blue pills in quite a while, nor have you told me what the red ones do," Treasure said, "which has made me crazy curious. Come on. Satisfy my curiosity. Tell me about the red pills. Not to play the 'you owe me' card, but you *do* owe me."

"Okay, I'll try. Firstly, they're not even for humans. The scientists here repurposed a lot of medications and techniques rather than research and develop their own," Electra said. "They're Appdurpin meds to assist in relational understanding. Appdurpins have three vaguely distinct sexes and any combination of the three can result in offspring, but there does have to be three individuals involved. So the concept of gender in other species, most specifically humans, always fascinated them since they didn't define their own genders. To that end, they started working on relationship-enhancing pharmaceuticals to capture some of the animal instincts they envied in humans and other similar species that created societal gender expressions to go along with inherent but often-defined gender identities. Depending on which sex of the three takes which color, a bunch of different stuff happens, but the basic goal is to create supercharged mating situations that will drive reproduction increases in their species. I guess they came really close to going extinct at some point in their distant past from lack of fucking."

"Pandas had that same problem in my time," Treasure said. "What happens when humans take them?"

"I don't know about all humans…"

"Fair enough… When *you* take them?"

"The blue pill gives me erections and an undeniable urge to use them," Electra said coyly.

"And the red ones? Why are you making me drag this out of you?"

"Because the red ones make me lose all higher function, they take a really long time to get out of my system and I pretty much have to be fucked and told I'm beautiful and loved then probably fucked again over and over and over," Electra said. "It's long, exhausting, I lose my appetite for several days and I typically have a hard time sitting for a week after — not to mention that being clingy, needy and sex-starved has scared away partners."

"Partners? You mean Essala."

"Fine, yes, one partner. After she left, I stopped taking the red ones."

"If I took a blue one and you took a red one…"

"We'd get married wearing purple," Electra joked. "I don't know what would happen. You're the only human I've slept with and I've never needed the pills with you."

"Do you want to, though?"

"I'm scared."

"Because I want to. I *really* want to. And, not to be 'that girl', but I'll require favors to make your apologies about lying to me feel valid."

"Okay, okay, we can, but only because you really want to and because you've made some valid points…and a lovely enhancement to wear," Electra said. "I'm up for it, but not here. I don't want to be in this room anymore right now."

They returned to the Cadillux before the light drizzle turned into a downpour. Instead of the all-white bedroom they'd started to share, they decided on the old-school lounge with the sectional couch, fake wood panel walls and hi-fi phonograph. Electra changed into her black silk robe with nothing underneath to cut back on opportunities to chicken out. She waited on the very edge of the red sectional couch, staring at the two shot glasses she'd taken from the bar to hold a red pill and a blue pill. She watched the pills just sitting on the coffee table, making her question things and began to wonder why she'd kept the red ones in the first place.

Treasure emerged from the guest room off the side of the lounge. She was dressed in a floor-length white satin robe with something of a comical tenting at the front over her crotch. "Okay, I've got to open this to show you and for another reason I'm kind of concerned about," Treasure said, undoing the tie on her robe to let the front slide open.

The pink Whippomorph phallus jutted out from the usual place, but it seemed to be held there by a tiny bit of pink mesh cloth dangling from a dainty black belt. The whole rig was lovely, delicate and looked more like jewelry or lingerie than anything else, but it also looked really flimsy.

"Is that going to stay on?" Electra asked.

"That's what's worrying me. I'm not sure it's ever coming off," Treasure said. "Check it out." She first waggled her hips back and forth to send it swaying. "It actually feels like I'm the one swaying." Next, she grabbed it and gave it a good yank. She immediately recoiled and started giggling somewhat painfully. "And that hurt like…"

"Like you pulled too hard on your own dick?"

"I don't know what that would feel like, but, yes, exactly like that."

"Give it a few strokes…for science."

Treasure quirked an eyebrow before sliding her hand far more gently up and down the lobes of the shaft. Her bemusement quickly turned to surprise. "I can feel this in my clit," she said. "Like really, really feel it."

"That must be transitive mesh," Electra said. "It's mostly used in prosthetics to move sensation from the remains of a missing limb to an artificial leg or arm. Don't worry. There's a tool to take it off when you want."

"Actually, the origins of transitive mesh were in the sex industry, Miss Electra," Ivy chimed in. "It was only later implemented in amputation replacement when the original patent lapsed."

"Ivy, we're going to need you to not listen in on this room for a while," Electra said.

"Ivy listening in on us never occurred to me," Treasure said.

"She's a virtual intelligence. She doesn't have consciousness or emotions or motivations or even the processing and storage power to develop them. I just didn't want her interjecting information based on what we're saying during," Electra said. "She's programmed to seem real, but she's not. Letterman, on the other hand…"

"Right, I'll keep that in mind for who I'm embarrassing around."

"Come here, quick, and let's take the pills before one of us loses her nerve." Electra lifted the shot glasses, one in each hand, and held out the blue pill to Treasure.

Treasure practically hopped over and accepted the glass. She shook out her free hand, bounced a little then threw back her head to swallow the blue pill in one quick gulp. Electra faltered, closed her eyes and downed the red pill as well.

"How long do they take to kick in?" Treasure asked.

"I'm usually super drunk or high when I take them, so I'm not sure."

"Wine, great idea. Yes, let's do that."

Treasure rushed to the wet bar, which was actually just a small, mobile fabricator that only contained schematics for beverages, and returned with two glasses of something approximating white wine. After the first glass went too fast, they each had another then sat together on the edge of the couch and waited.

"Do you feel anything yet?" Treasure asked.

"Your hand on my tit," Electra replied, looking down to Treasure's right hand that had made its way into the front of her robe to cup a breast.

Treasure looked down as well. "That is trippy. I did not consciously do that. It does feel really nice, though. Your breasts are so perky and responsive." She began randomly caressing and kneading Electra's chest.

"I'm glad you like them, because I love yours."

"Show them to me," Treasure demanded. "I want to suck on them. No, I *need* to suck on them."

Electra turned to Treasure and pulled open the front of her robe. It was what her body wanted her to do, not simply because Treasure demanded it but because her tits wanted in some primal way to be sucked on. Treasure took one nipple into her hot mouth, pulled at it with her lips and tongue, breathed hotly over it then moved on to give the other the same treatment — attention desperately given and urgently received.

"I've needed you," Electra said. "My whole life I didn't know what I wanted or needed until I started needing you." The words poured out unchecked. She wasn't typically a talker during sex, and she certainly hadn't given that level of thought to how much she wanted or needed Treasure. The words sounded so good and so true, though, so she couldn't imagine holding them back or regretting them.

"I need you too, and right now," Treasure purred. "I need your mouth on me."

Electra knew what she meant but also knew what she wanted and needed. She lunged across the distance and met Treasure in a deep, aggressive kiss. They pawed at one another, rubbing skin against skin while making love to each other's mouths. When the kiss broke, Electra's lips tingled from the intensity and her body buzzed with excitement. She plunged down onto Treasure's strap-on, the sense memory of the peculiar shape fading immediately into the old, familiar act until she had Treasure writhing and moaning with every stroke of her hand and lips. Treasure climaxed once, twice then halted the act on her way to a third, pulling Electra back up for another long kiss.

"I want to fuck you," Treasure said. "I've never wanted anything more than I want to fuck you right now." She roamed her hands and eyes hungrily over Electra's body, apparently building on her already overwhelming lust by devouring Electra through touch and sight.

"I want you to fuck me. I need you to." Electra fell back on the couch, her legs spread, her body taut as a bowstring from her nipples to her cock. She waited to be taken, but her lover didn't seem to know how to proceed. Electra popped a lubricating cap from its packet and slipped it over the head of the strap-on. "Go slow at first. I'll let you know when you can do as you like."

"Is there anything else I have to do?" Treasure asked nervously.

"Just stick it in me, beautiful," Electra said.

"Hearing you say that just sent a tremble through me," Treasure said.

"Imagine how it'll feel."

She didn't need to imagine, not for long. Treasure guided the head of her strap-on to the top of the line of Electra's ass until the lubricant cap settled against her rosebud. It slid in slowly at first, stretching until the head popped inside. Electra remembered the ache, the intense pain that subsided with every breath, then gave way to something else—a combined sensation, before turning into pure pleasure with more time, less friction and her body remembering what it was to be penetrated. Treasure held firm after the first push, letting her writhe onto the strap-on then grind until she felt ready.

"Fuck me," Electra moaned. "I need you to fuck me."

The unbridled desire was written clearly on Treasure's face, obvious in the way she strained and writhed, and coming off her in waves of heat. The blue pill had obviously influenced Treasure in the same way it always did with Electra. Everything about Treasure visibly spoke to the barely contained desire to ravage her. Inexperienced in how best to move, Treasure started first by holding Electra's legs and thrusting in long, slow motions, but that didn't appear to facilitate enough urgency, so she leaned forward and placed one hand beside Electra's head to support herself while she roughly kneaded Electra's breast with her other. From that position she drove into her harder and faster, which Electra craved.

When Treasure seemed to wane in energy from the rough exchange after climaxing twice, she pulled free and lay back. It hurt for a moment when the strap-on slid from Electra and more so knowing it was no longer inside her where she wanted it to be. Treasure was on her back, the pink phallus shiny and wet still, sticking straight up. Electra needed more.

She climbed atop her panting, sweaty lover, reached between her legs and guided the strap-on back into her. Straddled across Treasure's stomach, she began riding, hard and fast, grinding her hips down every few strokes to feel full and find every inch inside her that the strap-on hadn't touched yet. It felt amazing. With each rise and fall, tingling coursed through her. Then she came in heavy drips, flowing out of her onto Treasure's stomach each time she thrust herself down. It wasn't forceful in appearance, but she felt it in an entirely new and intense way. When she could no longer stand the sensation, she sat fully onto the phallus and ground her hips until she found the right spot to finish. Treasure reached up and milked the last of what remained within Electra in a few pleasant strokes of her soft hand.

Electra didn't want to dismount, even though she was completely drained. They were connected in an entirely new way, and her view was amazing. Treasure's dark skin, made shiny and beautiful from sweat, had a trail of perfectly white pearls from her sternum to her belly button, culminating in an almost iridescent puddle.

"You are so unbelievably beautiful right now," Electra murmured.

"I feel like a sex goddess," Treasure said, writhing a little and running her hands up her sides.

"You look like one." Electra closed her eyes, feeling the strap-on shift within her when Treasure moved. She leaned forward to kiss her lover roughly while she slid off the phallus. "Keep the strap-on handy. I'm going to need more of you."

"I love you, Electra," Treasure whispered. "I need you to know that, and I'm sorry I didn't say it before when you told me."

"I love you too."

"I'm never going to forget tonight," Treasure said.

"Neither will I."

"Care to join a sex goddess in the shower?"

Chapter Seventeen

Electra woke up deliciously sore and rock hard. She wanted to feel every inch of her against every inch of Treasure before she even opened her eyes. Once she found Treasure by feel alone, she would have another list of needs to fulfill. She crawled across the bed, found only cold sheets and blankets, crawled farther and found the edge. That bolted her awake and upright.

"Treasure?" Electra leaped from the bed. She checked the bathroom first. Empty. "Where is she, Ivy?"

"Miss Treasure is not currently on board, Miss Electra," Ivy replied.

Electra ran from the ship, naked since that was how she'd slept, and wild from panic. Rain fell in sheets. Wind whipped the ferns in waves. The surf crashed against the shore in the distance with unusual violence. Electra ran for the facility, calling Treasure's name.

From room to room, floor to floor, she ran and called out. There wasn't anything to take her on the planet. If the Glott pirates had found them, they would have taken the ship too.

A datapad sat on the bed of Electra's old room. She stared at the item from her ship, out of place on her bed from another lifetime, from another version of her. Swallowing hard would not remove the lump in her throat or the sting of tears at the corners of her eyes. With frightened, reverent hands, she picked up the datapad. The screen sprang to life on a video of Treasure at the desk in Electra's old dormitory room.

"Letterman and I had a long talk. He told me why I was created and studied in the first place. It's a bummer for Paul that I'm about to give him the dissertation supporting data I failed to provide for three centuries," Treasure said. "Let's be honest. I was never going to go along with your bullshit plan. You must have known that, right? I'm supposed to leave the woman I love alone on an empty planet for the rest of her life because she said so? Come on, Electra. You're smarter than that." Treasure tried to smile but couldn't make it stick. "Letterman apologized for trying to kidnap and sell me. I'm not sure how much of it was genuine and how much was the realization that he was completely vulnerable—a new sensation for him, I'm sure. Regardless, he was very deferential. You're the captain, he's the muscle but I'm in charge. I don't believe he likes that arrangement, but I know you do."

That made Electra smile and cry and tremble.

Treasure's tears in the video matched Electra's. "I know you lied to protect me, and I'm trying to remember your motivations were pure, even if your actions weren't. Let me protect you instead and tell the truth while doing so. After you saved my life, let me use your Spatronic and gave me the best sex of my life,

I think it's a fair trade for fifty billion units, which Letterman assures me is as much money as it sounds like. I gave him access to the ship's uplink. He summoned collection agents. He promised they wouldn't even wake you, since your debt was handled by what you'd already collected. I double-checked his math because I do not trust either of you when it comes to money at this point. It's close, but you should be out of debt. He even said he's not holding a grudge about getting his ass kicked by you — my words, not his." Treasure took a steadying breath and wiped tears from her cheeks before continuing. "I love you, Electra Rex. I love you too much to let you put yourself in danger for my sake. Get back out there, sweetness. The galaxy needs your spark."

The video ended. Electra clutched the datapad to her chest, curled up and lay on the bed. There wasn't a spark in her anymore, not without Treasure. *What is the point of any of it — the ship, the money, the freedom — if I have to live without love?* It was Letterman. He'd betrayed her. She hadn't trusted him, hadn't believed him, hadn't let him get close and he'd still figured out a way to fuck her over. *Kicked his ass? I haven't yet begun to kick his ass!*

She ran back to the ship through the gathering storm, bent on extracting some sort of retribution from Letterman. He'd brought agents to her ship. He'd lied about her to Treasure. If he thought the globauncher balls had been damaging, he hadn't seen anything yet. She'd rip out his CPU and show it to him. She'd put powerful magnets on whatever part of him equated to testicles. She'd blow rough silica crumbs into his cooling system. She'd get a club... That was what she'd do!

Electra stopped at the fabricator station directly off the gangplank and searched weapons for what would brutalize a bot most effectively – an electro-mace with a magnetic head to pull each swing harder into metal, the perfect tool to inflict pain on synthetic enemies. Armed with her newly printed electro-mace, naked, dripping wet from the rain and fuming mad, she felt like an ancient warrior woman from some forgotten Earthling fable, extracting retribution for her tribe, or country club, or clique, or whatever the name was for ancient warrior groups.

When she turned the corner to the cargo hold, her righteous fury turned into the most uniquely human of traits...impotent rage. The collection agents had gutted Letterman for his CPU and other valuable innards. All that remained were the damaged portions of his shell, the tracks he moved on, the flopping metal tentacles on top and a few bent collection chambers. She proceeded to beat the living daylights out of the shell all the same. The electro-mace made satisfying contact again and again without doing much damage to the hardened armor of the exterior. Electra pushed the door open farther to try to hit the collection chambers in the hope that they might be breakable. One good swing against them proved her wrong. The door rebounded and knocked her over. The mace bounced out of the door and down the hallway, making comical *ba-do-ing* noises whenever the electrified and magnetic head propelled the weapon away from the carpet. *Repulsed by organic matter to avoid self-harm* — she'd wondered what that description meant when she was printing the mace. *The carpet must have natural fibers. Stupid mace.*

She rolled into a sitting position to rub her shoulder where the door had struck her. Or maybe she was stupid for indulging in impotent rage against an inanimate object that no longer contained the essence of who she was mad at. Besides, she was a lover, not a fighter—a schemer, not a... Her train of thought derailed at seeing something out of place among the collection chambers. Her hit had managed to dislodge something...the data crystal containing Paul's research on humans. She'd been ducking Dr. Baarqua ever since she'd rescued Treasure, so she'd never had a chance to give it to him. A tweak of the interior release mechanism exposed by her mace had opened the back of the collection chamber so she could retrieve the undamaged data crystal. The wires to the port were severed and Letterman had already logged the crystal as acquired. Neither Letterman nor the collection agents would have known it was still inside without breaking open the damaged chamber to look.

She could lure Dr. Baarqua almost anywhere with the disk—and she could get some answers.

"You currently have fifty-five million unchecked hits on search parameters, Miss Electra," Ivy said.

"Later, Ivy, I've got an overgrown ape to extract information from."

* * * *

Threatening the good Dr. Baarqua wasn't Electra's style, nor did she think it would be particularly effective. She'd displayed a lot of various traits while working for Bi-MARP, but ruthlessness and violence weren't among them, the earlier mace incident notwithstanding. Meet for coffee... That was what she'd suggested, and he knew where.

When she arrived at Station 51's Tim Hortons, Electra found the eccentric Appdurpin doctor already waiting. He was drinking a cup of steaming coffee in a booth, nibbling on a bagel and reading something on a datapad. It wasn't necessarily a power move to make him wait while she got coffee. She was thirsty and wanted to say hi to Om. She knew she should be hungry, but the red pill was still in her system and nothing but more sex with Treasure sounded appetizing.

Order in hand, Electra made her way to the booth, set down her cup and sat across from the giant, shaggy blue ape in the crisp white lab coat. He put aside his datapad and attempted a weak smile.

"I had wondered why the data crystal was not among the eclectic gathering of valuables turned in by the collections agents on your behalf," Dr. Baarqua said. "A simple matter of absentmindedness on your part or inattention to detail on theirs?"

"A little of both," Electra said. "Is Dr. Paul super angry with me?"

"Quite the contrary, actually. And he is 'All But Dissertation', so it would be more correct to specify ABD rather than calling him a doctor…but I digress," Dr. Baarqua said. "You provided him with the only useful point of human data when you betrayed him to rescue Trish Miller from dissection. I believe you call her 'Treasure'. I find it somewhat vexing that you then essentially sold her to Bi-MARP, and I'm hoping you might shed some much-desired light upon the reason before I inform Paul that his data point might be corrupt."

"I didn't sell her," Electra said through clenched teeth. "Letterman betrayed me and she tried to save me…but it doesn't matter now. None of this went down how I wanted. I need you and everyone else to know that I was never going to give her to Bi-MARP."

"You're famous now, Captain Rex, and once you hand over the data crystal, your debts should be cleared with a little room to spare," Dr. Baarqua said. "Doesn't that please you?"

"No."

"Providing so many crucial pieces to the Bi-MARP effort to restore Earth does not please you?"

"No."

"Your name is synonymous with skilled treasure hunting and piloting. It wouldn't be inappropriate or inaccurate to describe you as a legend. Even this does not please you?"

"No, none of this shit pleases me. I am pretty fucking well *unpleased!*"

Dr. Baarqua pursed his lips and nodded. A pair of smaller hands emerged from his lab coat and began typing things on the datapad he'd set down.

"What the hell?" Electra demanded. "You have four arms? Since when do you have four arms?"

"Since always," Dr. Baarqua said. "There are a great many things my people did not disclose to your people when we sponsored you and granted access to the galaxy and beyond. We concealed our secondary arms and tails, a minor lie to appear more like the apes from your planet. Since I have already shared this secret with Bort and Treasure, I thought it only appropriate that I reveal the true Appdurpin form to you as well."

"What-the-fuck-ever… Have four arms, two heads, three tails for all I care," Electra said. "There are three tails, right? You're sitting down so I can't see, but I assume it's a weird cluster of three."

"Indeed, there are three. Quite astute of you," Dr. Baarqua said with a smile. His lower hands turned the datapad so Electra could see the historical images moving slowly across the screen. "For several millennia, my people studied Earthlings from afar, largely observational science until we decided whether or not to make a proper introduction. Over the millennia, a few humans hypothesized that we assisted in construction of the pyramids, but I assure you we did not. Indeed, we were quite taken aback when your ancient peoples commenced building marvels for no other reason than they evidently felt the urge to. Ultimately, after nearly ten thousand years of observational study, the consensus among the top scientists who oversaw our government was that your species was unfit for spacefaring society. Two centuries later, all life on planet Earth collapsed and the vast majority of humanity went extinct. Still we watched, vindicated to a degree at our initial decision but concerned more lives might have been spared had we intervened." The images on the screen showed the swift decay of Earth—the wars, the famines, the melting of the polar ice caps, the fires, the powerful storms that wiped cities from existence, and at long last a crack in the world so large the atmosphere filled with toxic gases and life ended.

"What changed your minds about us?" After seeing the pictures of what the planet had been like before humans destroyed it, then the ways in which they'd fought one another while the world had burned down around them, she completely understood why the Appdurpins hadn't thought humans were worth saving. The brief slideshow made her species look like a bunch of shortsighted shitheads.

"It took the death of your planet to change humanity's outlook," Dr. Baarqua said. "The Martians, Europans and Venutians all displayed admirable qualities not present in Earthlings — at least, not in significant rates. We resumed our study of your species with new fervor and your kind did not disappoint. Hardiness, kindness, cleverness… These were all traits present before Earth died, but now there was a marked increase in cooperation, emotional insight and self-awareness well beyond projections of typical societal evolution." The pictures shifted to the stations orbiting Venus, the large colonies on Mars and the people who'd banded together to strive to build a future for humanity. "Only after your species lost everything were they worthy of walking among the stars."

"If that's true, why are you letting the Jun'Tar screw up Bi-MARP so thoroughly?" Electra asked.

"Are they?"

"Yes! They screw up everything! Usually on purpose!"

Dr. Baarqua chuckled softly, which nearly incited Electra to throw her coffee in his face. If she hadn't still wanted to drink it, that coffee would have been on its way to splash blue-ape fur.

"They are succeeding at what they were meant to accomplish," Dr. Baarqua said. "Earth will become a grander spectacle and a far more effective warning than the Chamber dared to hope."

"The dire warning I get, but a spectacle without humans, since we both know Treasure and Bort can't produce a viable population alone and, aside from me, there aren't other humans to fill out the breeding stock."

"Aren't there?"

"No, there… Wait, are there?"

"What number is in your mind?"

"Three hundred eleven, but the other three hundred eight are gone."

"Are they?"

"Please stop doing that," Electra said. "I want to drink the rest of my coffee, but if you do it one more time, I will be honor bound to throw it in your face."

"To avoid that undesirable outcome, I will simply explain," Dr. Baarqua said. "Your species, excepting you, Bort and Treasure, has been purged from the rolls of spacefaring species. This does not mean your kind was purged from existence."

"The three hundred eight?"

"Are on Europa as we speak," Dr. Baarqua said. "The human colony, indeed, all of Jupiter and its moons, was designated a wildlife sanctuary by the Chamber before Bi-MARP began. It awaited only a new population to inhabit, which my people generously provided in the form of a cryogenically preserved small town formerly known as Urkhammer, Iowa. We 'borrowed' the town in 1928, forgot to give it back, then were too embarrassed to admit our mistake, so we simply kept them frozen. You recall that I did specify we only *largely* stuck to observational science. Because you were the only active human for so many years, the Chamber kept humanity on the deep census records as being spacefaring, even though only you and Bort technically fit that description for a significant amount of time."

"Then what is the point of Bi-MARP?" Electra asked, happy tears welling up and spilling down her cheeks. Humanity wasn't doomed. She wouldn't be the last, lonely member of her species, pointlessly wandering the galaxies until she died.

"Although it may be difficult to see now, I assure you, there was a twofold point," Dr. Baarqua said. "The first, I have given you part of. The Chamber wished a cautionary tale. The second reason I leave the deduction of in your capable hands." Dr. Baarqua slipped from the booth, dabbed at his mouth with a napkin and folded his lower arms over his stomach to hold the datapad in place beneath his lab coat. "Paul, ABD, implored me to thank you for assisting in his research and preventing the Glott insurgents from harming him or damaging his laboratory. He shared the security footage of your thrilling escape. Remarkable flying, Captain. I daresay you're the best human pilot alive."

She smirked. "What am I supposed to do now?" Electra reached into her jacket pocket and pulled the data crystal from it. She handed it to Dr. Baarqua, who slid it into the pocket of his lab coat without even inspecting it.

"Attend the grand opening of the Bi-MARP visitor center, of course," Dr. Baarqua said. "Your heroics are to be honored and your presence is most humbly requested."

Electra watched Dr. Baarqua leave. Her datapad link chirped after the door closed behind him. The transfer of units to pay for the data crystal had gone through. Drumming her fingers on the side of her cup, Electra watched ripples bounce back and forth over the surface of her quickly cooling coffee. She wanted to tip over the cup to be a little petulant, but Om would be the one who had to clean it up. Exerting a little control over her surroundings and indulging in snappish chaos weren't worth it. She was all but broke, and she couldn't imagine any other situation where having so little money was such great news. Between the interest and being charged for the significant damage she'd done to Letterman, the crystal put her a hair above zero units — not even enough to fix the scraped paint on her ship.

"Are you Electra Rex?" A soft, ethereal voice pulled her from her brooding.

Electra glanced up to find the glowing, willowy forms of two Ephemerettes standing at the end of the booth. Ephemerettes were comprised of gas-filled membranes, a very thin layer of chitin for support and bioluminescent light, which made them beautiful, but also kind of hard to look at for long periods. Ephemerettes could take almost any shape they bent themselves into, typically looking like floating orbs and tubes when no one else was around, or imitating a pleasing or threatening shape based on who they were talking to and what response they wished to elicit. In the case of the two speaking to her, they'd decided to shape themselves to buxom, curvy and highly feminine humanoid figures.

"Um…yeah, why?" Electra said.

"My friend and I are huge fans of yours," the one on the right said.

"You are?"

"The hugest!" the one on the left said, flashing brighter in excitement. "You're *the* face of Bi-MARP. The treasure hunter with the astounding ship who made a fortune rebuilding Earth — all the galactic net newsreels are talking about it."

"I'm Selestine and this is Chorrana," the one on the right said. "Do you think we could buy you a coffee or maybe get a tour of your ship?" Selestine leaned forward to place her hands on the table, using her arms to press her large, glowing breasts together.

"We've heard it's beautiful...and cozy," Chorrana added.

"I hate to burst your respective bubbles, but I don't have any of the fortune. To be honest, I've pretty much lost everything I care about except my ship," Electra said.

"Your ship is only the perfect symbol of style, speed and luxury dipped in glorious pink and dripping in chrome," Selestine said. "It must fit you perfectly."

"We could fit you perfectly," Chorrana purred, tracing the tip of her finger up and down the outside of Selestine's arm. "Any shape you like, we can make it happen."

"I...wait! *What*? How do you know...?" Electra pulled out her mobile datapad and typed her own name into the galactic net search. It exploded with stories, information and many, many interviews with the Bi-MARP staff, including one lengthy, popular exclusive given by Treasure. Through the Jun'Tar ability to pat themselves on their backs, the Chamber's skill in self-promotion and Treasure's remarkable story, Electra's fame had exploded before she'd even woken up alone.

"That's the one we watch most!" Selestine said.

"She was so lucky to get to fly with you," Chorrana said glumly. "I wish we could get so lucky."

"If we did, we'd be grateful," Selestine added.

"Grateful as many times as you could stand it," Chorrana agreed.

"If you'd made that offer weeks ago, I would have jumped all over it and both of you," Electra said.

"Yeah, but you weren't famous weeks ago," Selestine said.

"Or rich," Chorrana added.

"Why would we have cared weeks ago?" Selestine asked.

"I'm not rich now. What the fuck? Go away!" Electra yelled, not really sure why that bothered her as much as it did.

The Ephemerettes harrumphed, transformed back into swirling masses of orbs and tubes and floated out of the door. Electra thought they did a remarkable job of seeming haughty while holding no real defined form. It was impressive, at the very least.

Electra played the interview of Treasure on her datapad. All of Treasure's promises to retell the stories of what they'd done, where they'd been and the events they'd helped shape were accounted for. From time to time, the interview broke away to a different conversation to corroborate with another source or elaborate on something Treasure had said. Much of this secondary information had come from a bot-module, and though Electra didn't recognize the new voice, she spotted Letterman's obnoxiously stern attitude. Strangely enough, Letterman—for the most part—substantiated everything Treasure said, spoke glowingly of Electra's abilities in retrieving the Bort Pod and even gave a flattering retelling of how Electra had first rescued Treasure from the sociology simulation lab. A pang of guilt shot through her at trying to batter his shell with a mace. All he'd ever done was his job to the best of his ability and she'd been terrible to him the whole time. Bots weren't programmed to understand ethical and moral structures, like how wrong it was to sell a sentient life form for any amount of money. Letterman was physically incapable of knowing that what he'd done was abhorrent, and Electra knew it, even if she didn't want to admit to herself that in some truly fucked up way, Letterman had been trying to help her when he'd attempted to collect Treasure.

The only major difference in their accounts — and one the Jun'Tar interviewer spent a good deal of time highlighting — was how Letterman had come to be damaged and how Treasure had been turned over to Bi-MARP. If Treasure was to be believed, during the Battle of Station 111, Electra and Letterman had valiantly rescued Treasure from all manner of pirates. Sadly, Electra had to flee and go into hiding while Letterman had been badly damaged during their heroics. Treasure painted a beautiful picture of Electra and Letterman working as a team that was, despite being technically accurate, complete bullshit in spirit.

Letterman said his memory cells had been damaged in a fight with the Glott pirates and that he couldn't remember anything until after the collection team arrived to retrieve the goods Electra had amassed. He did admit that it was only through quick thinking, superior piloting and non-lethal combat skills on Electra's part that they'd been delivered from Station 111 without casualty and to a secret, secure location for the exchange with the lien enforcement agents. Again, his compliments needled Electra, and she had to face the fact that she'd vilified him more than he probably deserved.

The other videos largely functioned to support or wander down tangents created by Treasure's story. If anything, Treasure was even more of a media darling than Electra. Treasure was a product of one Chamber project completing another. The newsreels couldn't heap enough praise on the Chamber for the successful synergy of ventures that spanned centuries. Treasure was charming, clever, beautiful and enigmatic—a woman who had lived more than a dozen lives yet retained youth and vigor. The galactic net newsreels ate it up and begged for more.

Everything Treasure had said she'd do, she'd done. Across both inhabited galaxies, Electra was thought to be one of the greatest living pilots—daring, brave, stunning, equally brilliant at handling starships and women, the best humanity had to offer. The fifty-five million unchecked hits weren't for Bi-MARP stuff. It was the parameter for her own name she'd set up and largely forgotten about after the bounty notice had popped weeks ago.

"You are debt free, famous, fly the ship of your dreams and apparently have Ephemerettes begging you for threesomes, yet you look like you're on the verge of tears," Om said, rolling up beside her booth to re-form into a generally humanoid shape. "Didn't end up wanting what you wanted once you got it?"

"I guess not," Electra said. "No, wait. That's stupid. Yes, I want all of that stuff, but I also want Treasure, not the Ephemerette threesome. Okay, maybe deep down I want that too, but not now, not until I at least try to rescue Treasure for a third time." It only occurred to her after the fact that she'd rejected the Ephemerettes' offer of copious amounts of sex and adoration while still feeling the effects of a red pill. Her willpower rarely defeated pharmaceuticals and never so thoroughly and easily.

"I don't think there are enough globauncher balls to save Treasure this time," Om said. Electra gave Om a puzzled look. "I read some of the articles about your treasure hunting escapades. Clever use of catastrophic decompression preventative measures."

"Thanks. Every Embarker kid grows up thinking of a thousand new, unauthorized uses for globaunchers," Electra said. "I have a plan brewing. A plan this woman could pull off..." She turned the datapad so Om could see the artist's rendering of Electra for the cover of a galactic net magazine. "But probably not the real me. A very smart woman recently informed me that my plans tend to be shit."

"The only difference between the woman on that cover and the woman sitting across from me is who is doing the looking," Om said. "Also, maybe bra-cup size — the artist took some liberties."

"No kidding. She's got a couple serious zero-gravity mega torpedoes." Electra shook her head at the oversized ta-tas the rendering of her possessed. "Okay, and what exactly did the riddle part of your comment mean?"

"That woman on the cover is you," Om said. "That is the you Treasure sees. You're the one rescuing her, so be the person she thinks you are and ignore whoever told you that your plans are shit."

"Treasure told me that."

"Okay, yeah, you have to take that seriously, but try to prove her wrong."

"It's that easy, huh?"

"No, probably not, but you've got a fast ship, a few ride-or-die friends and a spike in notoriety right now, so you can probably pull together a daring plan or have fun trying," Om said. "Go get your girl, Captain Rex. Nobody at Bi-MARP knows that this wasn't your plan all along. They think you're thrilled with all these outcomes. They'll never see you coming."

"Good point. Okay, I've got an idea. It's incomplete, it's crazy and it's going to require help. Have you seen Fizan?" Electra asked.

"She's in her usual bay, throwing dice and talking about engorged genitals," Om said.

That was it. She was crammed full of caffeine and self-confidence, with only a slight drag of wondering if maybe her breasts weren't big enough. That was a fucked up, self-conscious thing to be wondering in such a moment, so she pushed it aside, mostly, and headed out to find Fizan.

After wandering the station for the better part of an hour among the stacks of starships and machinery in the queue for repairs, Electra finally heard her old Gromphra contact's voice and followed it to the empty slip used for gambling and clandestine meetings. A half-dozen Gromphra were collected around a game of dice that Electra only recognized upon coming closer. They were playing Yahtzee.

"I'm going for threes to finish out the row!" Fizan announced. "Come on triples!"

Electra cleared her throat.

A dozen insectoid eyes landed on her at once and a bombardment of sexual propositions followed.

"That's a nice top. Want to be nice on top of me?"

"Do those legs go all the way around someone my size?"

"Heaven must be missing a hot piece of ass!"

"Are your feet tired, because I'd like to lick them!"

"A threesome—you, me and my little friend." Followed by several thorax thrusts.

"Hey, shut it down, you mooks," Fizan said to quiet her nieces and uncles. "Don't you know who that is? That is *the* Electra Rex." The other Gromphra nodded and leered with new appreciation. "Sorry about that, Electra. They didn't know. But now that you're rich and famous, do you want to class up my bedroom by leaving your clothes all over the floor?"

"I'm not rich." Electra rolled her eyes. It was going to be next to impossible to make anyone believe a person could earn more than eighty billion units and end up flat broke. "Are you done?"

"We have more, but we can save them for later," Fizan said. "What do you need?"

"I have a disabled lien enforcement bot that I'd like repaired and modified," Electra said.

"No problem. Let me grab my tools, unless you see a tool of mine you want to grab," Fizan said.

Electra shook her head.

"Just the regular tools then," Fizan agreed.

A half-hour later, Fizan finally showed up, toolbox in hand. Electra had had ample time to clean the residual glob dust from the cargo hold, made all the easier by how empty it was after the collection agents had taken everything not nailed down. Apparently, the glob eventually turned into a fine gray powder. Her procrastinating about cleaning it up had ultimately worked in her favor.

Fizan let out a low, impressed whistle at seeing the state of Letterman's old frame. "Disabled was putting it nicely. That thing is fucked," she said. "Must have blasted it with that giant meat pole you're packing. Lucky bastard."

"Why do you do that?" Electra asked. "What's with the constant sexual harassment?"

"I shouldn't tell you, or anyone, and you're going to have to promise to keep it under your hat," Fizan said.

"I promise your secret is safe with me as long as the next words out of your mouth aren't about any part of my anatomy."

"All Gromphra that leave the home world are implanted with two things—a behavior modifier chip and a pheromone gland. The chip makes us say horrible, sexual things to everyone and everything and the pheromone gland makes us so repellent to every known species that even if we did get a comment to land, we'd still be too disgusting to do anything with," Fizan said.

"Seriously? Why?"

"It keeps us from forming romantic relationships that might compromise the hive mind's mission of collecting cash and goods for the Queen."

"But you're all sterile, right?"

"Sterile doesn't mean devoid of function and desire," Fizan said. "Our stuff still works for pleasure purposes, but with the way we act and subconsciously smell, nobody wants to touch us and we don't want to touch each other. The first few generations sent into the galaxies didn't come back and didn't send anything home. They found friends, lovers, formed families of their own and forgot why we existed. The implants make sure we remember."

"That's terrible," Electra said.

"Nah, that's what we exist for. If there wasn't the need for goods, the Queen wouldn't bother making us in the first place," Fizan said. "I know my exact purpose and goal in life, what I was born to do. I know beyond a shadow of a doubt what the meaning of my life is. Can you say the same, sugar-tits?"

"I'm getting there, I think."

"You'll love the feeling when you make it all the way to knowing," Fizan said. "Now, stand back while I work my magic on this clusterfuck."

The hours passed. While Fizan labored to bring Letterman's chassis back up to working condition, Electra set up the other parts of her plan. The first step was to get properly glamorous. She reset the Spatronic to go full-fabulous, ultra-glam and slid into the shell.

By the time the pinnacle in personal grooming accoutrement had finished with her, she looked better than the completely fabricated image on the front of the magazines to the point of hardly recognizing herself. The illusion took forever to achieve and apparently wouldn't last long. Electra only needed a few minutes and she wasn't planning on making a habit of going full super-starlet.

She sat in the lounge, prim, proper, glorious, and focused a camera on her to record a personalized message.

"Ready, Ivy?"

"Lights, camera, action, Miss Electra."

"To the incompetent, bungling, wall-eyed, pitiful excuse for a pirate, Sempa," Electra began. "I was surprised to learn you survived the minor scuffle with low-level collection bots on Station 111. I'm sure a massive amount of blind luck was involved in your continued, wretched existence. If you haven't already heard, the items you failed to steal from me were successfully delivered and I was paid an exorbitant amount of money. It's indelicate to talk about how much I have with someone as destitute and desperate as you, but let's just say I am worth billions now. That's billions with a capital B. They're throwing me a gala at the grand opening of the Bi-MARP station. You probably didn't get an invitation because you've fallen out of the top ten list of contributors. No doubt because you're worse at treasure hunting than you are at piracy. In a display of how much bigger of a person I am, I'd like you to attend the gala as my personal guest. Feel free to show up fashionably late, like you always do."

"Cut, Miss Electra," Ivy said.

"Save the message," Electra said. "I'll tell you when to send it."

Electra cleaned off most of the excessive makeup and undid the uncomfortable hair pins and ties creating the elaborate style spiraling up from her head. Timing would be important, especially with how much she had left to do before the grand opening.

She printed a six-pack of glass Coke bottles, had Ivy fill them with Coke Classic and headed down to the cargo hold. Fizan was putting the finishing touches on the Letterman conversion project when Electra arrived.

"Got your payment," Electra said.

"Or we could work things out the old-fashioned way."

"Nah, you've got an unfuckable pheromone odor turning me off."

"No more jokes about that where people can hear," Fizan said. "Not all of us Gromphra know that secret, and it might go badly if the wrong ones heard."

"Got it. That was the last one, stinkbug."

The electro-mace bounded past the doorway to the cargo hold, bounced off a wall and headed down the hallway toward the lounge in a series of *ba-zzzerp*s.

"What was that?" Fizan asked.

"That? That was…this whole other stupid thing. Don't worry about it," Electra said, really not in the mood to explain impotent rage and the silly things it could make humans do, especially not to a Gromphra who had thoroughly figured out the meaning of her life. "Hey, why were you guys playing Yahtzee earlier?"

"Earthling board games are all the rage now," Fizan said. "Everyone's buying licenses to print the things. Clothes, too, like the hat you gave Blix. I've got a friend saving up to buy an elephant."

"And Coca-Cola, I assume." Electra held out the six-pack for Fizan to take. If she didn't have her own private copy of the formula, she probably couldn't have afforded to print even a sip, let alone a six-pack.

"Worth a fortune, but I'm drinking these." Fizan took possession of the soda and ran her proboscis over the bottles to smell the glorious boon of carbonated sugar water in curvy, clear bottles. "Blix said it's heaven in liquid form."

"Yeah, it's the original formula with cocaine in it," Electra said. "So, go easy — or don't. You're a big girl. The cocaine made us fuck energetically and talk fast. Do with that information what you will — or what you can, I guess." Electra chewed sheepishly on the inside of her cheek for a second. "Is Blix cool with what happened on the Make-a-Wish con?"

"She'll get over it when I give her one of these…maybe half of one," Fizan said. "Sending her a few nude pics wouldn't hurt."

"If that's the price of smoothing things over, I'll just have to accept Blix being mad at me for a while," Electra said. "Walk me through the work on the collection bot."

"I've got the frame as straight as it's going to get. The door should close, but you're going to have to put your hip into it to make it stay. Don't bruise those luscious curves getting it locked or I'll have to come kiss them better." Fizan walked to the front of the repaired enforcement bot and opened the door. "I couldn't rebuild the servo motors. Whatever you did smashed them flat against the floor, ceiling and back wall of the main casing. If I had more time, I could use a torch to burn them out—or you could set that hot ass of yours on them and they'd melt like butter. The deployment tanks had to be a little smaller than you hoped because I needed the room for the new servos and the mobile VI module."

"Did you get the arms to work?"

"Only one, but that's all you'll need for what you've got planned."

"This is going to work," Electra murmured to herself.

"After all the work I put in, it better. Swing by and tell me how it goes." Fizan walked down the ramp out of the cargo hold, waving the two arms on one side in farewell.

"Watch the galactic net newsreels," Electra said. "You'll know when it goes down."

She hit the close button on the ramp and waited anxiously for it to finish buttoning up the ship.

"Ivy, set a course for Station 111," Electra said, "and print up another Dickies jumpsuit for me."

Chapter Eighteen

In a matter of a few days, Station 111 had transformed from a bloated, metal slug sitting in the middle of a nebula of vile gasses into a proper roadside attraction. Signs, flashing and lively, promised tours of the Battle of Bi-MARP, an all-elephant petting zoo and pictures with a genuine Electra Rex look-alike. Electra desperately wished she could turn to Treasure and have a laugh at the ridiculousness...except she was alone. She didn't even have Letterman to make snarky comments about anymore.

"Ivy, are you seeing this nonsense?" Electra asked.

"I am unsure of what you are indicating is nonsense, Miss Electra."

"Don't worry about it. It's all nonsense. Hey, we're friends, right, Ivy?"

"I am incapable of forming complex emotional attachments..."

"Please, just tell me we're friends and you're seeing the nonsense."

"We are friends, Miss Electra, and I am witnessing the nonsense at the same time as you."

"Great. That didn't make me feel even worse or anything." Electra shook off the melancholy feelings and zipped up her jumpsuit. Shit needed to get done. That was the second most popular Embarker motto behind *'never owe'* and she planned to embody it.

Ivy guided the ship to the designated docking point the landing authority had set aside for the Cadillux. Electra watched the exterior collision scopes that stated the private slip was reserved for *the* Captain Rex. At least her broke ass was getting free parking. A mob of adoring fans was already gathered outside the entrance to catch a glimpse of her.

As she descended the gangplank, the gathered throng erupted in dozens of different alien versions of cheering and applauding. At best, the noise was reminiscent of playing every type of music at the same time inside an active volcano. If they really loved Electra, they'd stop trying to make her ears bleed. She waved, even as she grimaced through the auditory discomfort.

Five Glott security guards, dressed in fancy new uniforms, created a pathway through the crowd. She stopped occasionally to take pictures with fans who asked. It was more of a reflex than anything, since 'have your picture taken with a human' was an option she'd offered as an activity back when she had been a professional party guest. She'd liked when her patrons had checked that box, since she could charge extra to sit and smile half the night—no forced conversations, no awkward dancing, just sit, smile and *ka-ching*!

There wasn't a compelling reason to take a tour to see where the Glott pirates had fought the collection bots. She'd been there for the start of the event and hadn't thought it interesting enough to stick around for all of it the first time. It wasn't even accurate to call it a battle, especially since nobody had died. Electra had looked it up on the galactic-news-net while she and Treasure had practiced nudism on their way to the far wormhole spawns. Five Glott pirates had been injured, seven collection bots had become disabled and a minimal amount of property damage had been reported. *Battle of Station 111 indeed.* What Electra was interested in seeing was who they'd found to be the genuine Captain Rex look-alike.

She followed the flashing signs through the crowd, pointing out her new destination to the Glott guards clearing the way for her. They seemed perplexed as to why the actual Electra Rex might want her picture taken with a fake Electra Rex. When the mob finally parted at the edge of the stage, Electra had her answer.

"Captain Rex, sweetheart!" Weisella screamed.

"You have *got* to be kidding me," Electra groaned.

Weisella, Electra's former employer and last owner of the Cadillux, looked nothing like her. For one thing, Weisella was a Panaeus and only vaguely humanoid. They'd dressed Weisella's shrimp tail in an Utopalex sleeve, put a brown wig on her and stuffed her tentacle arms into a reasonable facsimile of Electra's rarely worn leather jacket. The likeness was underwhelming.

Weisella rushed to her and folded her in an extremely awkward hug by wrapping all her tentacles around Electra from neck to belt. Eventually Electra had to pat Weisella on the hip. "Can't breathe."

"I knew you would come to see me once you heard where I'd landed," Weisella said, loosening the hug but not releasing Electra entirely yet.

"I didn't…"

"And you brought my ship!"

"I brought *my* ship," Electra said. "I also paid off *your* debt."

Weisella forced a giggle, looking around whimsically at the people gathered to have their picture taken with the Electra Rex look-alike. "Oh, you're so funny, Captain Rex," she said. "Let's call it a gift with a few minor entanglements."

"Whatever," Electra said. "How did you even get this job? We look nothing alike."

"Of course we do, silly! I showed them the picture of us at our last party and they couldn't hire me fast enough," Weisella said. "The Glotts declared we were practically twins."

"The party you stiffed me on? *That* party?"

"All irrigation under the overpass," Weisella said. "That's the Earthling idiom, isn't it? I've been practicing your kind's turns of phrase."

"I have no idea. I'm not an Earthling."

Weisella curled her tentacles to bring Electra closer. "I've thought a lot about this, a lot about you, and I'm willing to let you stick it in my nose. I may even like it."

"Gross. No, I wasn't trying to stick it in your nose," Electra said. "I thought that was your butt."

"How is sticking it in my nose grosser than in my butt?" Weisella asked.

"I don't know. It just is."

"Because my anus is on the bottom of my tail."

"That's really not…"

"I guess you can stick it there, but it's full of poisonous spines."

"Seriously, not what I was going for at all…not then, not now," Electra said, desperately trying to extract herself from Weisella's tentacles. After the struggling became a little awkward and their audience began grumbling, Weisella released her. "This is all a misunderstanding. Your nose is in the same place as a human butt and it's shaped like a very nice human butt."

"Exactly why I offered to let you —"

"I'm with someone," Electra said. "She's a prisoner right now, but that doesn't change the fact that I'm spoken for. And rescuing her seems to be a huge turn-on for both of us, so I'm saving myself up for... Why am I explaining this to you? Goodbye, Weisella."

Electra walked away from the whole encounter, both literally and figuratively, feeling like she needed two showers after visiting Station 111 to wash off the smelly air and the film of social awkwardness that Weisella had smeared all over her. The Glott guards, more confused than ever after watching the odd exchange, asked where she wanted to go next. Electra pointed them toward the mercantile area.

The spindly, greenish, mottled Glott at the window didn't seem to recognize her when she stepped up to the exchange booth, or, if he did, he didn't care. It wasn't like his job had ever hinged on the existence of tourism. "What do you need? What do you got? What do you want? Buying, selling, trading?"

"Buying," Electra said. "I need two of your least volatile, most odorous gases mixed with an agent to create sticky condensation."

"I got you. I see where you're going. Making a stink bomb. That's a thing we do. We'll do the hell out of that." The mercantile agent slid a datapad on a little chain across the counter to her. "Click the species you want offended by the smell and we'll get mixing."

Electra held her finger down and swiped the entire list.

"Tall order, but we've got the stuff. We've got the know-how. How much you need?"

"However much fits in these tanks, filled to the brim." Electra showed the mercantile agent her own datapad displaying a picture and schematic of the tank Fizan had installed in Letterman's old frame.

"You're going to ruin a lot of people's week, Captain."

"Counting on it."

"It won't be cheap."

"I've got a credit line." Electra handed her datapad over to have her account code scanned, and just like that, she was back in debt. "Never owe," she muttered to herself. "Sure, but shit's got to get done."

* * * *

Back aboard her ship, jumpsuit recycled and two showers taken, Electra finally relaxed in the captain's chair, sipping a Cherry Coke. She could still back out. The point of no return hadn't come and gone yet. Doubts might have gotten the better of her if she hadn't seen the final piece of the Bi-MARP puzzle lock into place on Station 111. Dr. Baarqua had been maddeningly coy about the purpose of Bi-MARP, assuming she'd figure it out, and she had, at least partly, since she still didn't know how it was going to serve as a cautionary tale.

Why had the Chamber decided to rebuild Earth? Why had they given the reconstruction contract to the frivolous Jun'Tar? Why had they poured almost limitless resources into the collection portion of the project? Why had they turned around and secretly set up a wildlife sanctuary on Europa rather than sending the humans back to the slowly rebuilding Earth?

Electra knew the answer the moment she put together the piece of Fizan playing Yahtzee to the seemingly unrelated clue of Weisella having a paying job. Bi-MARP was an economic stimulus package. It had nothing to do with restoring Earth to working order. The Jun'Tar had done their job perfectly, while seemingly bungling the whole affair. They'd collected mountains of easily commoditized items and provided an army of highly colorful characters to race around the galaxies to promote the project and build interest in the mystery of Bi-MARP while creating an alluring mythos about humans. Even if Electra, the only human treasure hunter on the roster, hadn't won the monetary prize — which she had, fair and square if not begrudgingly — they probably would have bounced her to the top in some other way to make her the face of Bi-MARP's success. A human saving Earth? Everyone could feel good about that and, by extension, the Chamber for making it happen.

There was just one problem with the Chamber's plan. Humans were chaotic and self-destructive, especially while under the influence of love.

"Send the video message to Sempa," Electra said.

"Sending now, Miss Electra."

"Plot a course to the Sol System. We've got a party to attend."

Chapter Nineteen

There wasn't really any way to prepare for what happened when Electra arrived in the Sol System and the now-complete Bi-MARP ring around Earth. Waste makes haste, an ancient Jun'Tar proverb promised, and apparently delivered often enough that people, the all-knowing Chamber included, still gave them contracts. Immediately upon exiting the wormhole, Electra found her ship surrounded by an honor guard of Jun'Tar construction vessels shaped like rings. They flashed lights, broadcast celebratory music that sounded like something ugly being tortured and flew happy patterns around Electra's ship.

All she'd had to give for such royal treatment was a screwdriver, a mostly complete Monopoly game, a partial Yahtzee set, a Volkswagen Beetle, arguably pointless data from a sociologist's dissertation, the fabled Bort Pod that contained an irate Martian, some reconstructed elephant DNA, oh, and the love of her life. Obviously, the last item on the list was the only thing she'd like to have kept. It wasn't even close when she thought about it. Monopoly was a frustrating game that took forever to finish, and the Volkswagen Beetle had no luxury amenities. The rest of it was junk she would have recycled for fabricator molecules. Except maybe Bort, although he might currently be trying to impregnate Treasure, in which case, she'd recycle him too.

She wasn't in the mood for pomp and circumstance, and the honor guard's music made her eye twitch, so she gunned it and left them to their celebratory nonsense somewhere near Saturn's orbit. A mission of prime importance awaited her on the third rock from the sun, a mission of love and betrayal and a whole lot of money.

Lights and a second cluster of Jun'Tar ships guided her to a docking port where even more wasteful nonsense awaited her. The Chamber wasn't perfect, even if they never admitted that anything they did was a mistake or failed. Projects ceased, changed direction seemingly at random, received entirely different staffs, mission statements, names and locations, but nothing was ever called a mistake by the Chamber. Everyone else could call many of their projects' mistakes. If the Chamber knew or cared what people thought—and Electra suspected they didn't—they never made it known. The basic premise of rebuilding a planet that humanity had destroyed long before they had other viable options… That wasn't something worth doing in the first place, especially since it was all just a scam to get the galactic economy chugging. The con artist in Electra did have to admit it was a pretty good grift. The mistake they probably didn't know they had made— but would find out soon—was assuming Electra would take the fame, fortune to clear her debt and luxury she'd always claimed she wanted and leave behind the lover who could make it all worthwhile.

Electra landed, steeled herself and made her way to the gangplank that was bracketed by two rows of Jun'Tar security guards in their funny orange helmets. Appdurpin and Jun'Tar workers cheered from behind barricades all around the docking bay. Letterman's shell, containing Ivy's mobile module and the party favor, followed closely behind her. The fact that Electra was once again in debt — only twelve thousand in the red, to be specific — shouldn't require the services of a debt enforcement bot. Perhaps they assumed Letterman was attending as her associate and friend. Regardless, the fact that she was escorted by the looming, omnipresent bot didn't seem to register with anyone.

The primary docking bay — the one that would receive the most traffic for the foreseeable future — bore her name in large, strangely glittering letters on the wall above the entryway to the rest of the space station. Below the sign, a ten-foot-tall statue of her stood, her hands on her hips, her chest thrust out grandly and her eyes boldly fixed skyward. Dr. Baarqua and Cog 2 waited her arrival at the base of the platform holding the giant Electra statue.

"My dear Captain Rex," Cog 2 said, "what do you think of your docking bay?"

"It's...super shiny," Electra said. And it was. Between the glittering lights used to spell out her name and the statue, which appeared to be made entirely of highly polished chrome, the whole bay kind of twinkled.

"And the statue? We made it based on the exacting specifications of Trish 'Treasure' Miller, the mother of the new world," Cog 2 said.

"Did you?" Electra examined the statue more closely. Knowing it had come from Treasure's imagination made it far more interesting. "She definitely remembered me fondly." From a purely objective point of view, the statue was gorgeous, not only because it was constructed of shiny chrome and crafted to perfection, but because it depicted a stunning, heroic woman of almost otherworldly beauty who Electra didn't remotely recognize.

"Empirically speaking, she did not," Dr. Baarqua said, clearing his throat. "The dimensions of your form were taken directly from scans when you first entered the station to deliver the Bort Pod. Treasure provided information regarding your behavior."

Electra's neck suddenly felt very warm. "Ah, I've never seen myself from this angle, I guess," Electra said. It was true. Why would she know what she looked like when depicted in ten feet of chrome and put on a pedestal? All in all, she liked the statue more than the artist's rendition of her on the magazine cover, even though both artists had attempted to capture a bold nature that Electra didn't feel she embodied anymore, if she ever truly had.

"Would you like the tour of the grand spectacle you helped create?" Cog 2 asked.

"That's what I'm here for."

Cog 2 led Electra through the halls, followed closely by Dr. Baarqua and the Letterman shell. A handful of VIPs were already inside the museum sections, although none had made their way to the 'Earth of the Future' wing yet. Some stopped to gawk and whisper at Electra's attendance, although none approached her—a much more subdued fan base than the throng on Station 111.

The older exhibits were little more than dusty rocks shaped like bones. Cog 2 assured her that they were fossils of giant beasts that once roamed the Earth. Over hundreds of millions of years, they'd evolved into birds, whatever those were. Electra only half paid attention. She wanted to see Treasure. She wanted to get her plan started. She didn't care that ancient Chinese people ate with sticks or that Australian aboriginals played a tube-like instrument that sounded like an FTL engine cooling tube about to fail.

Elk antlers, feta cheese recipes, stone tools, Craftsman brand tools, the Three Stooges, a portrait of Wu Zetian, two-and-a-half sperm whale ribs... It was all a slapdash pile of junk. Electra began to understand why her contributions were valued so highly in comparison to what other people had brought. Two living, breathing humans compared to a scorched, bulging tin of Jiffy Pop and a square of orange shag carpet someone claimed came from the Playboy Mansion.

"This was the game of baseball," Cog 2 said, at long last standing before a display that was actually kind of interesting.

A mannequin in a weird, white jumpsuit stood with a light wooden club, awaiting... Electra couldn't even guess what he planned to hit with the club based on his peculiar stance. There were pads that looked like uncomfortable pillows, unwieldy leather gloves to turn fingers into a semi-rigid scoop and a lot of 'innings' that contained smaller numbers of 'outings'. Most importantly, there was a vendor setting up to sell replica baseballs, baseball mitts, baseball caps and baseball bats.

"I don't suppose I could get a cap and bat," Electra said. "Maybe wear them through the visitor center."

"Yes, yes, absolutely!" Cog 2 procured one of each and practically threw them at Electra.

Electra slid the cap on and held the bat in the same strange manner the mannequin from the display did. "How do I look?"

"Perfectly Earthling," Dr. Baarqua said. "What was that delightfully bawdy phrase Bort graciously shared with us in regard to successful baseball execution?"

"Sock some dingers," Cog 2 said.

"Yes, that is the one," Dr. Baarqua said. "You appear perfectly equipped and arranged to 'sock some dingers'."

"If you say so," Electra said. "They had baseball on Mars?"

"A variation of it," Cog 2 said. "There is less than half the gravity of Earth on Mars, as you may know — perfect conditions for socking dingers, according to Bort. He really is the most charming man — his initial post-thawing outburst notwithstanding."

"Isn't that nice," Electra said through a forced smile. *Bort better not be working his charms on Treasure.*

The tour continued — sombreros, Alpine skiing, sloth skulls, Spiderman bed sheets, 2004 MTV Movie Award winner for the category 'Best Kiss'...Carmen Electra.

That stopped Electra dead in her tracks. A cardboard standee of a brunette woman in a red bathing suit was displayed behind glass. A screen beside the life-sized picture ran a loop of an ancient video reel of the same woman accepting an award of a black cup filled with small gold rocks fused together. The woman looked familiar — reflection-in-the-mirror familiar.

"My wondrous stars," Dr. Baarqua said, taking a step back to bring both Carmen Electra and Electra Rex into view at the same time. "You're something of a doppelganger for this highly decorated individual. A younger, more ordinary sister, perhaps."

"The scientists knew about her, the ones who helped me transition," Electra said. "I saw a picture on a screen once before a surgery. I was so woozy from anesthesia that I thought I'd dreamed it. I think I'm named after her and…modeled, maybe?"

"So it would seem. I'm sorry to say we can't tell you much more than what you've already seen," Cog 2 said. "She's something of a mystery since she came after the Encyclopedia Britannica fourteenth edition was published. We've learned she was a *Baywatch* slow-motion runner who excelled at kissing."

"Who brought these items in?" Electra asked.

"The Glott and his team," Cog 2 said. "What was his name, Doctor?"

"Admiral Sempa," Dr. Baarqua said. "I believe he and Miss Rex are well-acquainted."

"Admiral, huh?" Electra scoffed.

"Yes, he insisted we call him that after learning you were being referred to as Captain," Dr. Baarqua said, and they both rolled their eyes.

"Regardless… I can tell you it took some doing to pry the large portrait of her from his grasp," Cog 2 said. "It wasn't on the list, although it was obviously an Earthling artifact, so we had to negotiate vigorously. He wasn't overly eager to part with it until we brought out the proverbial mountain of units."

"Were she not a decorated award winner for the quintessentially Earthling activity of kissing, I daresay we would not have been so determined to acquire these items," Dr. Baarqua said.

"Speaking of kissing, should we show her the birds?"

"Oh my, let's!"

Dr. Baarqua and Cog 2 rushed Electra past several other displays to show her a cage with two small creatures inside — red and green with some sort of soft plumage and hard beaks. They quirked their weird little heads around then hopped to one another to meet beaks in something of a kiss.

"Those are birds?" Electra asked, only vaguely recognizing them from her skim of the Bi-MARP documents. For some reason, she'd assumed they would be huge — starship-sized or larger.

"Yes, well, animatronic versions, and they're kissing!" Cog 2 exclaimed.

"The big rock skulls from way back there... They turned into those?" Electra asked.

"Over tens of millions of years, yes!" Cog 2 nodded.

"What the fuck was going on with Earth?" Electra mused.

"We haven't the foggiest!" Dr. Baarqua said. "Isn't it wonderful?"

"Yeah, I guess. I don't know." Being human was something Electra had only given a lot of thought to lately. After her Embarker flotilla had died off, she'd actively worked not to think about her species in terms of what it meant for her identity. Humans hadn't been Earthlings, not in her mind, not for thousands of years. Humans were mostly Embarkers, and that she understood, full stop, no further need for consideration.

She hadn't enjoyed being an Embarker and never wanted to follow the lifestyle, but she'd understood it. Even while collecting for Bi-MARP, she'd worked not to think about the planet and long-dead civilizations that were the genesis of her species. The more she did learn of the humans who had inhabited Earth, the less she felt a connection to them. Real Earthlings were as alien to her as any species she'd ever met.

They passed through another archway into a new hall, a bleak corridor – the fall of humanity and the extinction of all life on Earth. These records came directly from the Chamber, no treasure hunters required. Electra could see the beginnings of the second purpose of Bi-MARP beyond economic stimulus. The cautionary tale was a harsh and powerful one.

Centuries of industrialization had led to a scarcity of drinkable water. Profiteers had stolen, hoarded, commoditized water, and wars had been fought over the life-giving resource. Temperatures on the planet had skyrocketed when human activity thickened the atmosphere, and sea levels had risen accordingly when the polar caps had melted. Life in the oceans had gone extinct from pollution and deoxygenating of the water shortly after. Breathable air had become scarce. Famines had followed droughts everywhere, resulting in starvation and violence. Brutal storms had decimated coastal cities. Wildfires had burned unchecked for years. Wealthier countries had fled the planet to set up colonies on the moon, then Mars, then orbiting Venus, eventually even the livable moons of Jupiter. They'd taken the last of the water and mineral resources when they'd left. Twenty billion people had remained on a dead rock with no food, no water, no way to escape. Without oceans covering most of the planet's surface to cool, calm and press down against tectonic activities, fissures had grown across every fault line. The largest was eventually three times the size of California, right in the middle of the dried-up Pacific Ocean. That had been the killer, the final, merciful blow to a dying world. Sulfur in a thousand different chemical forms had exploded from beneath the Earth's crust and the air itself had become an acid so corrosive that nothing could survive even minimal contact.

The full accounting of Earth's demise left only one clear conclusion. Humans had destroyed it all. Electra circled the hall, reading everything she could find, wildly scanning every chart, graph and historical recreation with desperate eyes. She couldn't find a single explanation for why the Earthlings had done it. The when, the how, the what, the where were all present, but nothing offered even a vague hypothesis as to why.

"They need to see this, Dr. Baarqua," Electra whispered, tears welling up. This was the other goal of Bi-MARP, the warning sent to the inhabitants of the Milky Way and Andromeda galaxies. Don't fuck up like the humans did. Don't destroy your world. We won't rebuild it, we won't save you and we'll tell everyone what you've done. Earth was the Chamber's cautionary tale to all other species, and the Jun'Tar incompetence in repairing what humanity had destroyed was the hammer to drive the point home.

"The colony on Europa? Yes, I quite agree, however..."

"The Chamber doesn't want them to."

"They do not."

Sadly, it made sense in the way many Chamber projects did. They couldn't tell the humans of the colony because they wanted to see if they'd do it again. The Chamber wanted to know if humans were actually a redeemable species, if humanity held value to the spacefaring society beyond what the Appdurpins had given them.

"Do you know why? Not why the Chamber is being obtuse—I think I've figured that part out—but why Earthlings destroyed themselves?"

"Appdurpins have many theories," Dr. Baarqua said. "The simple truth is we do not know. To ask me, personally, and not the entirety of my people, I would say the reasons were too numerous to make a proper accounting of them. All these reasons had one kernel of truth at the heart. Humans cannot conceive of large-scale concerns. Too much time, too much space, numbers too large, too many variables… Humans tend to shut down and return to focus only on the tiny details before them. These catastrophic events spanned generations across an entire planet. Grasping the enormity of the problem was something only a few could manage. When these special few attempted to share their hard-won insight, supported by decades of data, most humans couldn't understand or didn't want to believe and thus refused to see the truth."

"You're basically saying humans destroyed the planet because we're fundamentally selfish, stupid and stubborn?" Electra asked.

"Essentially, although I padded that explanation to fill a few hundred pages in my dissertation," Dr. Baarqua said.

"I can't say I like the implications."

"Nor did I, especially when I was invited to help establish the Europa Wildlife Preserve," Dr. Baarqua said. "Thousands of years ago, my people failed to help yours and a rare, special planet died. When Bi-MARP began, it seemed that both humans and Appdurpins were given another chance, but, as you've obviously figured out, that was not the case—at least, not on Earth."

"How do you think we'll do on Europa?" Electra asked.

"It is my hope that neither you nor I will live long enough to know," Dr. Baarqua said. "Such is the work we've begun."

"This is a depressing-ass museum we built, Doc," Electra said, forcing a chuckle.

"For Appdurpins and humans, at any rate."

At long last they came to the live mammals display. Unlike the room outlining the fall of humanity and all life on Earth, which was thorough, organized and complete, the living animals portion of the visitor center had a lot of empty space to grow into if anyone could find more critters to fill the slots. Two humans and a handful of baby green elephants comprised the entire exhibit.

Electra stopped first at the elephants, trying her best to be nonchalant. "You read the Encyclopedia entry," she said. "You know those aren't right."

Cog 2 grumbled, "You were the one to sell us the sample, and you made no mention of the errors it contained while you were getting paid."

"You know, now that I look at them, they're really, really close," Electra said, suddenly realizing her legal culpability if the display was pulled for inaccuracies.

"I think we can all agree that they're more elephant than anything else in the galaxy," Cog 2 said.

"Absolutely," Electra concurred.

"Perfectly stated," Dr. Baarqua concluded.

The tiny green elephants trumpeted at one another and bonked their heads against the walls.

At last they came to the crowning achievement, the seventy-billion-unit display—Trish Miller and Bort Thompson, a perfectly healthy mating pair of genuine humans, neither of whom was from Earth.

The habitat they occupied looked much like one of the lounges on Electra's ship. The décor of the kitchen and living room appeared to be from the early 1960s, heavy on the linoleum, brass and bright wallpaper. Treasure wore a green house dress, belted high on the waist and short at the sleeves. Bort was clad in khakis, a sweater vest and loafers, his dark brown hair shellacked firmly to his head. They both looked miserable. Bort sat at the Formica dining room table, reading a long out-of-date newspaper, while Treasure leaned back against the checkerboard tile kitchen counter and whipped silverware at the ceiling, trying to get the forks and knives to stick. She was as beautiful as ever and Electra couldn't help but press her hand to the glass and smile.

Several Jun'Tar security guards rushed into the room and began whispering frantically to Cog 2. Strange tremors and groans of metal buckling ran through the station.

"If you'll excuse me, there is an important, non-pirate related matter I have to attend to," Cog 2 said before rushing from the room with his security attaché.

"Sounds like there might be a pirate-related matter." Electra grinned.

"What did you do?" Dr. Baarqua asked.

"I can't let her stay here," Electra said. She shook her head grimly to Dr. Baarqua, tightened her grip on the souvenir baseball bat and swung as hard as she could at the center of the glass wall separating her and Treasure. The electrified security glass rejected the baseball bat and its swinger, sending the wooden club clattering across the metal floor and Electra tumbling ass-over-teakettle nearly half as far. From her newly seated position in the center of the room, Electra shook out her stinging hands and groaned. "I don't know why I thought that would work."

"This ruse of yours... I can assume it will result in calamity for the station?" Dr. Baarqua asked.

"A lot. A full kettle of calamities," Electra said. "I think that's a human idiom...kettle of calamities? Sounds like a thing."

Dr. Baarqua sighed and shook his head. He walked to a panel on the wall, pressed his ID badge to it, entered a code pattern with his fingertip and the glass lowered. Treasure and Bort at once looked to the opened wall from their perspective. Treasure ran from the kitchen, hurdled the couch on the way and threw herself across Electra, who was still seated on the floor after her multiple backward somersaults.

"Dr. Baarqua, what's happening?" Bort asked, emerging from the enclosure in a much more casual manner.

"It would seem the visitor center is prematurely closing for the...day, is it, Electra?" Dr. Baarqua said.

"Um...probably a little longer than that." Electra managed to peep amid the shower of kisses Treasure was raining on her.

"Did it work? Are you crazy famous?" Treasure asked.

"It did, I am and was this your plan all along?" Electra said.

"Like you would really leave me here after all we've been through," Treasure said. "I never doubted for a second you'd come rescue me...again."

"It's true," Bort said. "She's made it quite clear she did not intend to stay and breed with me."

"It's not you..." Treasure said.

"It's okay, Trish," Bort said. "My feelings might've been hurt if the first words out of your mouth to me weren't '*I'm desperately in love with someone else, so don't get any ideas, Martian.*' Hard to get one's hopes up after that sort of introduction."

"Come along, my boy," Dr. Baarqua said. "We are still men of science and there is much yet to be done in the Sol System."

Dr. Baarqua put his hand reassuringly on Bort's shoulder and guided him toward a service entrance. Bort looked back only once. Electra spotted the quick glance, but Treasure never did. Her eyes were focused solely on the love who had thrice rescued her.

"So, what's the plan?" Treasure asked giddily.

"Plan? I thought you had the plan!" Electra said.

"My part of the plan worked already," Treasure argued. "You're famous and hopefully debt free. Getting us out of here is all on you."

"Ah, well, I suppose I could improvise something." Electra stood and helped Treasure to her feet. She beckoned the Letterman shell over and tapped out a few command lines on the side panel. "Get the ship to the rendezvous, Ivy. The macros can handle the package delivery from here."

"Yes, Miss Electra."

"So that's not Letterman?" Treasure asked.

"It was Ivy for a little while, but it's not anyone anymore." Electra tapped the final command prompt and the Letterman shell rolled deeper into the visitor center. Before passing out of sight, its one functional arm opened the front panel and turned the nozzle for the gas feed. A putrid yellow fog began to leak out of every crack in the seams of the shell, even as the tentacle arm closed the front door. "Things are going to get extremely unpleasant in here. So we should probably take our leave."

"Where's your ship?" Treasure asked.

Electra consulted with her datapad. "About halfway to the moon by now." Electra grabbed Treasure's hand and dragged her back through the displays. Ahead, people screamed, weapons fired and alarms blared. Sempa and his pirates were doing a marvelous job of crashing the party. On the way through the human culture exhibit, a strange impulse overtook Electra.

She retrieved another keepsake baseball bat from the souvenir stand, braced herself for failure and swung it at the glass surrounding the Carmen Electra display. The bat crashed through the glass without triggering the same level of security. Thank goodness for the Jun'Tar propensity for cutting corners.

"Holy shit, that's why you look familiar!" Treasure exclaimed.

"Yeah, my transition was apparently somewhat patterned off her and my name half stolen," Electra said while grabbing the standee from the exhibit. "Was she pretty famous, important, revered, a woman of high society and respect?"

"She hosted spring break stuff on MTV and posed naked for *Playboy*," Treasure said. "So, no, not really."

"Not a world leader or competitive champion of some kind? That's a letdown." Electra positioned the standee in the middle of the room, scribbled a note across the front of a baseball jersey and wrapped it around the cardboard Carmen Electra. "Oh well, less to live up to, I suppose."

"Bygones?" Treasure read the hastily scrawled message.

"It's for Sempa," Electra said. "Hopefully he'll get what it means." Again, they were on the move, stopping only briefly to consult a visiting center map on the wall. The closest emergency exit was near the main entrance to the docking bay that bore Electra's name.

"I saw the statue, by the way," Electra said while they ran. "That was so sweet of you."

"Did you like the chrome? I thought you might like a statue in chrome."

"I loved it!" Electra said. "I'm told it's anatomically correct, although I have my doubts after seeing a few of the galactic net renderings of me."

"Hey, I tried to give my input on your body, but they weren't interested. The physical features are based on a security scan of you, sweetness," Treasure said. "That's you to double scale, no embellishments needed."

Electra's cheeks and neck felt hot with a flattered blush yet again. They ducked into the hall ahead of the docking bay just before an oncoming throng of tourists blocked their path. She thought she heard someone in the mob scream, "What the hell is that stench?"

In truth, Electra had no idea what the full chemical composition of the stink bomb was. Station 111 had proprietary rights to certain mixtures and she hadn't cared enough to pry. If it worked—and for what she'd paid, there wasn't any question it would—they could keep their formula secret.

"The pirates were more than enough of a distraction," Treasure said. "So why the mobile stink emitter thingy?"

They arrived at a long, curved room filled with triangle portals along the wall leading to escape pods. People were starting to file in, eager to flee the rampaging pirates and aggressively odorous cloud spreading through the station. Jun'Tar security attempted to keep the lines organized and succeeded to a degree. *What a polite bunch*, Electra mused. She almost felt sorry for ruining their little party...but not really.

"Partly, a backup plan in case Sempa didn't show up," Electra said. "Mostly, I'm pissed off at everyone in the Chamber and Bi-MARP right now. They were willing to buy and sell human beings. They're not being honest with anyone, least of all you and me, and they're turning a tomb into an amusement park, which is all just fucked up crap. Obviously, I'm happy about meeting you and getting out of debt, and I'm aware neither wonderful thing would have happened without Bi-MARP, but being conflicted has never stopped me from acting rashly before, so—"

"Wait, they aren't actually going to restore Earth?"

"Not in any meaningful way. I think they want to open the surface to tourism eventually, but no humans will live there. Even if they could make it the way it was, I don't think humans deserve it," Electra said. "We had a perfectly good planet and we fucked it all up for stupid reasons. Then we didn't do anything to warrant having it fixed for us. Even the Chamber can't undo what we did, not truly. It's a graveyard of twenty billion people down there and it should stay the way we made it. Fuck ancient Earthlings, fuck Bi-MARP and fuck the Chamber."

"After seeing the Chamber display of Earth's destruction...I'm with you. You know I am," Treasure said. "It's sad, but you're right, and there aren't people left to go back anyway."

"There are, but I'll explain that later." Electra dragged Treasure into one of the pyramid-shaped escape pods and closed the hatch behind them. A quick splice into the power supply and Electra had her homing beacon bleeping away for Ivy to find them amid the hundreds of similar escape pods all being sent to the moon as the emergency landing zone. "With any luck, Sempa and his buddies will stumble around the stench-filled station for hours looking for me."

In a hard lurch, the pod launched and suddenly they were shooting through space, one shiny pyramid amid a buzzing swarm of other little pyramids. The moment they left the artificial gravity, Electra and Treasure began floating around the enclosed space, giggling at the weightless sensation.

"I have been in space for weeks, and this is the first time I've actually felt like an astronaut," Treasure said.

They spun and clung to one another, ignoring the pleading of the onboard system to sit down, buckle up and behave reasonably. Electra couldn't remember a time where she'd wanted to behave reasonably, and she wasn't about to start because a low-level safety VI said she should. There would probably be blowback, consequences, perhaps even legal ramifications for what she'd done, but it was all worth it. She was young and in love with her Treasure.

Epilogue

A month later, Electra was back on Authrillia, but not in the tiny apartment she'd barely managed to pay rent on and not as a professional party guest scraping together jobs from galactic net postings. Treasure was the breadwinner, designing and coding replicas of human structures, furniture and food to sell fabricator licenses for. She called it her 'Intergalactic IKEA', a concept involving home assembly and meatballs that Electra still couldn't wrap her head around. They had a home, an honest-to-goodness house, something Electra had never had in her life. It was a small cottage by Authrillia standards — seven interconnected domes set on a hillside overlooking a beach in one direction and the village of Linjay on the other. The one-way mirrored exterior of the domes allowed panoramic views of the ocean, the beach, the crystalline forest to the north and the small municipal star port to the south where her Cadillux was docked.

Treasure spent much of her time in their new home decorating. Most of her complaints about their abode revolved around a complete inability to put furniture flush against the curved walls or hang pictures anywhere, since all the walls were concave glass. Electra tried to explain that the architecture on Authrillia was almost entirely Panaeus, telepathically floating, shrimp-tailed humanoids, so most of the furniture was globular and free floating. Treasure definitely did not want floating, globular furniture and vowed to design a new, human-friendly house. She was a former architecture student, after all.

"I really want to tell people what you did," Treasure said. "It was so cool the way you saved me, and everyone is getting it wrong." She was reading the galactic-net-news articles again. Every morning, Treasure woke up, made coffee and read the news. Sometimes she even checked outside the front door for a newspaper before settling into the familiar routine. Treasure explained that was how news used to come to people's homes—rolled up and thrown at the front door by a kid on a bike.

Electra laid her face down on the cool metal of the kitchen counter she'd been leaning forward on and let her hair fall in a curtain around her head. They'd been over it again and again. There was nothing to gain and a lot to lose by telling the truth. The authorities had determined Sempa had held some grudge against Bi-MARP for removing him from the top ten list of treasure hunters, uninviting him to the grand opening and swindling him out of a Carmen Electra standee he cherished. That was the galactically accepted explanation for why he'd attacked the visitor center. The Glott pirate captain had been apprehended while staring at an oddly placed cardboard cutout of 2004's 'Best Kiss' award winner. Electra still wasn't sure if she had any legal liability when it came to Sempa, especially if someone found her video 'invitation' to the grand opening. She'd thought it best not to correct anyone who laid the blame entirely on Sempa's infamous reputation for being quick to anger and long to hold a grudge.

"What would you tell them?" Electra asked.

"Maybe nobody needs to know about your catty fake invitation to Sempa. Still, the galaxy needs to know about your plan to have Ivy tether us into the cargo hold of the ship when our escape pod was mid-flight," Treasure said. "That was beyond clever."

"You mean the part of my shit plan that didn't work at all?"

Apparently, Ivy had a collision failsafe that Electra hadn't accounted for when programming the flight behaviors for the rescue. The cloud of escape pods was deemed far too dangerous to fly through by Ivy's risk-reward algorithms, so the rescue task in her activation queue was lowered in priority until such time as the search field was clear of obstacles. Electra and Treasure had landed on Earth's moon with everyone else. Their escape pod had tumbled across the dusty surface, bounced off a few other pods, and was then scooped up by a giant, rolling collection bot a while later, and they'd been brought back to a small lunar station in the first batch of refugees. It'd taken hours just to get to the landing zone where there wasn't a ship waiting for them. Ivy didn't have a command line for returning to the moon's secondary station, so she'd flown circles around the moon after the sky was sufficiently clear, looking for an escape pod that had already been emptied and dismantled hours before. They'd had to hire a tether-bot to retrieve the ship, and it hadn't been cheap, considering the Sol System only had Jun'Tar contractors available, adding even more debt on Electra's account that she didn't have gainful employment to repay.

"Yeah, that was kind of a tedious nightmare of inefficiency," Treasure said. "What about the baseball bat and the cardboard standee and... That doesn't sound all that heroic, hearing myself say it. You essentially broke a window and moved some furniture."

"It was a pretty big window, and I broke it even though it was only the second time I'd swung a bat," Electra said. "The first time didn't go as well."

"The stink bomb in the lien enforcement bot was a stroke of evil genius," Treasure said. "People would get a kick out of that."

"People would go to prison over that, and those people would be me," Electra said. "I contaminated a ton of Chamber-owned property using an illegally modified bot that wasn't mine to begin with. You really were correct back on Transition Island when you said most of my plans succeed in spite of me."

In a remarkable stroke of dumb luck, Letterman's automated shell spreading the stink gas around the station had fallen into a vat of experimental decontaminant while it still had some of the secret stench formula in the tanks. Electra didn't know what the decontaminant was or what stinky aerosol the Station 111 chemists had whipped up, but the two things did not get along at all. A highly energetic and foamy reaction had followed, filling a whole section of the ring with iridescent yellow bubbles. Bi-MARP had ground to a halt until the Jun'Tar could figure out what'd gone wrong, and they weren't exactly rushing into the disgusting foam to find the source. Why the bubbles hadn't popped over time was still a mystery.

"What does that leave?" Treasure asked.

"The way Dr. Baarqua helped break you and Bort out," Electra said, "but that wasn't heroism on my part, and telling people what he did would definitely land him in prison."

"How are they doing?"

Electra shrugged. "Being boring science-guys together, observing banal human behavior in the colony on Europa... I really only skim messages the Doc sends me. Did you know Bort is also a doctor?"

"Yeah, he's a gastroenterologist. We had plenty of time to talk about his medical practice in the habitat, so if I never hear about Martian irritable bowel syndrome again, it'll be too soon," Treasure said. "Maybe we need to make new stories for me to tell, because my head is too full of incredible things to say about you and my inbox is full of requests for interviews that I've been ignoring for weeks. It's hard, though. Two galaxies at our disposal, the most amazing ship ever to fly around in and all I want to do is spend the day in bed with you."

"The ship has beds, you know."

"Problem solved! But seriously, I don't want to go anywhere."

"I know what you mean." Electra walked to the dining room table, sat around the corner from Treasure at one end and wormed her foot into Treasure's lap in hopes she might caress it. "Do we spend the rest of our lives making love, sleeping late and reminiscing about the good old times back when we were interesting? I feel like humans have a reputation to live down and we're not going to do it with two thirds of the spacefaring population being homebody hedonists."

"It doesn't have to be all or nothing. Yes, we absolutely make love and sleep late for the rest of our lives," Treasure said, "but reminiscing is already boring and we've only had a month of downtime." Treasure began idly stroking the top of Electra's foot while she thought. It probably wasn't even a conscious behavior. Anything of Electra's that came anywhere near Treasure got a reflexive pleasant touch. "I've got an idea—something that will completely change our lives and be a huge departure for both of us."

"Do we have to go somewhere to do it?" Electra asked.

"Eventually, maybe, but not right away."

"Then tell me more!"

"Remember how you wondered if you 'threw genetic material' as you've called it?"

"Do you want to get me tested?"

"No need. I'm pregnant."

Electra could neither fathom the news nor function after she was struck by the completely unexpected and entirely overwhelming flood of joy that accompanied hearing that she would be a mother. Procreation hadn't been on her list of things to do, ever, even before she'd thought it was impossible, or improbable, or not remotely a good idea due to the ultimate extinction of her species. Now there was a new life, half her and half Treasure, human number three hundred twelve. They'd obviously need to come up with a better name than 'three hundred twelve'.

"Are you...mad? Okay, what? You've kind of just been staring at my stomach for a while," Treasure said.

"I'm deliriously okay with the news," Electra said. "There's a word for that…"

"Ecstatic?"

"Yes, I'm so ecstatic that I forgot the word for it! I'm going to be a mom. You're going to be a mom. It's a dream I never had that is all I want now."

"Then kiss me and help me think of baby names! Because we can't call her 'three hundred twelve'."

"I was just thinking that! Also, it's a girl?"

"Maybe — or maybe she'll be like one of her mother's and we'll need to head back to Transition Island."

Electra licked her lips and leaned forward to take Treasure's face in her hands. Their lips met and they melted into one another. In Treasure's excitement about telling her miraculous news, the front of her silken robe had fallen open a little, which was actually what Electra had been staring at and not Treasure's stomach, while she processed the joy-inducing realization that she'd be a mother.

"I want to play the game before we talk names."

"You always lose," Treasure said.

"I'm feeling lucky."

Treasure shrugged. "If you feel like challenging the Queen, I'll even let you go first."

"Green?"

"No." Treasure smiled and cocked her head to one side to study Electra. "Blue?"

"Yes." Electra sighed. And she'd felt so confident with the green guess. "Black and white?"

"Yes! Maybe you are getting better." Treasure leaned back and crossed her legs, bouncing the top foot a little while she thought. "Thong."

"Yes." Electra let out a long groan. "Same?"

"Nope," Treasure said. "Utopalex."

"How did you know I was building up my tolerance again?" Electra bounced angrily a little in her seat.

"You have so many crazy obvious tells, sweetness. I win again!" Treasure clapped excitedly. "Well, take them off and give them to me."

Electra stood and shimmied out of her panties — dark blue, thong-backed and made of Utopalex, as Treasure had correctly guessed. In the process, Electra was mindful to give Treasure only the briefest of glances at what was underneath the robe before tossing the prize to her lover. Treasure grinned like a Cheshire cat and twirled the tiny blue thong around on her index finger.

"You only won so many times early on because I didn't wear underwear and this is your game," Electra whined.

"And all the times you've lost since you started wearing panties specifically for this game?"

"Because you're better at it than me," Electra said with a sigh.

"How sweet of you to say!" Treasure feigned surprise at the required response of the loser to the winner. "Now, I'll give them back for…Carmen Electra's strip-aerobics."

"Oh, come on. I'm not very good yet."

"I disagree. You'd better start dancing, because we have to go see Dr. Bort about a prenatal exam and I'm definitely going to want to do things to you after watching you dance," Treasure said. "So make with the sexy, Captain Rex."

"Ivy, play Carmen Electra's *Werq*," Electra said.

"Yes, Miss Electra," Ivy said. "I'm sorry you lost again."

"What the hell, Ivy? I thought we were friends," Electra said, even as the upbeat song began to play.

"We are friends, Miss Electra," Ivy said. "As your friend, I am sorry you suck at the underwear game."

"You programmed her to say that!"

"I did," Treasure said with a grin. "I'm getting so much better at the command prompts."

Slightly over a minute into the song, Electra struggled to remember the dance routine from the ancient artifact of a DVD that demonstrated how to use burlesque dancing for fitness purposes. If the occasional halt and change of direction when she forgot a step bothered Treasure, it didn't show in the slightest. After the exceedingly brief strip tease, Treasure hopped up on the edge of the dining room table, spread her legs wide and beckoned Electra to her with a curled finger.

"One of these days we'll make it all the way through the song," Treasure said before pulling Electra into a deep kiss.

They'd need to come up with new maxims, since Electra couldn't care less about the Embarker wisdom of *'never owe'* and *'shit needs to get done'*. Owing had led her to a beautiful life, a future with a family, and shit would sort itself out, in her experience. 'Do better just because' had a nice ring to it. Maybe she'd write it down—after she did everything imaginable with Treasure.

Want to see more like this?
Here's a taster for you to enjoy!

Spotless: Heart
Bailey Bradford

Excerpt

Edie posed before the full-length mirror in her tiny bedroom. She stuck her butt out a little more, arching her lower back and trying to emulate the stick-thin model on the page of the magazine tacked onto the mirror's frame. "How do you even have a butt?" Edie asked the picture.

There was no way she'd ever be that skinny. Of course, she'd never have a vagina or full breasts, either.

Edie frowned, then scowled. "What idiot decided that's what women should look like anyway? Why am I even trying to look like you?" She tore the paper down. "You've got nothing on Marilyn, girl."

Edie preferred the curves and softness on a woman to those stick-straight lines she'd been trying to copy. Even with the parts she had, Edie was curvier than that model.

Well, okay, maybe they were equal on the lack of breasts part.

Edie pulled her dress out and glared at her flat chest. Breasts weren't ever going to develop there, and implants were out of the question. As a shifter, her body wouldn't tolerate anything like that.

She was okay with it, mostly, though. She had to be. A good bra fixed the problem, and anyway, while she'd felt a bit off in her body as a child, maturity had brought around a certain level of comfort with it.

The fact was there would be no altering her body from male to female, not since she was a shifter.

Edie had accepted that and now actually liked having the equipment she had. It was a pain to tuck and such, but yeah, she was content. *Mostly*. Okay, no, but she was learning to be happy with what she had.

With her body, at least. Everything else was…confusing and scary. Edie pushed a curl behind her ear. She flicked the clip-on earring dangling from that lobe. It was too bad pierced ears weren't possible either.

Although, maybe, if she talked to the shaman —

Edie shook her head. "No way."

There wasn't any chance she'd run into Rolly if she sought out Remus, and yet she couldn't get Rolly out of her thoughts. It seemed like any time she left her house, or even her bedroom lately, she carried the expectation of seeing the man again. It was giving her the creeps or something like that. *No, not the creeps. Rolly's not a bad person. He's just… I don't know. He's always unsettled me.* Edie couldn't figure it out.

Maybe Rolly had returned, and she knew it subconsciously? Though why would that be? The past year, she'd thought a lot about Rolly, though he'd always fascinated her, and scared her, too.

Rolly hadn't done anything to harm her. He'd only ever spoken a few words to her. Edie had always been too shy and nervous to give him a chance to do more. There was no reason for him to, anyway. Rolly had proven himself to be a very powerful shaman in his own right five years ago, almost on par with his father,

Remus. For all Edie knew, Rolly could have surpassed him in shamanistic abilities.

Why did she keep thinking of him? It was like she could feel him, not right there in her face, but in the background, somewhere, watching. Waiting. For what, she didn't know. It made Edie's belly go tight and hot.

Although, she mused as she looked at herself again, Rolly had yet to see her like this. All he'd seen was Erdwin, Edie's *blah* half — as far as Edie knew. She couldn't think of a time when Rolly would have had the opportunity to see her as her real self.

As Erdwin, Edie *did* feel even more out of place. Scared, timid, just out and out wrong in her skin. "Plain as that nasty vanilla yogurt," she murmured to her reflection. It was amazing how much confidence a subtle application of makeup and a change of clothes gave her.

"Not enough to go talk to Remus." Edie huffed and pouted. *Oh, she looked cute like that! Ducklips! Definitely going to have to try that on a cute boy in town as soon as I can work up the nerve.*

There was that strange tug in her gut again, warming her up.

"No, damn it." Edie dabbed at the beads of sweat on her brow.

"You okay in there?" Solomon called out at the same time that he tapped on the door. "I thought you were coming down for supper."

"Fine," Edie replied, giving herself another once-over. "Just got distracted."

Solomon snorted loud enough to be heard through the wooden door.

Edie grinned and hurried over to it. She was lucky to have the family she did, even if they were a huge clan of loud people. They were loving and accepting, and that was a lot more than many people in her situation had.

"Come on," Solomon said as he held out his elbow. "It's your birthday, and you've kept everyone waiting."

"It's embarrassing." Edie slipped her arm through her brother's. "I told you I didn't want a party."

"It's not a party," Solomon informed her. "If it was, we'd have invited people, but you aren't comfortable with that, so… It's only your family, celebrating the fact that they love you like crazy, and that you just started the long, slippery slope toward being an old maid."

Edie turned her nose up at her brother and huffed. "I'm only twenty-three! And that's just four years younger than you!"

"Yeah," Solomon agreed. "But I don't age. I just improve."

"Dork." Edie couldn't contain a snicker then. Solomon was a goofball. And she was glad there weren't any guests. Other people always made her uncomfortable. She was afraid to be herself around them. For that reason alone, Edie preferred to hide when there were any visitors.

"So I get the singing and cake, and presents?" she asked for clarification.

"Oh yeah," Solomon agreed. "Azil is hardcore about birthdays being a big deal. You know that."

Edie grinned. She did indeed know that Solomon's mate insisted on making every birthday into a full-blown party. Edie put that down to Azil having lived most of his life in a very oppressive society — and to him just being a sweetheart. "Well then, that makes up for the whole birthday acknowledgment, I guess."

Solomon cocked his head. "You knew you were getting a party. We weren't going to ignore this day."

Edie nodded. "Of course. Azil wouldn't let me get by without having a party, and that's awesome — Azil's awesome. I just get nervous around other people. It's so hard to even think about being my true self around them. It helps that you said no guests. As long as it's just family, I'm okay."

"Azil *is* awesome, I agree. As for the guests... I know, sweetie." Solomon brushed her cheek with a featherlight kiss. "But you should be proud of yourself and let everyone else see how you shine. Be yourself."

Edie bit back a sarcastic reply. Solomon was only trying to help. He didn't understand the depth of her fear and discomfort in social situations. Probably because it wasn't consistent. Sometimes she could go out in public with her family, but other times, she had to stay home and just hide.

PUBLISHING

Sign up for our newsletter and find out about all our romance book releases, eBook sales and promotions, sneak peeks and FREE romance books!

About the Author

April Griffith is a lesbian, a rogue academic, and a giant nerd. She's from Oregon, but calls San Diego her home. Her passions include LGBTQ+ political activism, creating safe places for women in Dungeons & Dragons, and writing the books she wanted to read when she was a kid. April worked on the Amazon Gladiator series (Anaxilea: Amazon Princess and Anaxilea: Gladiatrix) under a pen name.

April loves to hear from readers. You can find her contact information, website details and author profile page at https://www.pride-publishing.com